Also by Evelyn "Slim" Lambright

The Justus Girls

the
Sweethear-
of Soul

the Sweethearts of Soul

*

Evelyn "Slim" Lambright

HarperCollins*Publishers*

THE SWEETHEARTS OF SOUL. Copyright © 2004 by Evelyn "Slim" Lambright. All rights reserved. Printed in the United States of America. No part of this book may be used or reproduced in any manner whatsoever without written permission except in the case of brief quotations embodied in critical articles and reviews. For information, address HarperCollins Publishers Inc., 10 East 53rd Street, New York, NY 10022.

HarperCollins books may be purchased for educational, business, or sales promotional use. For information, please write: Special Markets Department, HarperCollins Publishers Inc., 10 East 53rd Street, New York, NY 10022.

FIRST EDITION

Designed by Nancy B. Field

Printed on acid-free paper

Library of Congress Cataloging-in-Publication Data is available upon request.

ISBN 0-06-018475-2

04 05 06 07 08 ❖/RRD   10 9 8 7 6 5 4 3 2 1

This novel is dedicated to
Mary Jones, my "adopted" aunt, who has guided me
through many a rough patch.

To Shirley Wyche, who is the matriarch in our family
and who is *not*, I repeat, *not* Bad Tooth Shirley
from *The Justus Girls*.

And again, to my beloved mother,
the late Thelma Moore Johnson, whose voice I can still hear,
whenever I am even tempted to go the wrong way.
"DON'T MAKE ME HAVE TO COME DOWN THERE!"
It worked then, it works now. I love you, Mommy!

Slim L.

✳

Acknowledgments

This street writer–fighter once again thanks her "corner girls": Alice "Pretty Girl" Peck; her skillful sparring partner, who wins at least six times out of ten, Victoria "Kick Ass" Sanders, who you wouldn't want to meet up with in an alley—even in broad daylight; and Carolyn "Cut Woman" Marino, who never leaves home without her red pencil in her pocketbook.

Be forewarned: these divas are DANGEROUS!

The Hummingbird

There is a story told about a bird, a beautiful
hummingbird, that sings but once in its life, and
the sound of its song is said to be so sweet, it has
been known to sometimes still the entire forest.
Then it dies, leaving only the memory of its
bright and brilliant voice behind.

Legs: Reporter's Notes

A lot of people were surprised by what happened at the Blue Moon Motel that night in May. Me? I should have seen it coming, should have known by then that when it comes to the Sweethearts of Soul, anything is possible. All I can say now is I wouldn't want to get on them sistahs' bad side. Damn.

See, I'm trying to be fair to all parties involved, I want to do the right thing here, to tell the truth. After all, I am a reporter, and everyone knows a reporter's job is to tell the objective truth.

A lot of people ask journalists, especially music journalists like myself, for the real story, the lowdown, you know, what's so-and-so *really* like. That kind of thing. As a professional, I usually try to accommodate them, to write the story the same way I would tell it.

But this one just won't let me go. I've heard of six degrees of separation, you know the drill, how everybody is somehow connected to everybody else by no more than six other people, but this is ridiculous! Talk about some hot mess! This is some *Rashomon* kind of shit going down here. I know they say that if you get ten black folks in a room, you'll get at least eleven opinions, but damn! This shit is just as deep now as it was when I first wrote it. Has it been three months ago? Four? Whatever.

So where is the truth? Is it contained in the pages of these beat-up comp books? Is it snaking its way through the spaces of the voices on the tapes? Is it somewhere in these notes I write tonight, hiding behind my own still-shaky and sometimes unreliable words?

Like I say, I'm trying to do the right thing by everybody, including myself. But everybody's got their own version of what really went down. Everybody sees things their own way. So what I've tried to do here is tell a tale of two stories. I guess you could call it the official story as written by me, and the real story as told to me by the people involved.

Like they say, to understand the mystery, you've got to know the history. So I'm flipping the script back to the beginning, back to that January. Back to the day I innocently began my trip down this haunted, hazardous road.

Okay, okay, not so innocently. Damn. Give me a break. I just ask that you hang on in there with me, and try not to blink; you might miss something.

Now, the official story you can find in the May issue of *Black Music Magazine* under my byline. But the real story, well, maybe it will someday see the light of day. But I doubt it. Just too personal.

I'm supposed to be the reporter, remember, the disinterested, objective observer, and all that shit. Yeah. Whatever.

Chapter 1

＊

The Sweethearts

"So what yall gone do? Are you with me on this or not? This Diamond broad say she want to talk to all the Sweethearts of Soul, not just me. She want to interview everybody."

Ruth Thomas leaned forward quickly, smashing out her Kool cigarette in the ashtray, narrowing her eyes as she looked first at Addie, then Venus, then Addie again. The two women stared blankly back at her.

"I swear to God, yall just don't wanna see me catch a break, no how, no way, do you?"

Ruth was glaring at Addie and Venus now.

"Ain't nobody say nothin bout tryin to keep you from catchin no break, if that's what you callin it. From what she said to me, all the woman want to do is talk to us about the old days, how it used to be, all that tired ole stuff. Hell, she can get that from the bio the record company keeps on file. I don't see why I got to interrupt my busy schedule just to go strollin down memory lane with her. The past is the past. Let it lay. I'm livin in the present, in the here and now."

Adeline Lights spoke slowly and casually as she stirred her tea, but her face betrayed her tone. Her dark eyes, the left one shining wickedly, were backlit and gleaming, and her mouth had twisted to the side, giving her an insolent, almost petulant, expression.

"Well, it does have somethin to do with the award and all, Ad," Venus Jones, the third member of the group, spoke up. "I mean, we never got an award before, and this seems to be a really big deal, and the publicity would be nice for us."

"Publicity would be nice for who? I don't need no damn publicity. I already got my own business, and Busy Bee Realty don't hardly need that kinda publicity. I'm doin very well these days, thank you, and Venus, you got your bridal shop and your rental property. You doin all right. What we need publicity for?" Addie, a satisfied smirk on her face, was talking loud enough for some of the customers at Gustine's Diner to glance over in their direction.

So there they were. The Sweethearts of Soul, together again. Well, three of them at least.

The women silently checked each other out. Now in their mid-forties, the Sweethearts were holding up well.

"Ruthless" Ruth Thomas, still slender, was wearing her trademark street "uniform," consisting of black jeans and turtleneck under an oversized black leather bomber jacket. She was hatless as usual, her hair pulled back tightly into a sleek dark knot at the nape of her neck, her only jewelry a pair of large golden hoop earrings. A vision in black, she was, but for her bright-red high-top leather Reeboks.

Pretty, plumpish, and practical, Venus Jones was dressed, on this cold Philadelphia afternoon, in a sensible beige heavy wool coat, which she had removed and carefully hung up as soon as she had entered the diner. She wore a cream-colored cashmere sweater and matching woolen slacks under one of her ever-present "working smocks," this one a bright pink, with "Gowns by Venus" brightly emblazoned in fancy gold script across the back. Soft auburn bangs peeped out from under her dark-brown beret, which perfectly matched her suede gloves and flat brown suede booties.

And finally, Adeline Lights. Last, but never, ever, least, Addie had what people called "a way about her," a certain style that all but screamed "I am the shit, and you better know it" to any and all who came near her. Today, Adeline was swathed in a full-length dyed blond ranch mink coat with matching hat, which she kept primping and adjusting, as if it were her hair. Under the hat, the hair—blond and straight, bought and paid for, thank you very much— flowed down to her shoulders, where it rested uneasily.

Beneath all that, Addie was wearing an ankle-length, blood-red sweater dress, the same color as her lipstick, and Dragon Lady press-on nails. There were rings on almost every finger (and probably bells on her toes), and when Addie moved her hands, the sound of jangling bracelets accompanied her every gesture like a band of triangle-playing monkeys. Adeline Lights definitely had *a way* about her.

"So, Ruthie, how's the show business comin along?" Addie asked pleasantly, all the while kicking Venus under the table.

Ruthie dropped her head and bit her bottom lip. *That fuckin Addie's really twistin the knife in now.*

All three knew that what was left unsaid before them was that nobody really needed this story but Ruth.

The Sweethearts of Soul had agreed to meet at Gustine's, a neighborhood diner (neutral ground), at four o'clock this afternoon to discuss whether or not they would be cooperating with Legs Diamond, a reporter from *Black Music Magazine* who wanted to do an in-depth story on them in association with the girls receiving the Rock and Soul Foundation's Pioneer Award.

Ruth was all for it, Addie was dead-set against it, and Venus, as always, was stuck somewhere in the middle.

"First of all, I ain't never even heard of this Pioneer Award before, and second, I ain't never heard of no damn Legs Diamond, neither. What is she, some kinda gangsta chick or somethin?" Addie sucked her teeth.

"Hell, no, she ain't no damn gangsta. The only reason you don't know is cause you don't keep up with shit in the music industry, noway. Too busy countin your money, I guess," Ruth said sharply.

"Hmph! Better than bein too busy countin my men! Or what's that you call em nowadays? Boy toys? Right! Too busy countin your boy toys!"

"So where's your next big-time gig at, huh? The flea market? The bingo parlor? Oh, no, no, wait a minute! I know, I know! *Ladies and gentlemen, coming to you live, straight from the neighborhood crackhouse, Ruthless Ruth Thomas, of the Sweethearts of Soul!* Yay, yay, yay!"

Addie was clapping her hands wildly, the clanging bracelets were adding percussion. People were turning around in their seats. Venus looked away, holding her hand to her mouth, trying desperately not to laugh. But laugh she did, loud and uproariously. Her and Addie. Ruthie was so furious, the veins at her temples were standing out, visibly throbbing, as she clenched and unclenched her jaws rapidly, simultaneously giving both women the Vulcan death stare.

"You know what?" Ruth slid out of the booth and stood up quickly.

"No! What?"

"I'm bout sick of you and your hifalutin, hincty, phony-ass ways. You gettin worse than Fluffy, only without the talent!"

Addie would have stood up, too, but was held back by Venus, who was sitting beside her on the aisle and would not budge.

"Now, wait just a damn minute," Venus yelled, spreading her arms like a crossing guard, simultaneously trying to push Ruthie back and keep Addie in her seat.

To put it mildly, the meeting was not going well. Gustine Blue, having observed all that had transpired from her usual seat at the corner of the counter, decided to step in just about now.

"Well, if it isn't the Sweethearts of Soul! Afternoon, ladies! Been a long time since I've seen you all in here together. Used to be my favorite regulars. I still got your picture on the wall there, you know."

Gustine, a short, petite woman, who somewhat resembled a light-complexioned Eartha Kitt, spoke quickly as she gestured toward her "Wall of Fame," where autographed glossy photographs of performers, from Louis Armstrong to Jill Scott, smiled out on the room. There, in the very center, was an eight-by-ten of the Sweethearts, taken somewhere back in the late sixties.

"Now, don't yall look nice," she purred, fixing them with a bright smile.

"You're your mama's girls, all right."

"Thank you, Miss Gustine," the Sweethearts mumbled sheepishly in unison, glancing downwards. Just like that, the three women, who only moments ago had seemed on the verge of turning the joint out in a knockdown fistfight, now grinned and nodded as Miss Gustine asked how they were doing these days, asked after their children, calling each by name, and had a sweet potato pie sent to their table.

"You know, the only woman who could make a better sweet potato pie than me was yall's mama, God rest her soul. Now, you girls eat up, and if there's anything else I can do for you, *anything,* just come see me. You know my hours."

With that, Gustine Blue swept off, trailing in her wake a mist of jasmine, magnolia, and something else, something strange yet familiar.

The Sweethearts of Soul, now properly shamed by the mere mention of MuDear's name, resumed their conversation in a more seemly manner.

"All right, listen up. You guys know how much this story means to me as far as gettin my career jump-started again. I'm askin you to please work with this woman. She's gonna feature our pictures and everything."

Ruth, usually way too proud to beg anybody for anything, spoke haltingly, as if her tongue were twisting around in her mouth involuntarily.

Addie, acutely enjoying Ruth's discomfort, glared at her with an undeniably wicked gleam in her eyes, especially the left one.

Venus anxiously looked from one to the other, then asked the question she'd wanted to bring up from the very beginning.

"Okay. Suppose we go along with this. What about what's goin on with the kids?"

Three pairs of eyes widened, shot quickly to the other two, then hastily away. For almost a full minute, no one spoke.

"How about this? How bout just for the interviews and the awards and everything, we keep all discussions about the kids off-limits? Just till this is all over with?" Ruth finally proposed.

"Seems fair to me. Lord knows, we gone have to deal with em sooner or later, anyway," Addie agreed, nodding.

"You damn right we gone have to deal with em. At least, *I* do," Venus muttered, her face now closed and masklike.

Ruth and Addie said nothing.

"And another thing: Birdie." Venus was whispering now. "What are we gone do about Birdie?"

What, indeed.

They'd do it. Addie and Venus had already made up their minds to do it before Ruth had even walked in the door. Hell, maybe it would turn things around in her "career." Who knows? Maybe even Birdie would snap out of that walking-wounded state she now seemed to live in permanently. Birdie. Maybe—oh God, please—maybe it would even save her.

Chapter 2

*

Legs and Roe

You know, Roe, I don't know who in the hell these old has-been, never-was, broke-down broads think they are. Got the nerve to be giving me a hard time! As if they get interviewed every day or something. Shit!

Well, I wouldn't call them never-wases. The Sweethearts of Soul at one time were stars, you know.

Damn, Roe, at least you could show a little love, a little support here for a sistah.

I'm trying to show some support. I'm trying to talk some sense into your damn fool head, Legs. Here, you've gotten an assignment to do a story on the Sweethearts, a nice little local piece which ought to be a piece of cake for you, being as they all live right here in Philly and—

All except for Fanya . . .

Yeah, well, you can save Fanya for last. She probably won't talk to you, anyway.

Hmph. As if. I don't want to talk to that stuck-up old skank, nohow.

Well, skank or no skank, you should want to talk to her. After all, she was there at the beginning and, as all good reporters know, the beginning is the nexus, the root of everything that comes afterwards.

Oh, so now I've got to listen to lessons on good reporting skills, huh? You think I need some kind of remedial course or something? Think you've gotta take me back to school?

You talking to me—LaVerne Diamond—remember? Me, Roberta, your best bud, your track teammate, college room-mate, godmother to your child. Remember?

I hear you, roadie. It's just these chicks—I mean, there's plenty of people who would just love to be written up in *Black Music*, something to show the kids, the grandkids, and these heifas are acting like they're doing me some kind of favor, just talking to me on the damn telephone. Jeez.

Yeah, well, maybe there's some things they don't neces-sarily want the grandkids to know. May be some things they don't even want to remember themselves. I know you, girl, running around shining your light of truth and justice in peo-ples' faces and all that good shit.

Well, what's wrong with that? At least I'm going to be interviewing one of the Sweethearts tomorrow.

One of them? Why not all of them?

Girl, don't ask me. For some reason, they refuse to be interviewed together. And the one they call Birdie, I can't even find her. It's some major drama going on up in there, chile.

Hey, well, it's a start. Anyway, make sure to tell them I caught em at the Uptown in the sixties, and they were sensa-tional! Turned it out with their singing, and their dancing. Those girls had some boss moves.

Yeah, yeah, yeah.

And get some autographs.

Okay, okay.

And, Legs?

For God's sake, Roe.

Take it slow and easy, roadie. Remember, everybody don't like that bright light shining on em.

Chapter 3

*

Legs: Reporter's Notes

I've always been the kind of person that people confide in. Not just friends or family, all kinds of people. Mere acquaintances, folks I've met on buses, trains, airplanes, in bars and beauty salons. Anywhere. I don't know, maybe I should have been a psychiatrist. Or a bartender. Or Oprah.

For whatever reason, I have been the keeper of secrets people never told their mamas, their daddies, their spouses, or their priests. And I just love to listen. I guess that's the reason I became a reporter. One of the reasons, anyway. Like anyone else, I've got my own secrets, too, which I'll keep to myself for the time being, thank you very much.

The conversation with Roe really pissed me off. The fact that she was dead-on right pissed me off even more. Roberta Johnson Willis is my best friend in the whole wide world, and she knows me sometimes better than I know myself.

The assignment from the Philadelphia African-American Cultural Commission had fallen into my lap like rain from heaven on a hot, parched desert. Having put in my twenty years as a general-assignment reporter for a major daily, I was locked down in the middle of a midlife crisis. I was sick to death of my job, tired and worn down by petty office politics, favoritism, and the debilitating feeling of fighting over every little crumb just to stay ahead in the game. I wanted out, I longed to retire, to throw my hands up in the air, curse my boss and his mama, and storm the hell out, slamming each door as I ran all the way through the front door to freedom.

But freedom to do what? I was far too young to be sitting at home watching the soaps all day, and not quite ready for the ladies' flower-arranging and sewing circle down at the Senior Community Center, thank you very much. Besides, I couldn't afford to just up and quit. I had a little money in the bank, but I was saving some of it for my prodigal son, should he ever decide to come back from California, where he had run off to "find my father and find myself." What he needed to do was finish college and "find himself" a decent job. Last time I talked to him, he was "bussing tables by day, and playing music on the streets by night." For money.

Jesus.

So there I was, stuck smack dab in the middle of the muck with no foreseeable way out, when two things happened:

First, my beloved father died, leaving me not only a tidy little sum of cash, but also two six-unit apartment buildings, fully rented.

Second, I received the assignment from the AACC to do a series of pieces on the lives of singers and musicians who are and were either native or "honorary" Philadelphians.

As for the first event, I am still grieving. For this motherless girl, Dad was the only parent I had ever had. Or needed. Or so I thought. But more on that later. I don't want to get ahead of myself.

As for the second event—JACKPOT, JACKPOT, JACK-POT! These people were going to send me, a writer who had specialized in music writing ever since I began my reporting career, they were going to send me out on music stories? And they were going to pay me to do it? Philly music? And on top of that, *Black Music Magazine*, for which I was writing freelance, had optioned the reprint rights to the Sweethearts' story. Double-bubble!

My daddy must have been whispering straight into God's ear.

Slightly beat down and brokenhearted from a recent love affair gone bad, not to mention the untimely death of my dad not even six months ago, I should be delighted at the prospect of writing the story on the Sweethearts of Soul. It would be, as Roe had so plainly put it, a "piece of cake," an easy A, a no-brainer.

The Sweethearts of Soul had been a big Philly singing group back in the mid-sixties, and though they had only had one record to reach the national charts—the double-sided "You May Not Know" and "Change My Mind"—they had managed to remain active well into the mid-seventies.

Like Roe, I had also loved both songs, and had considered them the definitive versions.

As far as the dancing Roe kept raving about, I had no memory at all of that. Dancing? Hmn. I remembered seeing them perform at the old State Theatre in West Philly as the opening act on a rock-and-roll show, but my recollection of their performance was hazy.

Back in those days, I had been too busy running track to pay much attention to anything else. Back then, I was convinced that I was destined for Olympic glory. But an ankle injury from a pickup basketball game put an end to all that, and the closest I ever got to the Olympics was watching them on TV along with everybody else. All that running got me two things: a full athletic scholarship to college, and the nickname that remains with me still. Wisely, I had majored in journalism—"something to fall back on."

Anyway, for the life of me, I couldn't figure out why the Sweethearts of Soul were being honored by the Rock and Soul Foundation, a prestigious organization of musical and cultural heavyweights whose primary goal was to honor the innovators and pioneers of rock and roll, soul, and rhythm-and-blues music who were so often overlooked by the larger, more established (i.e., white) music-awards associations.

Don't get me wrong. I'm all for giving people their due, their props, for the artistic contributions they've made, especially when they're still alive to appreciate them. Along with the honor of the award itself, there was a cash prize given to each recipient or group, which would shake out to a couple of thousand dollars apiece, and that was all good, for a lot of the honorees had fallen on hard times and could surely use the money.

Back in the fifties and sixties, recording artists were routinely cheated out of royalties, songwriting credits, and so forth, and they knew they were being cheated. But what could they do? It was strictly a take-it-or-leave-it situation, and it never occurred to these talented young originals, these children of sharecroppers and servants, of maids and porters, to question the status quo. A little bit of something was better than a whole lot of nothing, they reasoned. So they took it.

There were scores of young people, grandchildren and great-grands, even today, attending the finest universities in the country, their tuitions bought and paid for with money made from the sweat and talent of these pioneers. So if anyone needed to be honored, it was surely them.

But the Sweethearts of Soul? I just didn't get it.

The Sweethearts of Soul? Who dat?

Chapter 4

✳

There were four of them in the beginning: Ruth, Venus, Addie and Fluffy. And they weren't always the Sweethearts of Soul, oh, no. At Fire-Baptized Pentecostal Church, they were widely praised as the singing Sherwood Sisters, while at school they were ridiculed and teased, and jeeringly called the Home Girls. . . .

—from *Black Music Magazine*

Ruth

"She's a lyin sack of shit, and her nickname is Doodoo, and you can tell her I said so. Just don't look in that lazy left eye when you tell her. I can't be responsible, and that's the truth, or my name ain't Ruth!"

Aw, hell. I had started out on the wrong foot already. The first member of the Sweethearts I had contacted was Adeline Lights. She had seemed quite friendly when I called, informed her who I was and how I had obtained her telephone number, and explained that I wanted to do an article on them in connection with their being inducted into the Rock and Soul Foundation's Hall of Fame.

However, on the morning we were to meet, she had phoned me to postpone the interview for another time, mumbling vaguely about some sort of emergency at one of

her properties. Properties? She had offered no further expla-
nation, but had suggested that I call Cleo's Place, a bar
located on the Fifty-second Street strip in West Philadelphia
where Ruth Thomas, another Sweetheart, sometimes worked.

"Make sure you call sometime after twelve, one o'clock.
Ruthie will probably be in there by then. She's there just
about every afternoon, whether she's workin or not. It's
kinda like her office."

I had innocently relayed this exchange to Ruth, now
sitting across from me at a tiny table in Cleo's, wearing
what I hoped was an engaging smile. Miss Thomas was not
amused.

"See? That lazy-eye cow think she know my business.
All up in my shit wit no toilet paper. She don't know jack."

Uh-huh. I tried to clean it up, assured her that I had
meant no harm, but by now Miss Thomas had reared back
in her chair, crossed her legs, lit up a Kool, cocked her
head, and was eyeing me suspiciously.

"So, you drinkin?"

She gestured with a backhand in the direction of the
bar, which was half-filled with patrons seriously into the
Jerry Springer Show, cheering wildly and yelling things
like, "Sit down, hoe! Sit down, hoe!" and "Kick that sorry
bitch's butt" from time to time.

I'm drinking.

"You buyin?"

I'm buying.

A sly smile crept across her face.

"Hey, Hot Rod! Drinks over here. The lady's buyin.
What you havin, honey?"

She was leaning toward me now, fake smile still in
place. I asked for a Miller's Draft.

"Miller's Draft, Hot Rod, and I'm havin champagne."

Ruth Thomas stared at me hard then, daring me to dis-
agree. I shrugged, smiling weakly. We sat like that, her
smoking, me smiling, until Hot Rod, an old player if I ever
saw one, with Jheri-curled hair, a pencil mustache, and
blazing gold front teeth, shuffled over with the drinks.

"Is it your birthday or somethin, Ruthie?" Hot Rod
glanced over at me, smiling.

"Hell, no, it is not my birthday. I am being interviewed
by this nice lady from *Black Music Magazine*, if you must
know."

Ruth spoke loud enough for the whole damn bar to hear,
but the patrons were too engrossed in *Jerry Springer*—
which now featured two women engaging in a hair-pulling
fistfight over a man who looked to be at least eight months
pregnant—to pay any attention to her. Hot Rod was
impressed, though. Ruth smiled broadly up at him, knowing
that by tonight everybody at Cleo's would know that *Black
Music Magazine* had sent a reporter, in person, just to interview her.

This seemed to soften her mood a touch. But just a
touch. We sipped in silence for a moment, while I pulled
out my own cigarettes from my pocketbook and lit up.

"So, you wanna talk about the SOS, huh?"

"The SOS?"

"Yeah. The Sweethearts of Soul. We called ourselves the
SOS for short."

Okay, I get it. I explained to Ruth that even though a
brief article had appeared in our magazine concerning the
group in connection with the award, our editors wanted a
more in-depth piece chronicling the group from its origins
up to now.

"Ori-*what*?"

"The beginnings, the early years."

"Oh! You mean you wanna know how we got started?"

"Well, yes. I understand Fanya Dance was one of your original members."

"Oh, hell. Is this interview gone be about Fluffy or about the SOS? Because if this is all about Fluffy, you're wastin your time. I'm done."

And with that, Ruth Thomas rose abruptly, grabbed her champagne bottle and glass, and started walking away.

"It's *not* all about Fluffy! It's about the Sweethearts of Soul, each and every member of the Sweethearts of Soul!"

I hadn't realized I was yelling until the folks at the bar all turned in unison, staring from Ruth to me, waiting expectantly, as if they were about to see the two of us duke it out like the women on the television screen. Dayum. But no, Ruth whirled around, returned to her seat, and suddenly fixed me with a bright smile.

"Well, all right now. I'm ready. Shoot!"

It was then that I noticed, even in my now-rattled state, that Ruth Thomas was quite an attractive woman. Tall, broad-shouldered, and small-waisted—though solidly built— her slicked-back chignon accentuated her deep-chocolate, nearly flawless skin. Her eyes were dark, intense, and clear, and the only hint of her age (I knew she must be damn near fifty or thereabouts) was the deep furrow between her somewhat thick, closely knit brows.

Except for a light lip gloss, she wore no makeup, and her only jewelry was a pair of large hoop earrings. She was dressed in jeans, sneakers, and a short black leather jacket. I jumped right in and went for broke, asking if it was true that they had been expelled from the Fire-Baptized Pentecostal Church for singing rock and roll, a little tidbit I had picked up in my admittedly spotty research.

"Hell no, that ain't true. See? See how people just go round makin shit up? That *never* happened. Now, it's true that MuDear and PawPaw wasn't too happy with us for singin what they called the devil's music, and neither was the congregation at Fire-Baptized. But once they saw that was what we were gone do, and that we were bound and determined, they all gave us their blessing. We were always made welcome there. Still are, for that matter."

"MuDear and PawPaw?" Visions of Jed and Granny Clampett ran through my head.

"Yeah, our foster mom and dad. You say you did some research? Didn't you know we were fosters?"

"Yes, I had read something about that. But I thought it was kind of a temporary situation."

"Temporary? Hell, no. All five of us came to MuDear when we were small children, all less than five years old. Except Birdie—she was about five or six when we got her. MuDear and PawPaw Sherwood are the only parents we have ever known."

I sat still, letting that information digest, as Ruth stared at me quizzically.

"The Home Girls. That's what they called us, from the time we were little girls. First we were the Home Girls. Then, when we started singin gospel, we were known as the Sherwood Sisters. And after that came the rock and roll, and we became the Sweethearts of Soul. Look like the name stuck, huh?"

Ruthie winked, laughing softly.

"Tell me about those early days," I pushed. "Tell me about the Home Girls."

"Oh, God, the Home Girls. The holy terrors, the angels with dirty faces. Yup! Hangin out on the rooftops, kissin boys, gettin drunk backstage at the clubs, playin strip poker with the band! That was us, all right. Not! Well, at least not *then*.

"I swear, I wish we had done just half the stuff we were accused of doin back then! Trust me, if we hadn't been watched like chicks that shit gold bricks, I woulda been doin it all. And that's the truth, or my name ain't Ruth!"

Venus

"Oh, angels we were! Day in, day out, dawn to dusk, walkin with the Lord. Lil lambs of Christ, we were washed in His blood till we were white as snow! I do believe we must have been the purist, shiniest, whitest little black girls in Philadelphia!"

Venus Jones is laughing heartily, while pinning up a hem on a stunning white wedding gown. I am seated on a cozy little loveseat in her bridal shop, Gowns by Venus, sipping herbal tea with lemon, and it's the day after my brief meeting with Ruthie.

Things had been going quite well between Ruthie and me, until she stopped to take a telephone call at the bar. When she returned, she shrugged apologetically and promised to meet with me another time. As she rushed out the door, I thought I had heard her saying something about some "family problems," though I wasn't sure I'd heard her correctly.

"Oh, you probably heard her right, all right. Family problems means Sunni, and Sunni is definitely a *family* problem."

Venus now spoke through the pins in her clenched teeth, and her large eyes had narrowed considerably. Otherwise, she went about what she was doing. I said nothing, hoping she would elaborate, but no deal. Girlfriend was not giving up the tapes. Presently she came over and sat beside me.

"So, what did Ruthie tell you about us?"

She leaned forward, studying me in a casual but thorough manner. Venus Jones was a pleasantly plump, honey-colored woman with a moon-shaped face and large almond-shaped eyes that gave her an almost Asian appearance. Somewhat demure, she seemed like the last person you would expect to find belting out rock and roll in some smoky nightclub, and much better suited to a Sunday church choir. I told her so.

"But I *do* sing in the Sunday church choir. Yes indeedy, sweetie. I started out in the church choir and I ended up in the church choir. Didn't Ruthie tell you nothin?"

"Well, not much," I admitted, which was true. All I had picked up so far was that the girls had begun singing in the church their foster parents had belonged to.

"*Belonged to* was right—all of us, lock, stock, and barrel. Three nights a week and twice on Sundays. Good God. I can see us now, five little colored girls sittin side by side in the pew, brown-paper-bag-wrapped Shirley Temple curls, Dixie-peach shined knees and elbows. 'No dark, ashy knees and elbows in this house.'

"Bright ribbons in our hair, white-gloved hands folded, white anklet socks, and black patent-leather Mary Janes with matching little purses.

"We must've looked like a set of little black baby dolls on a toy-store shelf. MuDear was so proud of us, how we carried ourselves, our good manners. People complimented her all the time about her pretty, well-behaved daughters. And, Lord, when we started singin, child, that was it! We were stars! Oh yeah!"

"I want to know just how you first started, the moment when you knew you were something special."

"Oh, right from the beginning. We were members of the children's choir, and that was us and about fifteen other kids, and Miss Peat—she was our choir mistress. Miss Peat pulled us out from the rest and put us up front. She gave us all the solos and featured parts, and even kept us after she dismissed the other kids and worked with us alone.

"In fact, you could say Miss Peat was the one who discovered and created the Sherwood Sisters. We *always* knew we were something special."

"Do tell. And how did MuDear and PawPaw feel about that?"

"How did they feel? Hell, you would've thought they was Joseph and Katherine Jackson the way they strutted around, preenin like peacocks. You would've thought it was them doing the singin," she laughed.

"Anyhow, it was all good. We were pleased that they were pleased."

"So it really was one big happy family, huh?"

"Oh, absolutely. Listen, I know how you hear all those mommy-dearest horror stories about foster homes nowadays. But trust me, in our house we got nothing but love. MuDear and PawPaw couldn't have loved us more if we were their own children. Guess we just lucked out."

"Big time. And what about your own parents?"

"What about em?"

Venus shot the question back like a Ping-Pong ball, her face rearranging itself into a cool, masklike expression. I literally felt a chill enter the room. Treading softly, I pressed on, asking if she knew or remembered anything about her birth parents.

"I know all I need to know. I know they gave me away to the state, and the state gave me to the Sherwoods, who loved and took care of me. That's all I need to know."

"And what about the rest of the Sweethearts of Soul? Are any of them in touch or reconciled with their relatives?"

"We *are* our relatives. We are *sisters*. Always will be, whether we ever speak to each other again in life or not."

Venus clanked the teaspoon against her saucer, almost spilling her tea. The chill remained. So that was it! These women weren't even on speaking terms! Whoa! It was slowly coming together now, why Addie had suggested that I call Ruth instead of calling herself, why Ruth had told me where Venus's shop was located and given me the number, instead of setting up an appointment for me.

Well, I'll be damned! I made a quick mental note of this new information, and proceeded to change the subject.

"Did the Sherwood Sisters sing only in church, or did you venture out?"

"Oh, we sure did venture. We sang at churches, revivals, tent meetings, weddings, social teas, even on the gospel radio programs. We went wherever they would have us. We stayed on the go. What with school, church, and singin—shoot, we had our own bank account before we even finished grade school."

"Bank account? Bank account for what?"

"From our earnings as the Sherwood Sisters. You don't think we did all that performing, with MuDear and PawPaw draggin us all over town, for nothin, do you?"

A slight smile stole across her face as she poured herself another cup of tea. This time it was my turn to fake an inscrutable countenance. It had never occurred to me that the Sherwood Sisters were working for money way back then. Being that they were just a bunch of kids singing church music, I just assumed they had performed gratis.

"Grat-what? Are you crazy?"

Venus paused, teacup in midair, looking at me as if I were indeed touched in the head. I shrugged my shoulders.

"Girl, who you think was payin for those vocal coaches, music arrangements, gas, the musicians, and whatnot? I mean, the Lord's music was the Lord's music and all that, but business is business."

"So, all the money in the bank account went for these . . . ah . . . incidentals?"

"Oh, no. There was plenty left over for us. MuDear paid us an allowance each week, and even let us buy some decent clothes with some of it. But most of it was saved for us."

"Saved for you for what?"

"Well, for our futures, for college. MuDear always wanted that. Singin somewhere around town where they could watch over us was fine for the time being; but her and PawPaw always wanted us to go on to higher education. They really didn't see singin as a decent and proper thing for us to be doing once we got older. Even gospel music.

"The whole idea of runnin around the country, livin in strange hotels and what all, they didn't think that was a respectable life for ladies, especially young ladies."

"But there were plenty of female gospel singers around back then traveling the gospel circuit, quite a few of them from right here in Philly."

"Yeah, that was just it. MuDear and PawPaw knew a lot of those singers, and some of the stories they had either heard about or knew about would curl your hair, or straighten it out, whichever."

"About gospel singers?"

"Yes indeedy, sweetie. They just regular people, you know, just like the rest of us. Just because they sing God's words don't mean they are free of the same flaws as we all have. We all stumble sometimes, you know."

"Amen to that. So tell me about your school days. Did you all sing in the glee club, or anything like that?"

"We most definitely did. But that wasn't until we were in junior high school. Like I said, we had so much to do, what with schoolwork and practice and singin and church and homework, we didn't have much time for extracurricular activities."

"Did you all have any friends in school?"

"A few. We mostly stuck to ourselves. Until we got to junior high school, school was not the most pleasant place for us."

"And that was because of . . . ?"

Venus dropped her eyes, busily stirring her already stirred cup of tea.

I tried again. "School was not pleasant because of . . . ?"

"Because of the teasing. Constant teasing. You know how cruel kids can be. They made fun of our outdated long skirts and dresses, our sanctified church, our natural, kinky hairstyles, Buster Brown shoes, everything. They called us cootie heads. They knew we were fosters, so they always called us the Home Girls, jeerin and spittin that name at us like we had leprosy or somethin.

"Of course, all that was before we became the Sweethearts of Soul. After that, all the teasin and name-callin stopped, and everybody wanted to be our friend."

Venus Jones then gave me a beautiful, almond-eyed grin.

"Oh, lordy, look at the time. We'll have to continue this on another day. I've got to get home to my daughter."

She jumped up and began clearing the tea things from the table.

"So you have children?"

"Just one. The light of my life, my Raven."

She gestured toward a photo sitting on a desk across the room, a picture of a lovely young girl, sitting next to a huge golden crucifix.

"So here I am, again, from the choir to the Sweethearts of Soul and back to the choir again. See, when you're raised in the church, no matter where you go, the Lord never leaves you, and you can always go back.

"Hey, can I interest you in a bridal gown? No matter if you got a man or not, it always pays to be prepared. One never knows."

Addie

"Ha! As if *she* would know! Always a bridesmaid, always a bridal-gown maker, never a bride. Lost in the sixties. That's our Miss Vee."

"Say what?"

"Oh, nothing. So what did Ruthie and Venus tell you?"

I was now seated in the grand living room of Miss Adeline Lights. I use the word "grand" because, what she had done was knock down the dividing wall between two twin homes and made the whole thing into some kind of double-wide affair, with a huge staircase in the middle flanked by large white stone lions with twinkling emerald eyes standing sentry-like at the bottom of each banister.

Adeline was the only member of the Sweethearts of

Soul who had invited me into her home so far, and I was impressed, in spite of myself.

Now, I might not be the one who would stick a carpeted double staircase in the middle of a block of twin houses. I might not plant a bunch of pink flamingos and seven stone trolls in my front yard. And I certainly wouldn't want to have matching cut-glass chandeliers on either side of the staircase. Or deep pile avocado carpeting, setting off the obviously custom-made identical French provincial double living room suite in the same vomit-inducing Pepto Bismol–pink shade as the flamingos.

As far as the heavy gold brocade drapes are concerned, I won't even go there, and it's a safe bet that I wouldn't have fake fireplaces built into both sides of the staircase.

But, hey, that's just me.

As I adjusted my eyes to the riot of color that was Adeline Lights' "sitting room," the woman of the hour busied herself with the tea sandwiches and grape Kool-Aid she had set out on the glass coffee table. Well, the tops of the coffee and end tables were glass, but they were supported by alabaster cherubs, or something that you would expect to see somewhere in Greek sculpture.

I explained that I hadn't gotten too much from Ruthie or Venus, as Ruthie had had to postpone her interview and Venus had given me a rain check after talking a little bit about the school glee club, and about how they had been hassled in school.

"Hassled, huh? Uhm-hmn. Did she tell you about the Bonner sisters?"

I was shaking my head in the negative when I first noticed it. Oh, God! Adeline *did* have a lazy eye! It wasn't really noticeable unless you looked at her dead on. I tried my damndest not to be distracted as she sat facing me, her right eye looking into mine, her left veering somewhere over toward the wall. I explained that Ruth and Venus had mostly talked about how the girls had stuck to themselves and were kind of outsiders at school.

"Oh, yeah, all that's true. We were kinda treated like freaks until we joined the glee club. Once they heard us sing, we were in, just like that. Well, that and the Bonner sisters."

Addie snapped her fingers in between polishing off one tea sandwich and reaching for another.

"Don't you want something to eat? Don't be tryin to be cute, chile, eat up. My housekeeper didn't go through all of this trouble for nothin."

"Housekeeper?"

"Heck, yeah. See, I'm a busy woman nowadays, what with overseeing my properties and everything."

"Your properties? Do you work for a real estate company or something?"

"Honey, I *am* a real estate company. Busy Bee Realty, that's me. I *own* rental properties in West, North, South Philly, Germantown, and Mount Airy. I'm gettin ready to branch out into New Jersey."

Adeline Lights spoke in a casual, nonchalant manner, but I could hear the pride in her voice, could see her sit up a little bit straighter when she spoke of her "properties." Dayum.

"So I don't be havin no time for housework and cookin. I pay somebody to do that kind of stuff for me nowadays."

"Oookay."

"So they told you all about our glee club days?"

"Not everything. Who are the Bonner sisters?"

"Oh, yeah, Katrina and Katora Bonner. Everybody called them Herculina and Herculetta, behind their backs, of course. I swear to God, they were built like Sumo wrestlers, and I ain't nevah lied! Carried these big ole Jethro Bodine picnic lunch baskets to school, ate like horses, and could whip everybody's ass in the whole class, boys and all."

Both of us were laughing now as Addie, with surprising agility, jumped up from the sofa and started lumbering around the living room like a gorilla, swinging her arms about, mocking the infamous Bonner sisters.

"Ooh, child, let me sit down here and catch my breath. So anyhow, everybody in the school was scared of em. Up to that time, they had never messed with us, and we had no reason to mess with them. Then, one day, here they come, stompin into the music room, where our glee club was rehearsin.

"See, the Christmas Pageant had been held a couple of weeks before, and that was the first time everybody at school had heard us sing. People were still talkin about it, comin up to us, sayin how good we sounded and all.

"So the Bonner sisters decided they were gone join the glee club. Good God. Now, these chicks were tone-deaf as fence posts, couldn't carry a note in a suitcase, but some-how they had convinced themselves that they sounded good! So Miss Welles—that was our music teacher and glee club director—tried them out, you know, runnin the scales with them and everything, and I swear, we had to keep our heads down to keep from laughin out loud. Some of the kids did laugh, and pretty soon, all of us were laughin.

"Everybody was scared of em and everything, but they sounded so *bad*, we couldn't help it! Sounded like the damn Lollipop Kids in *The Wizard of Oz*. And I ain't nevah lied! Anyhow, Miss Welles rapped on the blackboard with her ruler and made us all shut up. She ushered the Bonner sisters out into the hallway and talked to em for a little while.

"But not before we saw the glares of pure hatred the sisters shot back at us on their way out the door. And by next period, everybody in the whole school knew that the Bonner sisters would be whippin somebody's ass from the glee club when school let out."

"Whipping whose ass?"

"They didn't say. 'Somebody's ass' was all we heard. Now, since me, Ruthie, Venus, and Fanny Lou had been, in a way, the stars of the Christmas show, since we all had done a solo turn, everybody figured it was gonna be one of us."

"Fanny Lou?"

A quick smirk settled over Addie's face at my question. There was a wicked gleam in her right eye, the good one.

"Yes, Fanny Lou."

"Are you talking about Fanya Dance, the singer?"

"I'm talking about Fanny Lou Philpot, a.k.a. Fluffy, a.k.a. Fanya Dance, a.k.a. my sister. You can call her whatever name you want. She got plenty."

Addie refilled our glasses while I sat scribbling this new information into my notebook. Fanny-fuckin-Lou Philpot!

"Do you mean the great, the fabulous, the legendary Fanya Dance was really named Fanny Lou Philpot?" Oh, Jesus. I tried hard not to laugh, but it was no use, and when I looked up, Addie was reeling, tears streaming down her face.

"I seem to remember some vague allusions to her supposed Latino parentage . . ."

"Yeah, right. Just like my vague Latino parentage, or Ruth's, or Venus's or Birdie's. Truth of the matter is, *none of us* know what we are. Latino? Huh! Two years ago she was callin herself half-Indian. Like I always say, a rose by any other name stinks just the same!"

I broke up again, as did she. After regaining some type of composure (and jotting down that play on the Shakespeare quote) I urged Addie on.

"So what happened with the Bonners?"

"Okay. So anyhow, we were all terrified. Even Ruthie, who was the bravest of all of us and the one who talked the most trash and sold the most wolf tickets. Me and Venus had a class together and we was makin plans on how to jump Katrina and Katora before they got to us.

"Fanny Lou, as usual, was worried about gettin her hair messed up. Even though we weren't allowed to straighten our hair back then, Fanny used to put all this Dixie Peach hair grease and water on her hair, brush it a hundred strokes, slick it back into what we called a French twist, and tie it down with a head rag every night. Every night! And the next morning, honey, that girl's hair would be so slick and shiny, it used to look like a process! I mean to tell you, that do would be layin down like black licorice! So with all her hair drama goin on, we figured Miss Priss wasn't gonna be no good in no fight. No way.

"And Birdie—she's the baby, you know, and we knew if MuDear found out the four of us was fightin, we would be in enough trouble as it was. If she found out we let the baby take any part in it at all, well, it would have been better for Katrina and Katora to just go ahead and kill us and save MuDear the trouble."

"Birdie. She's the only one I haven't been able to contact. Do you know how I can reach her?"

"Yeah, well, Birdie's like that, you know, like a bird, flyin around from this place to that."

Addie dropped her eyes, busying herself with arranging the leftover tea sandwiches.

"Sure you won't have another?"

I was sure. I had already eaten two. Caviar, cream cheese, watercress, and grape Kool-Aid. Not bad. I explained to Addie that upon Ruth's suggestion, I had left a note at Cleo's with my name and phone number for Birdie, leaving out the part about slipping a twenty-dollar bill into the envelope along with the note.

"Oh, good. Ruthie will make sure she gets it, and if I talk to her, I'll tell her to call you, too."

"If I could just have her phone number or—"

"I'll tell her what you said. She'll call *you.*"

Well, that was that, for the time being, anyway. Addie's tone had made that clear.

"So, back to the Bonner sisters."

"Back to the Bonners. So that afternoon, we all gathered under the tree where we met up each day after school. A crowd had started to form around us, ready for the big fight. I was so nervous, I was about to piss my pants.

"Me and Venus quickly let Ruthie in on our plans to jump Katrina first, since she was the biggest one, and when Katora joined in, Ruthie was supposed to smack her upside the head from behind.

"So, we started walkin home, holdin our books in our arms, heads high, on through the crowd, scared shitless. I took little Birdie's hand and held her close to me. She didn't have a clue, and when she asked what all the excitement was about, we just told her to keep her mouth shut.

"We had walked about a block away from the school when there on the corner, right in front of Miss Mabel's candy store, stood the Bonner sisters, surrounded by their gang, a bunch of girls who were also scared of them and did everything they said.

"When we got up to where they were, we just walked around them, followin Ruthie's lead, and kept on walkin. Well, then the Bonner sisters started walkin behind us, followed by the crowd, who was yellin and hollerin at us by that time. I pulled Birdie even closer.

"After walking about a block, Ruthie had had it. She glanced over at me, I glanced over to Venus, and even Fanny nodded her head. We was like, whoa! Fanny Lou's gonna throw down with us!

"'On the count of three,' Ruthie said under her breath, cause we was still walkin and wanted to catch them by surprise.

"'*One.*' Chile, I could feel my knees commence to quiverin.

"'*Two.*' Venus was mumblin the Lord's Prayer like she always does when she gets nervous. Ruthie was hummin 'We Are Soldiers In The Army Of The Lord,' and I wouldn't even look at Fanny Lou.

"'*Ready, set, go, and a one, and a two, and*'—before Ruthie could say three, Birdie broke away from me, ran back to Katrina, and bashed her right in the face with her Mickey Mouse lunch box! Knocked the girl to the ground! Now, this is Katrina, mind you, the *big* one!

"'Nobody messes with MY sisters!' Birdie chirped in her high soprano voice, while she stood over the girl like she was about to whack her on the head again.

"Chile, all hell broke loose then. Katrina was lyin flat on the ground like Goliath. The girl's nose was gushin blood and her right eye was swellin up. Her dress was up to her waist and her big ole pink bloomers was showin. The boys was havin a field day over that! Her sister was crouched down beside her, tryin to stop the blood.

"Somebody ran down to the school and brought back the school nurse, who must have called for an ambulance, because they were there within minutes. By this time, the principal had walked down from the school, along with Miss Welles, the music teacher.

"I grabbed hold of Birdie and we all stood together as the ambulance folks lifted Goliath—I mean Katrina—onto a stretcher and into the wagon, followed by the school nurse and Katora, who was pointin and screamin in our direction.

"'*They did it, them Home Girls did it!*'

"Katora was still screamin as the ambulance closed its doors on her and sped away to the hospital. The principal then whirled around, lookin all of us over.

"'*Just who is responsible for this? I demand to know immediately.*'"

Addie was leaning all the way back in the sofa, eyes nearly closed, looking inward, back to the day she was so vividly describing.

"So what happened? Did the rest of the kids dime you out?"

"Not a peep. Not a word, not a name was spoken. He demanded, again and again, the names of the people responsible for what happened to Katrina. Nuthin. Finally, he turned and walked on back to the school. Miss Welles stood there for a few more minutes, givin the five of us a brief glance. Then she turned and walked back to the school with the principal."

"You think she knew it was one of you?"

"How could she? And who would think Birdie, out of all of us, would be the one to coldcock Katrina? Skinny little Birdie, the baby, wasn't even half that girl's size!

"Now, Venus and Ruthie will swear to this day that they saw Welles smilin just before she turned back to the principal. I don't know. I ain't see all that."

Addie giggled. "After that day, we never had no more trouble with the kids in school. *None* of us.

"Ruthie could have a point. The singin might have helped. But I think Birdie droppin that giant is what really did it. Like she told em, nobody messes with *my* sisters!"

Chapter 5

*

Legs and Roe

So anyway, Legs, give me the 411. What are the Sweethearts of Soul really like?

Interesting. But strange.

Strange how?

Well, Roe, they seem real guarded. I kinda get the feeling that they're tiptoeing around me, leaving something out.

Like what? Give me a for instance.

Okay. For instance, why aren't they speaking to each other? I only found that out when I talked to Venus, and I think she let that kinda slip. I tried to follow it up, but she wasn't having it.

Well, that's not so strange. They are family, you know, and sometimes members of a family won't speak for years over some trivial thing.

True, but somehow, whatever caused the riff, I don't think was a trivial thing. I think it's bigger, something important.

Really? Why?

Just a feeling, I don't know. And that Fluffy/Fanny Lou/Fanya Dance business. Do you know they're *still* pissed off at her after all these years? Incredible!

Well, the jury's still out on that one, but I hope you get to the bottom of that story. Nobody else ever has.

Hmph! The time comes when you just gotta let shit go or it will destroy you, eat you up.

Uhm-hm. Well, do the Sweethearts of Soul seem ate up to you?

Not at all. In fact, just the reverse. Venus has a lovely bridal shop down on South Street, and Addie is a real estate queen, owns rental properties all over the place.

Great. And Ruthie?

Ruthie. Yes. Ruthie barmaids in West Philly, at a place called Cleo's, when she's not doing show business.

Doing what? Do you mean she's still singing?

She's still out there trying, still believes she might catch that big break, or the gold ring, or the brass balls, or whatever it is everybody talks about catching.

Lord Jesus.

I know. She invited me to one of her gigs, scheduled for Friday.

Cool. What club?

No club, honey. It's at the Rock and Sockit Bowlerama.

What? She's singing at a bowling alley?

Yup. Don't laugh. Last week, she appeared at BeBe's Barbeque Joint. See what I mean? Interesting, but strange.

Jeez. And what about that Birdie, what's she like?

I wish I knew. So far I haven't heard a word from her, and I've left messages everywhere she's supposed to be hanging out. Birdie is a whole nother story of strange. I mean it's weird enough that the woman has not responded to my requests for interviews, even if it's only to tell me that she's not interested. But on top of that, it's the way the SOS act whenever I make mention of her.

The what?

Oh, sorry. That's shorthand for the Sweethearts of Soul.

Oh, well, excuse me! First with the nicknames, now with the shorthand. Girl, you must have been touched by a celebrity!

* * *

Phone Message
for Legs from Birdie

*Hello. My name is Brenda Wade. I understand you're look-
ing for me. Both Ruthie and Addie asked me to return your
call, and that's really the only reason I'm speaking to your
machine now. I appreciate the twenty dollars you sent, but
I really can't see how I can help you. Ruthie, Venus, and
Addie can tell you everything you need to know about the
Sweethearts of Soul, and I really can't think of anything I
could add, except to tell you a little bit about my sisters
and me.*

*It's so kind of you to do this story on us. You sound like
a nice person. They told me all about your leather miniskirt
and red cowgirl boots. Girl, you were the talk of Cleo's bar
all week. All the men are still talking about your long legs,
and, between you and me, any woman wearing red cowgirl
boots is all right with the SOS!*

*Addie and Venus like you already, and Ruthie, well,
Ruthie's sometimes a little slow to warm up to new people.
She can be a tough one. Don't let her put you off, she's just
got to get to know you better, that's all. But Ruthie is the
bravest of us all, and the most successful.*

*Now, Addie, she's the businesswoman of the family,
and she's the most practical. Addie's the one who can figure
out how to solve your problems quicker than anybody else.
Anybody!*

*And Venus, Venus is really our mother, now that MuDear
is gone.*

She's the one to talk to when you've got the blues, when

you need somebody's shoulder to lean on, somebody's arms to rock you and tell you it's gonna be all right. But not just for bad times. Whenever you have good news in your life, Venus is the first one you call. The first! Venus has the joy.

I hope what I've said tonight can help you in some way. Gotta go now. Bye.

✳   ✳   ✳

Legs: Reporter's Notes

Whoa! Finally, a message from Birdie! I can't believe it. I've got to play it back, right now.

Okay. I'm sitting up on my bed having a cold Miller's Draft. A digitally remastered version of "You May Not Know" is sailing from my speakers through the air. I found it on the Net as part of a compilation of sixties girl groups. It is simply beautiful. Birdie's sweet soprano soars over the lush foundation laid down by Ruth, Addie, and Venus. The voices themselves are so stark, so distinct and clear, I believe I can pick out who's singing what. It's just a simple moon, June, spoon, doo-wop tune, nothing special in the melody or the lyrics.

It's the voices, their clarity—pure, rich, bell-like, and so strong that at times, they almost sound like men! These girls got skills! As I sit here listening to the song over and over (I have it set to repeat), I am also listening to Birdie's message, to the soft, quiet whisper of a voice that still bears the vestiges of the young, gifted Black Bird blaring from my speakers tonight. How old was she then? Fifteen? Sixteen?

This marvelous, supple sound made a fan out of me immediately, this voice so full of—what's that word Birdie used? Joy? Yes! That's it. This voice so full of joy!

Ruth

"Wait a minute, wait a minute! Hold up! Hold up right now! If you're gonna stomp all over my voice like that, thanks but no thanks. I'll do it a cappella."

Ruth Thomas, perched atop the tiny stage of the Rock

and Sockit Bowlerama, had turned her back to the fairly good-sized audience and now stood, hands on hips, glaring at the members of her four-piece pickup band.

"Now, let me have that intro again, and this time, play it like you mean it."

With that, Ruthie, now facing us again, swept seamlessly into "Misty," smiling, winking, and flirting shamelessly with the mostly male audience. I sat mesmerized. In the time it takes to blow a kiss, she had us all in the palm of her hand. Ruth Thomas still had it.

I must admit that upon entering the Rock and Sockit I had my doubts.

"Still hangin out in them ole rundown bars, still buyin hot clothes from them fast-finger boosters hangin out on the corner, still actin like it's 1966," Addie had said, sucking her teeth disdainfully.

"I don't know when that girl is gonna grow up. Showbiz! What kind of showbiz is that? When is she gonna realize that it's over, been over for decades? Her big break done come and gone," Venus had commented, shaking her head.

At the time, I was inclined to agree. But as I sat in this cozy, low-lit lounge tonight, dressed in my short black velvet minidress, black-diamond patterned stockings, and the red-, yellow-, and orange-striped Bozo the Clown bowling shoes that fool at the door had forced me to rent, I thought of something Birdie had said in her telephone message to me, something about Ruthie being the bravest and most successful of them all.

Her remark made no sense to me at the time, but tonight I sat there totally hypnotized, as caught up and carried away as anyone else in that room by that rough-and-ready, bad-whiskey voice. Ruth Thomas sounded like a woman who had been to hell and back, and lived to sing the story.

Dressed in a full-length emerald satin gown, accentuated by gold cloth heels and matching gold drop earrings and necklace, she segued easily from pop standards to light jazz to straight-out rock and roll. We cheerily followed her along, line by line, song by song. We sang the melody along with Ruth, filled in the background, supplied the handclaps and foot stomps, jumped up from our seats, and shook what our mamas gave us.

People who had come there simply for an evening of bowling abandoned the lanes and walked over to the lounge, captivated both by the singer and her loud, lusty audience.

The Rock and Sockit Bowlerama lounge seated about seventy-five. When I had arrived—about fifteen minutes before the first set—it wasn't even one-third full. I took a table toward the back of the lounge, hiding my clown shoes under my chair, nervous about this sparse crowd and fearful that Ruthie wouldn't be able to fill the room. After all, this *was* a bowling alley.

I needn't have worried. By the time that bourbon-colored voice had finished the first verse of "Misty," it was on! The distraction of the bowling balls began to recede into the background as the tables quickly filled. Ruth sailed through "They Can't Take That Away from Me," vamping around the little stage as if she were playing the Palace.

By her third song, "Something You Got," she was actually on the floor, dancing between the tables, placing the mike before individual members of the audience, challenging them to sing. Spotting me trying to hide behind the menu, Ruth laughed out loud, strode over, pulled me out of my seat, and forced me to sing.

Now, people who have heard me actually attempting to vocalize can testify to the horrific, chillingly awful sound of my singing voice. I'm sure I made even the Bonner sisters sound like the Supremes. But Ruth had everybody, including me, feeling so good that it didn't matter. I raised my voice with gusto, singing heartily, "Somethin you got, baby, you oughta know-o-o-o-o . . ."

I was so seriously off-key that it probably hurt Ruthie's ears to listen. But she just laughed and urged me along, just as she did with five or six others in the crowd.

Onstage again, she went through an up-tempo "Satin Doll," then closed the first set with a heartfelt, gospel-tinged "Change My Mind," leaving the audience misty-eyed and crying for more. I've got to admit, the Ruth Thomas of the Sweethearts of Soul show was much more than this jaded, old been-there, seen-that reporter had expected.

"So you made it, huh?"

Huh? I looked up into the grinning face of Ruth Thomas, who was now seated across from me at the tiny table at the back of the room. I quickly woke myself out of my trance and grinned back.

"Sorry about havin to go off on my musicians, but you got to put your foot down with these guys. They will walk all over you and wipe their shoes off on your back if you let em. So what you think? Are you enjoying the show so far?"

I nodded, still spellbound.

"Great. Catch you after the second set."

With that, she was off, sliding into the crowd of fans and well-wishers who had come to pay their respects, signing old album covers, and posing for photos. Every inch the star!

* * *

"Oh, God. Katrina and Katora? Jesus. I had almost forgotten that one."

Ruth Thomas sat across from me at the Blue Bird All-

Night Diner, laughing like a loon as she dug heartily into her scrapple, home fries, and scrambled eggs. She'd suggested that we do this interview at breakfast after the last set, in which she had absolutely torn down the house.

I was trying to be cool, but, truth be told, I was having more than a little trouble reconciling *this* Ruthie, now sans makeup, dressed in jeans and a turtleneck, black boots, and a black leather jacket, with the glamorous, satin-clad and bejeweled figure that I had been so thoroughly thrilled by two hours before.

And though I'd never admit it to Roe, I guess I was a little bit starstruck. What a talent! What a voice! This woman ought to be somewhere making recordings. But even as I entertained the thought, I knew that at her age, getting signed to a recording contract was as unlikely as a blizzard on the Fourth of July. Not in these days of prepackaged, cookie-cutter, one-name, one-dress, one-note wonders.

The Hummingbird

She would not make a sound, no matter what.
She could hear them out there, screaming, yelling,
drunk, high, and cursing her name. But they wouldn't
find her here.

Alone. In the dark. She tried to lie sideways on the pile
of dirty clothes so the welts and bruises on her legs and
backside, where she had been struck that morning,
wouldn't hurt so much. She tried to keep from going to
the bathroom on herself. She failed in both efforts.

But that was okay. She would wait until they fell
asleep. Then she would clean herself up. And she
would not make a sound.

Chapter 6

Venus

"Ruthie was telling me about what happened with you all and the Bonner sisters, and when I asked her why nobody told the principal on Birdie, she mentioned something about what she calls school-yard rules?"

"Oh, yes indeedy, sweetie. Same rules for the park, the playground, or anywhere else.

"Let's see: '*Nobody likes a squealer*' was one. '*If you come together, you leave together*' was one. '*Everyone in the group had each other's back*' was one. And, of course, there was the '*Me first*' rule."

"Me first?"

"Sure. My rope, my ball, my jacks, me first. Or else I pack up my shit and go home."

"But then nobody gets to play."

"Exactly."

"I see. My friends and I had some of the same rules, with the exception of that squealer thing. No way were any of us going to do time for anybody else."

"Oh, yes, sweetie. In our neighborhood, at school, at church, nobody squeals. Did Ruth or Addie tell you about Simon Hall?"

I shook my head no before taking a bite of the best

chicken and dumplings I had ever tasted. Venus and I were in the right-hand window seat at Miss Tootsie's, a soul food restaurant on South Street, not too far from Gowns by Venus.

"I know our don't know/don't tell code sounds silly, but what went down with Simon Hall is a real good example of just how that thing works."

Venus was speaking between mouthfuls of a cheese steak that looked and smelled so good I was tempted to ask for a bite.

"Addie told you about Miss Welles, our music teacher in junior high, right?"

"Right," I managed to mumble through a mouthful of dumpling.

"Well, Miss Welles had picked the four of us, me, Ruthie, Addie, and Fanny Lou, along with three guys, Al and Ty Chestnut and Simon Hall, and made us into a little group. She called us her Youth Ensemble. She took us all over the city, had us singin downtown to the white folks at social events, at cultural programs, just all over.

"Well, we just loved it, especially singin with the boys. Now, we knew Al and Ty already. They lived right around the corner from us. But Simon, Simon was the kind of boy, if you were passin by him in the hallway at school, you probably wouldn't even look at him twice, and not because there was anything wrong with him. In fact, he was tall, dark, handsome, and built like Hercules. Yes indeedy, sweetie.

"The reason you wouldn't notice him was because he seemed to be doin everything he could to make himself invisible. He would be hurryin through the halls, head down, not makin eye contact with anybody. Even though he had that great physique, he hid it under these big old shirts and sweaters. Seemed like he was tryin to make himself small, you know?

"But Lord, when he sang! Good God! A voice like black gold! When Simon sang, you could feel the vibrations through the floor, right through the bottoms of your feet. Simon sounded like a full-grown man, and he was only fourteen, fifteen years old. Whole, complete, fully finished. Know what I mean?"

I nodded, though I wasn't quite sure.

"Anyhow, one Saturday afternoon, Miss Welles picked us and the Chestnut brothers up for reharsal, and we headed over to Simon's house to get him.

"As soon as we pulled up in front of his house, before Miss Welles had even stopped the car, here comes Simon tearin ass out the front door, down the steps, almost runnin into our car. He was wavin his arms and yellin for us to *open the door.* The Wicked Witch was only a few feet behind him and—"

"The what?"

"The Wicked Witch. See, Simon lived with his grandmother, and everybody on the block said she was a witch. And she was!"

"Get out of here!" I was laughing, but Venus was serious as cancer.

"I'm tellin you, if you had seen this woman, hair flyin all around her head, snaggle-toothed, eyes lookin all wild and red-rimmed, you would say the same.

"We opened the car door, scooted over, and pulled Simon in. The witch was at the window now, still cursin and what all. Miss Welles got out, walked around the car to where the witch stood, and started talkin to her.

"We could hear Miss Welles tryin to explain that Simon was part of the school music program and so on, and the witch was yellin that Simon wasn't goin nowhere, that he had work to do. I don't know what Welles said to her to make her change her mind, but finally, she walked back around the front of the car, got in, and turned on the ignition.

"'*We're going now. It's all right, Simon.*'

"That's all she said about it. Now we understood why Simon always came to the Chestnut house to be picked up, why he hurried through the school and home each day."

"Wow! So did Simon get to stay in the ensemble?"

"Heck, yeah. Simon was one of us, as far as we were concerned, especially on the night of the Christmas Pageant. Yes indeedy, sweetie."

"Christmas Pageant? So this story is leading to something?"

"Of course it is. I ain't just tellin you all this for my health's sake!"

"Okay. The Christmas—"

"Yeah, yeah, the pageant. See, the Christmas Pageant was a big deal. It was held each year at the neighborhood high school, and about four or five junior high glee clubs and choirs participated. It was a best-of-the-best kinda thing, you know? So even though we, the Sherwood Sisters, were used to singin in front of people in church and everything, we were almost as nervous as the rest of the kids.

"It was real competitive. Every year, everybody, and I mean *everybody*, would show up to see who would turn the show out. Anyway, we had three numbers to perform: 'Christmas Is Here,' 'Away in a Manger,' and, for our big finish, 'O Holy Night,' which was lead by Simon."

I found myself leaning forward, pulled into the story.

"So, the night of the pageant, everybody showed up on time and ready to go. Everybody but Simon. Chile, we panicked! Everybody was checkin the doors and hallways between acts, but nobody had seen him all night. All we could think about was the evil-witch grandmother, chasin him down with her broom, beatin him back into the house.

"Miss Welles told us that we would go on whether he showed up or not. One monkey don't stop no show, you know, but it just wouldn't be the same. We wanted Simon. That big voice of his was like our anchor. Plus, we wanted this for him. Simon had opened up a little bit to us by then, and we knew how much it meant to him.

"We knew he had to sneak out to be with us every time we rehearsed. The kids on his block told us how the Wicked Witch used to beat him with boards, electrical cords, whatever was on hand. We wanted it for him. Anyway, when the principal announced us, we took our places on the stage, and the curtains parted—"

"So you went on without Simon after all?"

"Wait a minute, wait a minute. Don't be so fast, Miss Thang."

Venus sat back, calmly sipping her iced tea, clearly relishing my anticipation.

"So we opened with 'Christmas Is Here,' and we did great. Then we segued into 'Away in a Manger,' lead by our own Fanny Lou. They even had fake snowflakes falling from the rafters onto the stage. It was really beautiful.

"When we finished Fanny's number, the audience stood up and applauded. You know Fanny was eatin that up, takin bow after bow. So after the applause had died down, we looked over to Miss Welles to see what to do next.

"But Welles was gone, disappeared from her piano bench. The stage curtain closed on us, leavin us standing in the dark. As the principal mumbled something over the microphone about a brief intermission, Welles appeared backstage, motioning to us. Not knowin just what was goin on, we followed her to the back. And then we saw him."

"Saw who? Jesus?"

"Saw Simon, fool. Girl, you crazy!"

I already knew that, but I nodded in agreement, anyway.

"'I am ready to sing,' was all he said. There was a large open gash on the right side of his head that looked to be almost an inch wide. His once-white shirt collar was soaked in red. There was blood on his face and in his eyes, and I swear, that boy stood there just as nonchalant, ready to sing.

"By this time, Welles and the principal were goin at it, while the school nurse sat Simon down on a nearby cot and treated his wounds.

"'I will not allow that boy onstage in that condition,' the principal was yelling as Miss Welles begged him to reconsider. 'Absolutely not.'

"Finally, Welles walked over, stood in front of us, turned back to the principal.

"'*This is my glee club, my ensemble, my show. And if Simon Hall does not go on that stage tonight, the show ends now.*'

"We was like, '*Whoa, Wellsie! Go head with yah bad self!*'"

"Dayum!"

"Dayum is right. Welles talked to Simon for a few minutes and then told us to take to the stage again. When we heard Welles play that intro, and when that curtain went up, Simon Hall stood out front of the choir. At first, you heard the people in the audience gasp. The school nurse had cleaned his wound and placed a big old white bandage around his head, but the bandage was turnin red. They had a dimmer light on him, but you could still see the blood.

"I'm tellin you, I don't think I ever saw anything like that in my life. We, the glee club, everyone there, all began to applaud, louder and louder, stompin our feet on the bleachers, whistlin and cheerin. Simon Hall got a full three-minute standing O before he even opened his mouth.

"'Give him that spotlight,' Welles yelled to the stage crew. 'I said, give him that *spot!*'

"We was yellin, '*Spotlight! Spotlight!*'

"And suddenly, there was Simon, a single spot shinin on him, bloody head and all, singin that song. I'm tellin you, 'O Holy Night' never sounded so good. The dance club girls were floatin around in front of us, the snowflakes were fallin, and it seemed like we were all risin up out of that school auditorium. We felt like we were standin on clouds, baby! Clouds!

"You know how the old folks say sometimes you can find angels in the strangest places? Well, I want to tell you that we all saw an angel sing that night, and turn that mother out!"

Other diners glanced over at us as Venus pretty much yelled that last sentence at me.

"Dayum! So what had happened to Simon? Had the Wicked Witch beaten him up?"

"Nah, not the witch this time. This time, it was some boys from one of the other junior high schools who figured if they messed Simon up, they would win. They had won the year before, and they had heard all the buzz about how good we were. Simon was taken to the hospital right after his performance. We all went down to see him the next day, and gave our prize trophy to him. He deserved it."

"Were the boys that beat him up expelled or anything?"

"Oh, they were dealt with, all right. They were taken care of by boys from our school. I don't know how they thought they was gone get away with that crap in the first place."

"But what about the school authorities? Didn't the boys at least get suspended?"

"Why would they?"

Venus looked at me, a puzzled look on her pretty face.

"I mean, once the school found out they had beaten Simon up, didn't they take any action against them?"

"Who said they found out? Our boys took care of em, and that was that. Like I just told you, school-yard rules. *Nobody* likes a squealer."

Addie

"Simon Hall? Wow! That's a name from the past. Last time I saw ole Simon was about ten, fifteen years ago. Still singin like thunder and lightning. Still built like Hercules. And I ain't nevah lied!"

Addie and I were cruising around West Philly in her long silver Lincoln Town Car, looking for Birdie. We had already covered the Fifty-second Street strip area, Addie parking in the streets, popping in and out of the car, honking the horn, running up onto porches, ringing doorbells.

"I seen her on the north side two, three nights ago, over there round Baby Dobbs," Tony G, the neighborhood number man said, leaning in the car, flirting outrageously with both Addie and me, offering to buy us a drink at the White Devil, his main hangout.

"Thanks, anyway, Tone. But I'm on a mission now," Addie said with a smile.

"Well, when you finish your mission, you bring your fine self on back here, and bring your fine friend, too."

We were now cruising up and down Lancaster Avenue.

"Nice ride," I had said when I hopped out of my slightly worse-for-wear Mustang and smack into the seat of luxury. Smooth and easy, it felt as though we were gliding. Snuggling into the butter-soft leather seats, I marveled at the computerized dashboard and individual climate control, amenities which had not even existed when I bought my 'Stang.

"When you can afford the best, always get the best.

That's something Fluffy used to say a long time ago, and it took me half a lifetime to learn it. But that was Fanny Lou for you. That girl always did dream big. You gotta give it to her. That's why she's somewhere up in the Hollywood Hills right now, and I'm ridin around West Philly.

"Ole Secret Simon. That's what we used to call him. Of course, that's not the name he goes by now."

"He has different names? Whatever for? Is he a fugitive from the law or something?"

Addie glanced over at me.

"Just how much did Venus tell you about Simon?"

I filled her in on everything from the glee club up to the "O Holy Night" performance.

"Oh, I see. Well, no, he's not a fugitive. Once he became a big star and everything, he took on a brand-new name for his brand-new life, moved to New York, and—"

"Wait a minute, wait a minute. Big star? What kind of big star?"

Addie cocked her eye again, as if she thought I was pulling her leg. I guess she could tell by my expression that I was not.

"Oh, I see. So Venus left out the fact that Simon Hall is now professionally known as—hold up! Hold up! This is off the record now, so turn that tape off, and let me see you do it."

After she had literally taken the tape recorder from me, made sure it was turned off, and thrown it into the back-seat, Addie whispered a name that caused my jaw to drop so wide open, I could have gotten a job catching flies.

"Get out of here," I managed to gasp. "Not him! Not the Love Man!"

"Uhm-hmn. That's him, all right."

Oh, my God. She was talking about one of my teenage

idols, a man so golden-boy gorgeous that even after all these years, my heart still skipped a double-dutch two-step at the sound of his name. Oh, no.

"I was so in love with that man, I had plastered his posters all over my bedroom walls."

"Yeah, probably you and a million other girls."

Addie was now turning left, off of Thirty-eighth, onto Lancaster.

"Oh, my God! Where does he live now? Is he married? I would give anything to meet him. Could you introduce me?"

Blah blah blah. I was gushing like a schoolgirl, and Addie was laughing her head off, but I just couldn't help myself.

"Well, as I said, I haven't seen him myself in a long time, but I guess I could put a few feelers out and find him. Now, listen. If you just want to meet him as a fan, or you want an interview or something like that, that would be just fine. But if you got anything in mind other than that, girl, you are soooo wastin your time."

"Anything like what?"

Addie was now pulling up, parking in front of Baby Dobbs's, a well-known bar and poolroom.

"Wait here."

"Fine. Anything like *what?* What would I have in mind other than—now, hold on just a minute! You're not trying to tell me that my man is gay or something, are you? *Are you, Addie?*"

I was yelling from the passenger seat just as Addie reached Baby Dobbs's front door. She turned, smiled, nodded slowly.

"As fireworks on the Fourth of July! And I ain't nevah lied!"

The Hummingbird

These folks seemed nice, these big clean girls who fussed over her hair and petted her up, who saw the bruises on her spare, naked, malnourished body and began to cry.

She liked them. She liked it here. Plenty of food to eat, a bath every night, and best of all, no fighting and cursing. Nobody getting a beating all the time for nothing. And she loved the lady already, the one who held her tightly in her arms at night, who read her bedtime stories, who rocked her and sang her to sleep, the one who called her "the baby."

The man didn't say much, but he always had a smile, a twinkle in his eye, and a pocketful of peppermints just for her. Nothing like that other one. Nothing at all.

But she worried about how long it would last, worried that she would wake up one morning and find this was just like one of that lady's bedtime stories, just a dream, that these nice folks would be gone and she would find herself snatched back with the bad people.

So she would not talk, but she could not help humming. Humming was safe; you didn't even have to open your mouth. And when the bad people came back, they would see that she had not told anybody about what they had done to her. She would not speak. But she could not help humming.

Addie

"I'm startin to get just a little bit worried now."

We were still cruising up Lancaster, Addie pulling over just about every other street corner, inquiring about Birdie. Me, I was still trying to swallow the news that a man I once would have proposed marriage to and gladly worked like a mule for every day and every night of my life wasn't ever gonna be the least bit interested in me, or any other woman, for that matter.

Damn it to hell! So fine, so built, so, so . . . masculine! Damn!

Reluctantly sweeping mental cobwebs out of my head, I forced my attention back to what Addie was saying.

"This is strange. I haven't heard from her in almost two weeks. Nobody's seen her since day before yesterday. I hope she hasn't gotten herself mixed up in no mess."

"Mess? Like what?"

"Well, sometimes that girl acts just like the nickname MuDear gave her. Just takes off, without a word to anybody. Here, then gone. Small and thin like a bird, and just as helpless. A hummingbird. Yep, that's our Birdie, all right. Think I'll swing past Fortieth."

We had been riding around for over an hour now and I was dying for a smoke, but Addie's ashtray was closed, and probably every bit as spotless as her living room floor. I had spoken earlier about having heard from Birdie only once, via telephone message, and that even then she had mostly talked about them, offering up very little about herself.

Addie giggled softly as we made a left onto Forty-eighth Street.

"Birdie came to us last, you know. She was about five, maybe six years old, all eyes, and she wouldn't speak a word. Not a one! Just hummed to herself all the time. MuDear took her to the doctor, but they couldn't find nothin wrong with her vocal chords.

"The social worker said she seemed to have been traumatized earlier in her childhood."

"Her childhood? Didn't you say she was only five?"

"Five or six, yes, but you'd be surprised what young children will remember. Anyhow, the first time we took her to church was the first time we knew for sure that the chile could talk."

"So what did she say?"

"'DRACULA!'"

"What?"

Addie was laughing so hard, tears were streaming down her face. I waited, somewhat impatiently, for her to compose herself as the big Lincoln swerved onto Market Street.

"See, we were walkin to our church, Fire-Baptized Pentecostal, and on the way, we were passing Our Mother of Sorrows, the neighborhood Catholic church.

"A morning mass was just lettin out, and a couple of the priests and a few nuns had also come outside, and they were standin at the top of the steps talkin to some of the parishioners. Because we stopped for a minute to let some of the people pass by, Birdie probably thought this was *our* church. Well, she took one look at those priests and nuns, and, chile, girlfriend commenced to throwin a fit you would not believe!

"I mean, she let go of our hands, me and Ruthie's, and laid out on the ground, kickin and screamin, holdin her hands around her neck. 'Dracula, it's Dracula. Don't let him bite my neck!'

"See, we used to watch *Shock Theater* on Saturday afternoons, and the movie they had shown the day before was *The Brides of Dracula.* Well, when Birdie seen them white-faced priests in them long black gowns, she thought they were Dracula."

"Oh, no! And the nuns were the brides?"

I was laughing along with Addie now, imagining the terrified little child kicking and screaming.

"You got it! It wasn't until we dragged the chile past the church and were about a half-block away that she settled down and took her hands from around her neck!"

"And after that, she began to talk?"

"Hmph! Talked like she'd been talkin all along. When we asked her why she hadn't spoken before, she just shrugged her shoulders. Then she went right on back to hummin, and she hummed all the way to church."

I wondered aloud what could have traumatized a six-year-old so badly that she would stop speaking.

"Who knows what happened to her before she came to us?"

Having circled the block once, Addie was pulling into a parking spot on Fortieth. I looked at her, and this time I cocked *my* eye.

"I know. Even if you knew you wouldn't tell me, right? Because nobody likes a squealer."

"And I ain't *nevah* lied."

This time I went along with Addie, mainly so I could

light up. We stopped at Natalie's, a funky little jazz spot on Market, sat down at the bar, and ordered beers. Addie introduced me to Mitch, the bartender, then proceeded to inquire about Birdie.

"Naw, can't say that I've seen her. At least, not in the last week or so. Did you go by her place?"

Her place? Staring at my reflection in the bar mirror, I pretended not to see Addie quickly cut her eyes in my direction, then back toward Mitch, the almost imperceptible shake of her head. I busied myself by making a big deal of fumbling around in my pocketbook, digging out my smokes and lighting up. I waited until we had had our beers and were back in Addie's Lincoln to ask the obvious question.

"I thought you told me that Birdie moved around a lot and you didn't know where she was staying now?"

"So you caught that, huh? Well, yes and no. Yes, it's true, she goes from pillar to post. When you get to know Birdie, you'll see. She's always lived a temporary kind of life, changin from one place to another, just as easy as she changes clothes, especially since Butch died. She couldn't make herself go back to his place, bein as he died there, in that bed. But her *place*, what Mitch was talkin about, is a property I own, a three-unit building. So Birdie has a permanent little apartment there. At least, as permanent as anything could be for her."

Addie slowed down and came to a stop. When I looked around, I was right beside my trusty old 'Stang again.

"Later, Legs. Got things to do, places to go."

Addie was smiling as she unlocked the automatic door on my side, and the next thing I knew, I had gathered up my tape recorder and was out of the car, standing in the street, and waving good-bye to the rear of the silver Lincoln. Well, so much for that. At least, for today.

Chapter 7

*

Ruth

"Dracula? Oh yeah, I remember that one. I'm tellin you, that girl had more shit with her than a lil bit. And that's the truth or my name ain't Ruth!"

Ruth and I sat across from each other at her table in Cleo's, or at least, what I assumed to be her table, since she was always sitting there.

"Birdie and Fluffy. I swear, between Birdie's round-the-clock weirdness and Fluffy's round-the-clock drama, it was about all I could take. One more like either of em would have killed me."

Ruth smiled at the memory. She seemed more relaxed and a bit more open today. I guess Birdie was right when she said it would take a little time. And Fluffy was the name I had been waiting to hear. I treaded lightly this time, recalling what had happened when I had broached the subject before.

"So Fluffy was a drama queen even back then?"

"Aw, hell, yeah! That girl was a serious diva from the day she was born. Always threatenin to do herself in if she didn't get her way, upsettin MuDear and PawPaw, gettin everybody worked up in a tizzy over nothin!"

"Do herself in? You can't be talking about suicide?"

Ruthie signaled for the bartender, ordered a second round, then leaned forward, fixing me with a smirk.

"Yeah, right. I wish. She really had MuDear and PawPaw fooled, though, knew just how to press their buttons. One week, she was gone jump out the window if she didn't get a felt hoop skirt. Then she was gone jump off the roof the next week if she couldn't have a crinoline slip to wear under the felt hoop skirt. Then she threatened to drink bleach if they didn't buy her a pink poodle pocketbook to match the pink poodle on the stupid-ass hoop skirt. Chile, please!"

Ruth took a drag off of her cigarette, rolling her eyes in an expression of exasperation.

"But it worked, didn't it? Did she *get* the skirt, and the slip, and the pink pocketbook?"

"You damn right, she did. Worked every time. Fluffy always got what she wanted. *Always.* That treacherous heifa will outlive us all. Can we change the subject now?"

Ruth finished off her vodka rocks, quickly chasing it with a Miller's.

"Fair enough."

"One of the girls, or maybe it was both of them, talked about how you earned money as the Sherwood Sisters gospel group even before you went pro as the Sweethearts of Soul, and that the money you made was earmarked for your college educations. So what happened with that? Did any of you actually attend college?"

"College educations? What college? Oh, I know. Venus and Addie must have their heads together again."

Ruthie blew smoke rings, studying me with narrowed eyes. Uh-oh.

"No, no one's done anything like that."

"Maybe I misunderstood."

"Maybe, yeah. Probably not. It's true, they did save

money for us. And it's true we were supposed to go to college with the money. One day. I can't say for sure, since none of that happened."

Ruthie paused, sighed, and stared into her drink as if making up her mind whether to continue along this line.

"Ah, what the hell. What happened was, we had been workin as the Sweethearts of Soul for about three or four years, and we were livin large. Venus had bought herself a triplex, same one she's livin in now, I was livin in a penthouse apartment downtown, luxury, you understand, and Addie was still stayin on the third floor at MuDear's house. Birdie was, well—you know, flittin around from one place to the other, sometimes with Venus or Addie, sometimes with me."

"But why? You all had money then. Why didn't she buy a place of her own? What did she do with her money?"

"Gave it away, chile! To every Tom, Dick, Slick, and Trick with a sad story. We tried to make her stop. But what are you gonna do? She was a grown woman, she had earned it, she had the right to spend it as she pleased. Besides, she didn't like livin alone. She liked havin somebody around. And we liked havin her around."

Ruth sighed, and took a long drag.

"PawPaw passed away sometime around '68, '69, and although MuDear seemed to be gettin a little forgetful at times, her physical health was fine. Everything seemed fine. So Addie moved out, and moved in with a guy she was goin with at the time. The four of us stayed on the run so much, we hired a lady to come in to clean and cook for MuDear. Of course, whenever we were home, we all checked on her and spent time over there. Everything was workin out just dandy. Or so we thought.

"One night, we were playin an engagement at the Fox Theater in Detroit, and we get this telegram from Reverend

Nichols, from our church. We called the good Reverend, and all he would say was for us to come home immediately, that MuDear's house was bein sold.

"Well, we caught the first thing smokin back to Philly, got a cab back to the house, and there's people all over the place, I mean top to bottom! The neighbors, the people from the church, some of our school friends, and worst of all, the press! We push past everybody, run into the house, and find MuDear sittin at the kitchen table, sippin from a cup of tea, as if this was all a perfectly normal thing.

"The Rev called us into the dining room, and showed us the papers. MuDear was bein evicted from the house for failure to pay back taxes. Seems she had not paid taxes on the house since PawPaw had died, some two, three years before. When we tried to question her, all she would do is shake her head blankly, then commence to sip her tea again. It took hours before we finally got to the truth.

"The bottom line was, MuDear had been tellin each of us that the other was takin care of her house and business affairs. I thought Addie was doin it, since she was the last of us to leave. Addie thought it was Venus, Venus thought it was me. It was our fault, plain and simple. All of us had dropped the ball. We had been so caught up in bein stars, we had almost let the taxman snatch our mama's house right out from under her."

Ruth looked as if she were going to cry. I nodded my head sympathetically.

"So, were the taxes supposed to be paid from the money you girls had earned as the Sherwood Sisters?"

"Hell yeah! That was the plan. MuDear was gettin a pension, and we had told her that if there was ever any need for any extra money, to feel free to take it from our Sherwood Sisters' account."

"So the Sherwood Sisters' bank account was still there? You were able to save the house, weren't you?"

"We saved the house, all right. But not from the Sherwood Sisters' account. There *was* no Sherwood Sisters' bank account. Not anymore."

At this point, Ruthie looked like she was either going to burst out crying or laughing, one or the other.

"No money? What happened?"

Ruth tried to suppress a grin, but couldn't quite pull it off.

"Mattresses and clocks!"

"What?"

"Mattresses and clocks. That's what I said. We were lookin all through the house because our lawyer had advised us that if MuDear had never been properly served with a Sheriff's notice of intent to foreclose, they could not take the house. MuDear was tellin us over and over that she had never seen no notice. So we had started in the attic and worked our way down. Birdie was the one that found the notice, and I'm the one who found the mattresses and clocks."

"Ruthie, please! What mattresses and clocks?"

"Well, Birdie had gone into the freezer to get ice for soda, and that's when she found the Sheriff's notice, stuck to the inside of the freezer."

"You mean MuDear had stashed the eviction notice in the freezer, in the ice?"

"Hell yeah! But that wasn't the worst of it, not by a long shot. Something told me to go downstairs to the basement. PawPaw had built a little shed down there where we used to keep canned goods and things like that.

"So I go back there, turn on the lights, and there's mattresses and clocks all over the damn place, all stacked on top of each other! You would have thought you were in a damn department store or somethin! You know those gold-tinted tin wall clocks they had out in the sixties that had a clock in the middle, and a picture of the Kennedy brothers and Dr. King on the sides?"

I nodded. Seemed like every black family owned one.

"Well, MuDear must have had thirty, thirty-five of em, stacked on top of each other. Then in the other corner, she had about ten or twelve mattresses, each stacked atop the other. Seems there had been some travelin salesman passin through the neighborhood about once a month or so, and this guy must have really had his charm goin on, because MuDear had bought just about everything the man had for sale!"

"Well, I'll be damned."

"'Damned' is the right word for it. We all knew that MuDear had been gettin a little slow, but we had no idea that she had become absolutely senile. But then again, bein her daughters, we should have known. Right?"

"I guess so."

"Yeah. That's the way everybody felt. The press had a field day with us, makin us look like selfish, ungrateful children who had hit the big time thanks to the sacrifices of their foster mother, then left her to the wolves. That wasn't true, but it might as well have been.

"We each pitched in and paid off the taxes, keepin the house. But after that, MuDear's health got worse and worse, physically and mentally. We canceled the tour and took turns stayin with her. But it was like she had lost the will to live. No kids to take care of, no PawPaw by her side. She was a very giving soul, you know, a woman who had to feel useful. In less than a year, we buried her."

"Mercy."

"After that, Addie moved back in. So, like I said, we did save the house. But we lost our mama. All the Sherwood Sisters got out of that deal was plenty good nights of sleep, perfect time, two dead Kennedys, and a King."

Ruthie's laugh was contagious, I couldn't help joining her.

"So this is the house where Addie lives?"

"Oh, no! I live in MuDear's house now, me and my daughter. You know Addie is the real estate queen. Oh, hell, yeah! And do you know some years after we saved that house, she almost lost it again, to another smooth-talkin fancy man? Oh, she got it goin on now, but it wasn't always that way. She done got all hincty these days, wearin fur coats in the summertime, servin the church ladies them fancy French cheese pies, makin white folks' potato salad and all—"

"White folks' potato salad . . . ?"

"Yeah, chile! Usin Miracle Whip instead of Hellmann's, shit like that. Now, you *know* she crazy."

I had to agree with her on that one. Miracle Whip? Jesus.

"I gotta give it to the girl, though. She sure learned her lesson. Miss Addie don't mess with nobody except men old enough to be her father, with plenty money in the bank. All these years, she still lookin for that daddy. You see that man she got now?"

I shook my head.

"Suppose to be some kinda businessman. Hmph! Must be the eatin business! You shoulda seen his big ole wide-load ass waddlin down the street. He's fatter than the butcher's dog, and just a couple of biscuits away from bustin clean outta them clothes altogether. And if you add syrup and butter, just one. I ain't lyin! Just one biscuit. Butter that bad boy up, let him sop it up with a lil syrup, and stand back, watch out! And that's the truth, or my name ain't Ruth.

"Look like he smells, too. Now, you know that old-ass goat got worms."

Ruth and I both collapsed with laughter. This girl was too much.

"Something else I want to ask you about, since you seem to be in such a good mood today."

"Shoot."

"What's this I hear about you sneaking out of the house when you were a teenager to sing with the boys?"

"Hell, yeah! That was me, all right, the only girl on the corner, doo-woppin with the boys! First, me and Fluffy used to sneak out on the porch roof at night when we were supposed to be up in our rooms doin our homework. We just loved that doo-wop sound. In the beginning, we would just be sittin upstairs at the bedroom window, harmonizin along with em, singin real soft.

"Then one night, they were singin one of my favorites, a song called 'Wind,' by the Jesters, and I got carried away and started singin loud as you please. And they heard me!

"'Who's that up there?' they yelled. 'Come on down, come on down and sing!'

"So I did! I tried to get Fluff to come along with me, but she was too chicken. Huh! Not this girl. I put my wool overcoat on over my pajamas, snuck down the back fire escape, tiptoed down the alley, and ran out into the street. To sing!

"After that, you could find us under a streetlight most any night of the week, in any kind of weather, with our arms stretched wide, heads thrown back, and eyes on the stars, singin to the heavens. We would stand in the cold, stand in the snow, stampin our feet on the ground to keep the blood flowin, blowin cold breath on our fingers.

"And to this day, I really can't explain why. It was just somethin inside you, somethin you had to let out. We just *had* to do it, you know? We just *had* to."

Ruth dropped her eyes shyly, then looked up at me again, and I could swear there were tears in them.

"You see, our music is our art. It's the original creative expression of black city street kids who had no music lessons, no fancy instruments to work with. But we did have the voices. So we sang the love songs of the city, sometimes makin em up on the spot, and we made a form of art that's not like anything else in the world.

"*We* made rock and roll. And don't let nobody tell you no different. That so-called Rock and Roll Hall of Fame be damned. It wasn't them white boys up there in New York. It wasn't no Elvis. It was *us* who made rock and roll. Couldn't nobody else have done it!"

It was almost an hour later and Ruthie and I were polishing off some hot sausages along with our third beers, when there was a bit of commotion toward the entrance to the bar. I was sitting with my back to the door—something I rarely do—when I saw Ruthie suddenly freeze, her sandwich poised in her hand in midair.

Before I could turn completely around, there they were, Addie Lights and Venus Jones, standing at our table.

"We gotta go."

This from Addie, whose left eye appeared to be rolling around in her head even more than usual.

Both women nodded to me, then turned directly to Ruthie again, ignoring the slightly elevated buzz of conversation circling around them.

"We gotta go," Venus repeated, then turned toward the door, followed by Addie. Ruthie jumped up immediately, laid a ten on the table, and with a quick "Talk to you later" rushed out behind them.

I sat there, slightly dazed. I was well aware by now that these ladies were barely on speaking terms—hadn't been in quite some time. What could be the matter? Having suddenly lost my appetite, I picked up Ruthie's money, and walked over to the bar, pulling out my wallet to pay my share of the tab. Hot Rod, our friendly waiter from my first time at Cleo's, was working as the bartender tonight. He shuffled over to me, smiled.

"Take a load off."

I sat at the bar, then handed him the money, aware that I was being watched by the other patrons. I could hear the word "reporter" and "music" being whispered around me. Hot Rod came back with a fresh Miller's.

"This one's on me."

I really didn't feel like another, but not wanting to hurt his feelings, I accepted and thanked him.

"Don't worry. Ruthie will get back to you when she can. They probably got some news about Birdie, and that's where they goin now."

He smiled at me and winked.

"Yep, they on a mission to find Birdie."

This coming from a man seated next to me at the bar.

"You *know* that's the only time you see em all together nowadays."

The Mission

"Somebody said something bout her bein up there on Market, messin with them people's bingo game, tryin to turn that big wheel over again. They put her out, and they say she was wanderin around out there, yellin and preachin at people, almost got hit by a car. I swear, she's actin more and more like Butch every day."

Addie was talking fast as she rolled the Lincoln up the strip toward Market Street.

"Who said all this?" Ruthie, sitting in the backseat, searched anxiously out the window.

"One of Bobby's buddies saw her and called Bobby. He called me. He's up there, ridin around, looking for her now."

Addie was visibly worried.

"Oh, God. I don't know, yall," Ruth said. "I hate to say this, but maybe, like Pastor Nichols said, maybe we should be lookin into puttin her away somewhere, so she'll be safe."

"Put my Birdie away?" Venus screamed. "Put her away where? No effin way! We're just gone have to get together and find a way to watch her ourselves. We can take turns, we can—"

"Oh, Lordy! Birdie!"

Addie swerved the car to the side of the street, her right-of-way blocked by both a police squad car and a wagon parked in the middle of Market Street. Two policemen were trying unsuccessfully to handcuff a flailing, resisting, half-naked Brenda Wade, and place her inside the police wagon.

"Officers!" Ruthie and Venus jumped out of the Lincoln while Addie looked for a place to park.

"It's my sisters! My sisters will tell you who I am! I ain't no criminal! I was just tryin to tell them people—"

Birdie chattered nonsensically as Ruth, Venus, and then Addie joined in, trying to persuade the police to release her into their custody. A small crowd had gathered.

"Let her go! Let her go!" they began to chant.

The Sweethearts hastily explained that their baby sister had emotional problems, recently had lost her husband, and so forth, while the cops sized up the situation.

"Well, ladies, this woman was disturbing the peace inside the bingo parlor, and after they got her out of there, she started removing her clothes, right here on the street."

It took some mighty fast and fancy talking, but presently the police agreed to let Birdie go. The crowd was beginning to get ugly, and they didn't want an incident.

By this time, Birdie was leaning on Addie's car, contentedly putting her blouse, jeans, and jacket back on, chatting with the Sweethearts as if nothing had happened.

"Hey, yall, I know what let's do!" She said excitedly, after they were all inside Addie's car, Birdie riding shotgun. "Let's stop for pizza!"

"Okay, Bird. We'll stop for pizza, honey," Addie said gently, heading in the direction of Atlas Pizza, over on Spruce. As soon as they had parked and Birdie stepped out of the car, Adeline turned toward Ruthie and Venus in the backseat.

"Not a word about this to that damn reporter—yall hear me?"

"Not a word," Ruth answered, shaken.

"Not a word, Ad," Venus repeated, weeping softly.

"Don't worry, Venus," Ruth murmured, reaching over to pat Venus on the arm. "We'll take care of her."

"Yeah. Right. Just like we took care of her the last time." Venus spat out the words, pushing Ruthie's hand away.

Chapter 8

*

Venus

"Yeah, she's just fine. Spoke to her last night. I don't know why that girl can't remember to tell somebody when she plans on going away."

I was seated in the living room with Venus Jones on the second floor of her triplex apartment house. Large, spacious, and comfortable, it reflected the same bright optimism I had seen in her bridal shop. Lush, cream-colored wall-to-wall carpeting covered the floors. Gigantic sofa and oversized chairs in soft peach-tone colors. Soft, salmon-colored walls. Blindingly white floor-length lace panels covering the windows. Cute little love-bug knickknacks rested on glass coffee tables. A distinctly feminine room, a woman's abode.

Venus Jones lived on a large, tree-lined street in Mount Airy, an upper-middle-class, multicultural neighborhood, but she was still a practical girl. The first- and third-floor apartments of her triplex were rented out, as well as the two apartments above her bridal shop, which she also owned.

"Well, I'm glad to hear she's doing all right. You all had me really worried, the way you stormed out of Cleo's."

"Oh, chile, please. That's not the first time we had to go find Birdie, and I doubt it will be the last."

I saw an opening and took it, hoping to finally get the 411 on why the Sweethearts of Soul weren't on speaking terms.

"Somebody in the bar said that's the only time the three of you are ever seen together."

"Well, when the situation calls for it, you gotta do what you gotta do."

I held my silence, waiting for her to elaborate. Nothing doing. Venus Jones sat back on her satin chaise lounge, her body covered in a head-to-toe white terry bathrobe, feet encased in fluffy pink house slippers, looking rested and relaxed. I sat across from her in a matching armchair, feeling pretty good myself. We were halfway through a bottle of champagne, and enjoying the Wynton Marsalis CD playing in the background.

"So, where did you say she was again? Some kind of retreat?"

"She was out on one of them so-called wilderness retreats she goes on every now and then with one of those church groups. Ah, I don't know. Birdie's kinda lost in the wilderness these days, anyway. Sometimes she can be so childlike, just a big ole kid.

"Though, for the life of me, I can't figure out why she's goin to all these different kinds of churches these days, especially considerin the way she acted when she was a child."

Venus's face dimpled into a bright smile. "They told you about the Dracula thing, huh?"

I nodded, smiling.

"Nah, Birdie wasn't too big on church. The only thing she loved about the church besides the singin was the work we did for charity—you know, collectin soup cans, makin Thanksgiving and Christmas baskets for the needy, participating in the coat and clothing drives, that kind of thing. She always did have a soft heart.

"I mean, this is a girl who cried for weeks and weeks after we went to see that movie, *Bambi*. Every time she thought about Bambi's mother being killed, she'd start up again. Talk about depressing? We thought she'd never stop. Truth be told, that movie got next to all of us. As much as we loved MuDear, we were aware that we were all orphans, really. All motherless girls. Just like Bambi."

Just like me, I thought to myself.

"And she's kinda like that now. She really hasn't been the same since Butch passed, you know."

"Butch?"

"Yeah. Her man. Butch Taylor."

"You mean . . . the singer?"

"That's the one."

"You mean . . . the beautiful one?"

"That's the one."

"So it was Birdie and Butch Taylor, huh?"

"Yes indeedy, sweetie."

"He was one fine-looking man," I offered.

"Fine? He was beautiful, he was gorgeous. Women used to purposely try to get pregnant by him, just so that they could have pretty babies. I've never seen anything like him, before or since. And he was Birdie's one true love."

"How long has he been dead now?"

"A little over a year. We expected her to be pullin out of it by now, but it seems like she's goin deeper and deeper into it. Addie took her to the minister for grief counseling, but after a few sessions, she just stopped goin. We've all tried to talk to her, but it don't seem to be doin her no good. Maybe this wilderness stuff just might work, might be the best thing for her after all."

"Let's hope so. You know, maybe you could find some charity work for her to do, since she likes that kind of thing. I've heard that doing things for others can sometimes pull a person out of his own pain."

"Good point. I'll look into it. Charity. Every time I say that word, I remember how much Birdie loved it, and how much Fluffy hated it."

"Charity?"

"Fluffy couldn't stand the word! I don't know if you know anything about foster care, but each season MuDear would take us down to the Christian Bureau, where we would pick out our clothes. Sometimes we got somethin new, but most of the time, they were old hand-me-downs. Used to drive Fluffy crazy.

"I mean, none of us was crazy about wearin hand-me-downs, but you would have thought somebody was takin Fluffy outside to be shot or somethin. She couldn't stand the thought of even bein a foster child, let alone wearin somebody else's clothes. Fluffy wanted glitz, glamour, beautiful shiny things. She wanted to light up the room like a diamond.

"But, you know, as much as we laughed at Fluffy and called her Miss Priss and everything, it wasn't entirely her puttin on airs. I mean, none of us wanted to wear ugly Buster Brown shoes. But if Fluffy had to wear em, the girl would actually get physically ill! If she had to wear anything that didn't fit her just right, she would look as if she was gonna die. And then she would start to spinnin."

"Spinning?"

"Spinnin. She would start slow, then go faster and faster, until she finally would fall down in a heap on the ground. Then she would lay there for a while, looking for all the world like a dizzy Raggedy Ann doll.

"Once, when nobody else was around, I asked her why she did it, what did spinnin do for her. She told me that the more she spinned herself around, the more everything else would fall away. She would spin until she was no longer the home girl in a too-big ugly coat, the long plain dresses, and the horrible shoes, but a star, slinking across some imaginary stage in red satin, trailing white ermine behind her, wrists wrapped in diamonds, taking her third encore.

"And I've seen her on TV sometimes, lookin just like that, just like that vision she told me she got from spinnin, before she was even twelve years old. To anybody passin by, she was just a lil black girl, amusing herself. They just didn't know. But I did. I knew that when Fluffy was spinnin, Fluffy was gone."

I sat there, dazzled.

"Oh, my God! I forgot all about the butt!"

I looked over at Venus, who was now laughing and waving her arms around excitedly.

"The butt?"

"The butt, chile! The Frederick's of Hollywood butt! Oh, Lordy! See, this is what happened. You know how skinny Fluffy was. Still is, for that matter. And at the time, Ruthie and Addie were pretty thin, too. I was the only one that had any kind of real curves goin on, if you know what I mean.

"So, one day, this big package in a plain brown wrapper arrived for Fluffy. She took the package upstairs, tearing it open as fast as she could. And when she opened it, the butt was inside! The Frederick's of Hollywood butt.

"It was really this long-line girdle kinda thing, but it had a fake butt and fake hips attached to it. Fluffy had saved her allowance and ordered the thing. Well, we spent the whole afternoon takin turns tryin on the butt. I, myself, really didn't need it, but Ruthie and Addie wanted one, too, and threatened to tell MuDear on her. So Fluffy made a deal with them, that they would take turns wearin the butt! And they did!"

"Girl, stop it! You have got to be lying now!"

"I ain't lyin! I ain't lyin! You just ask them. And when Fluffy left, she took that butt with her!

"Ooo, chile! We sure had some fun in those days! Now, you can see that Ruth and Addie had filled out by the time we were grown. But I seen Fluffy on the *Tonight Show* about a month ago, and I swear to God, I believe she still wearin that fake butt!"

Addie

"Oh, I knew I'd find her. I was wearin red, so it was just a matter of time."

I was sitting in Addie's so-clean-you-could-eat-off-the-floor living room, and the color scheme alone was already making me a bit queasy.

"Say what?"

"Red. I was wearin red. You don't know nothin about that?"

"What's to know?"

"Girl, don't you know that red is a woman's power color? It's the color of everything female, the color of everything a woman goes through in this life."

Addie was looking at me as though I were daft.

"Uh, care to elaborate on that?"

"Chile, red is the color of blood, the color of birth, of death, love, and hate. Didn't anybody ever tell you that?"

"Uh, no. I must have been out to lunch that day."

Addie Lights was looking at me, shaking her head slowly as if she felt sorry for me.

"Okay. I'm gonna tell you one of my first red stories. And I want you to listen carefully. You might learn something.

"I guess the girls told you that we used to sing at different churches sometimes."

I nodded.

"Well, one Sunday, we was singin over to Bibleway Baptist, a church not far from where we lived. We were all sittin up in the choir while the minister delivered his sermon. So, first, this man ran into the church and took a seat in one of the middle pews. He was sweatin, breathin hard, kept lookin over his shoulder.

"Then this woman wearin a red dress and carryin a big-ass lead pipe burst into the church in the middle of the service, sashayed up and down the aisles, just as calm as you please, apparently searchin for somebody in the pews. The man who had run in there before stood up and tried to sneak outta the church, but she had already spotted him.

"Chile, that woman bolted across the room, and brought that pipe down on his head with a backhand blow that would have made both Venus *and* Serena Williams jealous!

"Knocked that sucka out cold!

"Then she ran right back on out the church. About two or three of the deacons and three or four of the younger men from the church followed after her. Of course, we had to stay up in our choir seats. But we found out later that a police car saw the men chasin her and joined in. Just about the whole congregation ran outta the church at that point to see what was gone happen.

"I tell you, it was some Sunday morning! Well, she

stopped runnin finally, whirled around, lifted that pipe, and fixed them men with a stare, one hand holdin the pipe, the other restin on her hip. And them men backed off! Do you hear me? Backed . . . off!

"Just goes to show you—never mess wit a woman wearin red. And I ain't nevah lied!"

"But what does this have to do with you all finding Birdie?"

"Chile, listen: whenever you go on a serious mission, it pays to wear red. *Everybody* know that. Just like Fluffy on that *Tonight Show.* Now, she may have been dressed in head-to-toe white, but I'll bet you dimes to dollars that underneath all that white she had them red panties on!"

I mentioned Venus having referred to Fanya as a drama queen.

"Yeah, that Fluffy was a mess, but, truth be told, none of us was exactly angels. Well, Birdie, maybe. But the rest of us did our little devilment, too. Like the time me and Venus got drunk at church."

"What? At church?"

"Oh, yeah, honey. We was about thirteen then, and one night, they were servin Holy Communion at the evening service. So me and Venus had gone downstairs into the church basement to use the bathroom. Well, when we came out, we noticed—you know them lil glasses that they put the Communion wine in and serve on them lil round trays?"

I nodded.

"Well, somebody had left some of those trays on a table down there. So you know what we did, now, don't you? We both of us lifted a lil glass, counted to three, and downed the whole thing. Man, that stuff was so goood! So we drank another one. And a couple more.

"I don't know how many glasses of that Mogen David wine we drank before one of the church ladies came downstairs and caught us.

"We're like, 'Naw, naw, we wasn't drinkin no wine,' lyin through blue lips and purple tongues, right there in the church!

"Well, by that time, both of us was havin a fit of the giggles, pointin at each other and laughin, but we did have enough sense to know that we didn't want to embarrass MuDear any more than she already would be when that ole loudmouth busybody finished tellin her and everybody else in the church what we were up to. So we decided to sneak out.

"We were flyin through the park, still gigglin, when we heard the sound of the singin. We followed the music over to a group of boys standin just outside the park, and I don't know if it was because we was high or what, but nothin we had ever heard sounded as good as those guys did that night.

"It sounded like they was hittin notes nobody else had ever even heard of, sound like they was snatchin them notes from the sky. Me and Venus joined right in. We knew we were goin to get in trouble the next day, knew we'd probably be put on punishment until we were twenty-five.

"But I'ma tell you something. That night, drunk on wine, drunk on music, we didn't even care. We sang out to the heavens that night in the park the same way we sang up to the heavens in church. From our lips to God's ears!

"And that was just the beginnin of us sneakin out at night, takin PawPaw's car, drivin down to the Market Street subway, just to sing wit the boys! Chile, we was sangin! And I ain't nevah lied."

Legs: Reporter's Notes

Okay. I'm sitting here on my bed, fighting sleep as I make these notes. Let's see what we've got here so far.

Number one, Venus and Addie snatching Ruthie out of Cleo's, a place Addie claimed she'd never set foot in. These three ladies who never speak, all walking out together, like it was the most natural thing in the world. The customers in the bar whispering about them being on a *mission.*

Number two, Birdie, needing to be rescued from a *wilderness retreat.* What the hell was up with that? And why did Birdie need such protecting, anyway? Is the girl slow? Is she brain-damaged from drugs or booze? Why do the other three act so secretive about her?

Birdie and Butch Taylor! Butch Taylor, a man once so beautiful that even men turned to look twice when he walked by, a man who lost his looks, his talent, and his money to—to what? Booze? Drugs? Madness? Him and Birdie, the innocent, the *baby?* Hmn. I can't even imagine those two together.

Addie. What did Ruth mean when she warned me not to look into her left eye? Exactly what was supposed to happen to you if you did?

"Aw, that's only supposed to work on men. Unless you're gay, I guess," Venus told me, laughing and waving her hand dismissively when I had tried to pump her about it. *What* was only supposed to work?

And then there was the matter of the Sherwood Sisters' money. All gone? Clocks and mattresses? Dayum.

Chapter 9

✳

Ruth

"Well, once we started sneakin out the window to sing with the boys, everything changed. We went straight from singin in the choir to singin on the corners."

Ruth Thomas and I were sitting at her table in Cleo's on this cold, rainy Tuesday afternoon. The regulars—of which I was starting to feel like one—were seated at their usual places at the bar, this time yelling at the guests on the *Jenny Jones Show.*

"Would you look at that stank hoe? If she knew she was gone come on TV and strip down, you'd think she'd have enough sense to at least wear matchin bra and panties."

This, from a little old lady one might expect to see on any Sunday, sitting up there and nodding her head in church.

"Hmph! She don't know no better. She think she lookin *good* in that mix-match shit," an elderly man piped in.

I sat pitched forward, elbows resting on the table, chin resting in one hand, marveling at the fact that the Sweethearts had managed to sneak out of the window without getting caught, night after night, risking possible injury, or worse, just to sing.

"You mean you all never got caught?"

"Never. Girl, we had it down to a science. We would

climb out of that window, slide across the back porch roof, climb down that fire escape, run down the alley, right on out to the street.

"I think that's how we really learned to sing out, to do that hard kind of singin. When you sang against boys, you had to sing forcefully, sing strong, or you would just be drowned out, and those boys were good. But we were better. We had had years of training by then, so we had it all over them."

"So you would say your earliest influences, besides the church, came from singing with the boys in the park and on the corners?"

"Oh, yeah. And the radio, of course. One of them cow-eyed boys who was in love with Fluff had given her a little transistor radio, and every night we would turn on the Georgie Woods radio show, the "guy with the goods," and listen to all the hits. We played it down real low, you know, under the blankets. We got to hear them all, everything that was going on. I guess we were influenced by everybody.

"And there was Petie's, the store everybody hung out at after school. We would stop in there every day, and the jukebox would always be playing all the latest sounds.

"Later on, when we were finally allowed to buy our own records, we studied all the great ladies singin at the time. We would mimic the hiccup at the end of Ruth Brown's 'Mama, He Treats Your Daughter Mean.' We would practice going from the deepest, lowest register, straight on up to the highest one, like Della Reese did. We would try on Dinah Washington's phrasing for size, Etta James's growl. Chile, we did Etta's 'Trust in Me' to death.

"We practiced pleadin like Connie Francis, even blowin kisses like Dinah Shore!

"And the great girl groups! Motown! Martha and the Vandellas doin that 'Heat Wave' and 'Dancin in the Streets.'

"Now, 'Heat Wave' was a great dance record, but 'Dancin in the Streets,' that was a revolution song. I don't know what they was thinkin bout at Motown, but we took that song to mean 'Takin It to the Street'! And we did! The civil rights movement was goin strong then, cities were goin up in smoke and riots, and we was right wit em, dancin in the streets!

"Gladys Knight and the Pips, stepping to 'Givin Up'! Gladys, with that great stone gospel voice, and man, them Pips were so together, they even blinked in time. I practiced Darlene Love and the Crystals's 'He's Sure the Boy I Love' until I was hoarse!

"And you know we were crazy about our own Patti LaBelle and the Blue Bells. Them girls was strong, baby, strong!

"And the great Shirelles! We sang 'Blue Holiday' so much, people thought *we* had made the record instead of them! And we knew all the Marvelettes' songs by heart. Gladys Horton ruled!

"But the one group we really adored was the Chantels. Their sound was so clean, so pure, and for my money, even today, nobody sings like Arlene Smith of the Chantels! Nobody!

"We did the guy groups, too. In fact, the first rock-and-roll song we ever learned was Smokey Robinson and the Miracles' 'Tracks of My Tears.' We covered just about all the Temptations' material. We used to bring the house down doin 'Old Man River.' Our arrangement wasn't all that much different from theirs, except, of course, nobody did Melvin Franklin's bass parts. But people loved us to do that song, just because nobody believed that a girls' group had the nerve to even try it. And then when we did 'Dorma,' that would really blow em away!"

"Who?"

"'Nessun Dorma,' the song Luciano Pavarotti uses as his signature song today, the Puccini song. Miss Welles had taught it to us in glee club. Somebody gave us the record, by Mario Lanza, and when Bird heard it, she fell in love with it, plus everything else Mario Lanza ever sang. She was crazy for Mario! So she made us teach her the song. Honey, we could turn out a joint any day of the week with 'Old Man River,' followed by 'Nessun Dorma.' People would be cryin and and hollerin and everything!

"Chile, we even tried purring like Eartha Kitt. We took a lil bit from everybody. Pretty soon, we were showin up at basement parties and playground talent shows, competing against other groups, and winning! Again and again.

"And I'm tellin you, there's nothin like it, that moment when you're all singin hard and strong and beautiful. It's the payoff for all those hours and hours of practice. It's the moment all singers live for. Better than chocolate, better than sex.

"Girl, we beat the Cupcakes' butt so many times, they stopped showin up when they knew we were on the show."

"The Cupcakes?"

Venus

"Oh, you mean the Hoecakes? That's what Ruthie used to call em. Sure, I remember them no-singin hacks. Girl, don't even get me started."

Venus Jones and I, back at our familiar window seat at Miss Tootsie's, laughed out loud. Venus was doing a job on some smothered pork chops, while I, of course, just had to have the chicken and dumplings again.

"Honey, you wouldn't believe them heifas. First, we

beat them at a couple of basement parties. Then we kicked their butts at a few rec center talent shows. That's when they started with their dirty tricks."

"Dirty tricks?"

"Oh, yeah, chile. One time, we had a show down at the playground on Fifty-eighth and Vine. So we got there early and hung up the blouses and skirts we was goin to sing in. Well, come time for us to sing, and you know what them skanks had done?

"Them Hoecakes had taken our blouses, wet em, then hung em back up. We didn't even notice til it was time for us to go on, and they were drippin all over the floor. Another time, they mixed up our shoes so we were late gettin on the stage.

"Oh, yeah. I'll never forget em. Cherry Cake, Coco Cake, and Chocolate Cake."

"You mean, they actually called themselves that?"

"Yes indeedy, sweetie. Used to come out onstage with these big ole ribbons on their heads, carryin giant lollipops and Teddy bears, wearin those stupid-ass Mary Jane shoes. Oh, wait a minute. Did Ruthie tell you about Tricky Ricky Starr?"

"Don't believe she did."

"Oh, chile, you should have seen him. Dressed like a Disney cartoon—and, girl, you shoulda seen that hair.

"See, in the mid-sixties, we were some of the first girls in Philly to wear our hair natural, in Afros. When we first met him, Tricky Ricky never missed an opportunity to rag on us, tellin us we needed to chip in our money to get straightening combs and home perms. He was still wearin his hair in a process, which everybody called a recess even then.

"I myself was hypnotized by that hair, chile. He had this combination Little Richard/very early Diana Ross kinda thing goin on, hair hangin down over one eye in front, like Diana's, and pouffed up in the back, like Richard's. Know what I mean?

"Chile, I started to hold out my hand like a Supreme and yell, 'Stop! Stop! Stop in the name of decency and good taste!'

"But that wasn't the worst of it. You should have heard him sing. Ooo, chile. Bad. Real, real bad. I don't mean bad, like real good. I mean bad, like sucks. Big time. And the Hoecakes had the nerve to back him up. Sounded like the damn *Omen* Choir or somethin. I ain't lyin.

"So this was about a year afterwards, and everybody was wearin Afros by then. Ricky had tried to get one, but his hair was so soft and fine, he couldn't get it into an Afro. So he had taken to wearin this big ole jet-black Afro wig. And you know we never let him forget it. Between that monster bush and them loud-ass, tacky clothes he wore, he was a sight to behold. One night, Fluffy and Cherry Cake almost got into a fight over that no-singin fool. I mean, they was ready to throw down."

"You mean, have a real fistfight?"

"Yes. Girl, you should have been there. First, Ricky come strollin backstage before the show started, orderin everybody around, actin like he was in charge and every-thing. We didn't pay him no mind.

"Then he yells somethin about '*You bitches better get over here and line up for the show.*'

"Well, Fluffy took exception to that. She walks over to Ricky, wags her finger in his face, and tells him about how common he is, how uncouth.

"Well, Ricky hits the roof over that, starts yellin, '*Who the fuck you callin uncoof, bitch? I'm just as coof as anybody else up in this motherfucker.*'

"Then, of course, Ruth had to jump in. Then here come Miss Cherry Cake, gettin in Fluff's face, talkin about she don't preciate Fluff callin her man uncoof. You *know* she ain't say nothin to Ruthie. But it was too late then.

"I still don't know who threw the first punch, but I'm tellin you, everybody, the musicians and all of us, had to jump in and pull em apart."

Mercy.

"So when did the Sweethearts of Soul get to the point where you went from playing rec centers and parties for free to actually playing professionally?"

"Actually, it wasn't too long after that. What happened was, one day, on the Fourth of July, they had a big talent show at the playground, and asked us if we would appear. We agreed to do it. So that afternoon, here we are up on the stage, just singin our hearts out. I think we was singin some Marvelettes, or maybe it was the Chantels, something like that.

"Anyhow, we was just tearin it up, bringin down the house. Oh, yeah, I remember now. It was a Patti LaBelle and the Blue Bells song, 'Down the Aisle.' Well, Fluffy was singin the lead, so she was on one mike by herself while me, Ruth, and Addie shared the other. So we get to the part in the song where Fluffy's supposed to hit the high note and all of a sudden, we don't hear nothin.

"We look over, and Fluffy is just standin there, frozen like a statue, mouth wide open, lookin down into the audience. So we look down and there's MuDear, big as you please, sittin right up there in the second row.

"Well, we like to died, chile. So we went on and somehow managed to finish the show, and by the time we had got backstage, changed into our street clothes, and come back out, MuDear was gone. Now, you know we was all scared to go home. We didn't know what was gone happen. So we hung around the playground for the rest of the afternoon, just tryin to work up our nerve."

"I guess you all did. So what happened? Were you grounded for life?"

"You would have thought so, wouldn't you? But let me tell you how it went down. We finally got home and tried to tiptoe upstairs, but MuDear was too fast for us.

"*'RuthAddieVenusFannyLou! Yall get your hind parts back in this kitchen right now, and I mean right now.'*

"So we slinked back down the stairs and walked into the kitchen like some prisoners goin to the chopping block. MuDear and PawPaw was sittin at the kitchen table, having coffee and cake.

"*'Yall set your lil narrow butts down here.'*

"So we sat down. For a few minutes, nobody said nothin. MuDear and PawPaw just kept on eatin that cake, while me, Addie, and Fluffy looked over at Ruth, expecting her to speak up, since she was the one that always had something to say. Ruthie was lookin up at a crack in the ceiling, like she expected the house to fall down on us.

"Finally, it was Fluff who spoke up.

"*'So who told? Who dimed us out? Cause I just know it had to be somebody who told yall what we was doin.'*

"*'Just don't you worry bout who told, Miss Lady. The point is, I know now. I know all about how yall been sneakin all over town, singin that rock-and-roll mess. How long did yall think yall was gone get away with it? Yall know I know everybody round here, and sooner or later, I was gone find out.'*

"MuDear was biting her lip, shakin her head. She looked like she was about to bust out cryin. We all looked down at our hands.

"'*All this time, I thought I was raisin good, decent Christian girls to sing the Lord's music, and here yall are sneakin around behind my back, singin for Satan, singin the devil's songs.*'

"'*We have not. It's not the devil's songs, MuDear. It's our own music, and the devil ain't got nothin to do with it.*'

"Well, me, Ruth, and Addie just stared at first, as Fluffy went on and on, defiantly defending our music. We couldn't believe it, chile.

"'*I can't speak for Ruth or Venus or Addie, and I'm not tryin to. I can only speak for me, and I'm tellin you I believe God gave me this voice to sing this music. He gave me this voice to use as a way out and a way up. I'm going to be a star. I've always known it. And nobody and nothing is gone stop me from singin my music.*'

"'*Don't you dare bring God's name into it. God ain't got nothin to do wit it. We taught you gospel music, music that glorified His name, not Satan's.*'

"'*What do you mean, Satan's? All we sing is love songs. What's so wrong with that?*'

"I don't know if they told you or not, but the first hard, fast rule in MuDear's house was no back talk. Uh-uh. We might roll our eyes or mumble somethin under our breath every now and then, but that's as far as it went.

"But Fanny was leanin forward all up in MuDear's face and everything. Her mouth was all poked out, and she had that look in her eye, what I call that killer look.

"It's the same kind of look you see on the faces of top athletes sometimes, just before they get ready to do their thing, the kind of look that tells you to get out of their way cause they don't wanna kill you but if they have to they will cause they mean business.

"It startled MuDear so bad that she actually backed off, leaned back in her chair away from Fanny. Me, Ruthie, and Addie sat there, afraid to breathe.

"'*So you bound and determined to do this thing, huh, no matter what we say.*'

"This was the first time PawPaw had said anything. PawPaw was what you would call the strong, silent type. Usually, he went along with whatever MuDear said, but every now and then he would speak up. And when he spoke, everybody listened. This wasn't even a question, it was a statement.

"'*Yes, sir,*' Fluffy tells him. '*If God hadn't wanted me to sing this music, He wouldn't have given me this voice, this talent, and He wouldn't have made me so good at it. And with all due respect, sir, nobody's going to stop me from singin it. Not you, not MuDear, nobody.*'

"Fanny was talkin so quietly now, she was almost whisperin. I was scared. The chile looked like she was gonna start spinnin or somethin, and MuDear was lookin at her like she was speakin in tongues.

"'*And how about the rest of yall? Do you all feel the same way?*'

"PawPaw was lookin from Ruth to me to Addie. Ruth grabbed my hand under the table, I grabbed Addie's.

"'*We all feel the same way, sir. We don't see no harm in singin about love. Only difference is, in church we sing about the love of God. In the streets, we sing about the love of people. We don't see no harm in that.*'

"With Ruthie having drawn her line in the sand, PawPaw looked over at us. I nodded my head, agreeing with Ruth. Addie did the same.

"So there was the four of us, standin our ground for the first time against MuDear and PawPaw. I was so excited my hands were sweatin. We didn't know if they were gone kick us out of the house or what. They could even have sent us back to the Children's Bureau if they really had a mind to, and they would have been within their rights.

"God knows we didn't want that to happen. This was really, when you came down to it, the only home we had ever known. But like I said, singin, there's nothin else like it. Nothin else in the world. Specially singin rock and roll.

"'Yall go on up to bed,' PawPaw said.

"He started to say more, but, for whatever reason, he let it drop at that. The four of us filed out of the kitchen, up the stairs, and into our bedrooms. None of us said another word about it that night.

"The next day was a Sunday. We went to church and sang in the choir, as usual. After church, we came home, got our clothes ready for the next week, and had our dinner, as usual. Nobody said anything about what had happened the day before.

"Now, on Sunday nights, we usually went back to church at around seven for the evening service. But when we started upstairs to change back into our Sunday dresses, MuDear told us to hold off on that, that they were expectin a visitor.

"Well, I don't have to tell you how nervous we were, do I? We just knew they had called the people from the Bureau on us, and we were about to be taken away, separated forever.

"We heard the doorbell ring, heard MuDear answer it, then heard an unfamiliar male voice speakin. We sent Birdie downstairs to spy and see who it was. She was back in no time, cryin and carryin on, talkin bout MuDear and PawPaw tellin this man all about us, about how we had been sneakin out and singin at the playground, and on the street corners with boys, just everything.

"Seems MuDear had received an anonymous call from somebody who claimed to be a 'concerned neighbor.' Everybody knew it wasn't nobody but them damn Hoecakes who did it. I'm tellin you, those chicks would do anything to take us out. Birdie blathered on about MuDear tellin the man that she was at her wits' end, that she didn't know what to do with us, that we was out of control, blah, blah, blah, you know, all that kind of stuff, before her and PawPaw realized that Birdie was in the room, and made her go back upstairs.

"*I don't want yall to go, I don't want yall to go. If they take yall away, I'm gone run away, too.*'

"Birdie was workin herself up into a real fit. We were doin our best to calm her down, but truth be told, we were every bit as upset as she was.

"Finally, MuDear called us downstairs and into the kitchen. Seated at the kitchen table between her and PawPaw was this man. He was old, and by that, I mean anybody over thirty was old to us in those days. But he was handsome. Looked a lil bit like Billy Eckstine.

"He nodded pleasantly as he was introduced to each of us by MuDear. We sat down side by side, holdin hands under the table again. PawPaw cleared his throat.

"*All right, girls. I'll get to the point. As you know, MuDear and me really don't hold no truck wit that rock-and-roll stuff. We don't have no use for it at all. But we had a long talk about that last night after we sent yall to bed.*

"*And after seein the way yall all lined up behind Fanny like that, we made a decision. If singin that music means so much to yall, we're just gone have to get with the times.*

"*As much as we might hate that mess, we love yall, and we don't want yall runnin round out there in the streets, gettin yourselves mixed up with the wrong kinds of people, and gettin taken advantage of.*'

"The four of us stared at PawPaw in stunned silence. Chile, we couldn't believe what we were hearin. Then MuDear spoke up.

"*And that's why we decided to call Mr. Dunn, cause if anybody knows about that worldly music, it's Jimmy Dunn.*'

"She was right. Jimmy Dunn was a classically trained musician who had started out singin and playin piano in our church years ago, before branching out into what the church folks called 'worldly' music when they wanted to be polite. Now, he wasn't no rock-and-roll kinda guy. He was more into standards, jazz—you know, that Nat King Cole, Joe Williams, Johnny Hartman kinda stuff.

"But he and his trio had played some of the top supper clubs in the country during the fifties, and they had backed many famous singers. His act had played all over Europe, all around the world. He had worked with some of the best. When the music started to change in the sixties, he quit performing and opened a small studio in his basement, where he gave piano lessons and did vocal coaching.

"Jimmy was polished and polite, and he knew just how to talk to the old folks, to calm their fears about the so-called devil's music. So he became our vocal coach and manager.

"Now, we still continued to sing gospel in church on Sundays, appearing at teas and socials and the like, but now, in addition to that, we were coached every week by Jimmy Dunn, who saw us as some sort of potential supper-club act and was groomin us to play the country club resorts, the Catskill Mountains, the Poconos, places like that.

"That sounded boring as hell to us, but, hey, it was damn good money, and it was a start. So we sang gospel at church and standards at Jimmy's—and *still* snuck out on the corners to sing rock and roll with the boys. You know we did, chile!

"Jimmy was a good manager, and within about six months we were actually playing nightclubs. That's right. Nightclubs! Fifteen-, sixteen-year-old girls, singin in the clubs. Now, I know what you thinkin. You thinkin we was runnin round with this one and that one, havin wild affairs, goin round town with dangerous men and all, huh?

"Come on, now. You can tell the truth. That's what you thinkin, ain't you?"

I had to admit that's exactly what I was thinking, and it must have shown in my smile, in my eyes. Teenage girls living a rock-and-roll life at an age when I couldn't even stay out past ten on a school night. Wow!

"Ha! A rock-and-roll life, huh? Not! Girl, Jimmy was so tight on us, we couldn't even go to the bathroom without him walkin us there, then standin outside waitin for us until we finished. Almost as bad as havin MuDear with us. Couldn't do shit."

"Oh, come on now, Venus. First of all, here it was the wild, wild sixties. Second, here you all were, young, gifted, and Black, singing all over town. I've seen some of those old eight-by-ten glossies of all the local music guys who were playing the same clubs you were playing at the time. Are you trying to tell me that not one of you managed to get with any of those fine singers and musicians?" I cocked my eye at her, my disbelief as broad as my smirk.

"Oh, don't get me wrong. We met all the other singers and musicians on the local circuit, and there was some fine men in Philly music circles, let me tell you. We met em, we grinned and winked at em, all right. But that was about all.

"A typical show for us back then went down somethin like this: Jimmy would pick us up in his van, and when we would arrive at the venue, he would promptly usher us backstage, where we had to wait in so-called dressing

rooms that were really nothin more than dingy, window-
less storage rooms filled with cases of beer, broken-down
tables and chairs, cracked-up mirrors, and stuff.

"At showtime, we went out, did our act, left the stage,
and went right back to the dressing room until the next set.
After the show was over for the night, we changed back into
our street clothes and still hung around in them funky so-
called dressing rooms, waiting for Jimmy to get paid, after
which he would hustle us right back out of there, back into
the van, and then straight home.

"That was that, as far as our rock-and-roll life went in
those days. And it was the same ole same ole, every place we
played, and things never changed. Until we got the record
deal, of course."

"Ah, the record deal. That was it, huh? I bet the stuff
really hit the fan then, huh?"

"Wellll . . . yes and no."

Venus had finished her meal and was now leaning back
in her chair, staring out the window, a faraway look in her
eyes. I waited for her to continue, but she said nothing. I
cleared my throat.

"Uh, yes and no?"

"Oh, God. You have to excuse me, chile. I was lost in the
sixties there for a minute. So where was I?"

"You were getting ready to tell me about the record deal."

"Oh, yeah. The deal. Well, like I said, Jimmy had us
performing all over the place. We played all the nightclubs
in the Philly, New Jersey, and Delaware areas, and back
then, there were plenty of nightclubs, honey. It's not like
today. This was before disco killed the live music. We used
to work sometimes straight through from Wednesday night
to Sunday night. And we *still* sang in the choir on Sundays.
Oh, yeah.

"Girl, we stayed busy, and the more dates we played, the better we got. We might have been still in high school, but we were polished pros. Not only did we play the clubs, we played all the local colleges and social functions at the downtown hotels, sometimes at places where we would be the only Black people in the room. Well, maybe the janitor would come in later, to clean up. And this was in the mid-sixties, chile, and we didn't even have a record out."

"Dayum. I'm impressed."

"Well, after doing that for about a year or so, Jimmy decided the time was right for us to shop around for a record contract. So he set up an audition for us with Chance and Lane. Well, not really an audition. He set up a showcase for us."

"A showcase?"

"Yeah. Back in the day, if you wanted a record producer to see your act, you invited them to see you perform at a local club. This gave the producers a chance to not only hear how you sounded but also to see what you looked like onstage. You know, to see if you were marketable. They called it a showcase.

"Now, Chance and Lane were just starting out then. They only had a couple of groups and artists signed, but their music was young, it was hot. It was soulful and slick at the same time, and they were developin a reputation for bein up-and-comin major players."

"Hey, tell me about it. Musically, those guys put Philly on the map. So you girls were right there at the beginning, huh?"

"At the beginning? Hmph! We was right there when Carl Chance and Ronnie Lane's so-called offices were right behind this lil record shop they used to run. We helped out workin in the store when they were in a jam sometimes, and also worked at their Under 21 Club. Were we *there*? Hell, we practically pressed up our own records. I know they're all slick and sophisticated now, but it wasn't always that way, trust me.

"Anyway, Al and Ty Chestnut were already signed with them, and a lot of the musicians we had worked with around town were on board as session players. Musically, it was the place to be.

"But anyway, like I say, back in those days they were just gettin started. So we were playin a local spot in South Philly, Emerson's Bar and Grill, and the—"

"Emerson's? You mean the place where all the old-time greats played? Billie, Dinah, Ruby Raines, and them?"

"That's the place. Honey, everybody who was anybody played Emerson's. So anyhow, we had a four-night gig there, and Jimmy had invited Chance and Lane to come down and catch our show. So we do the show, and thank God it was too dark in there to even see the people at the tables, cause we was plenty nervous that night. We was used to playin for all kinds of people, but just knowin that Chance and Lane were sittin in the audience, just knowin that these two guys could make us stars, had us stoked to the max.

"And, girl, we burned the stage down that night. Set fire to the motha! Killed! After the show, Jimmy ran backstage, and I do believe he was more excited than we were.

"'*Girls, girls, you were fabulous! They loved you! Now, hurry up and get into your street clothes, because Carl Chance and Ronnie Lane are out there waiting to meet you.*'

"Well, you know we were thrilled, just floatin on air! And you know, Legs, I would like to tell you that we were surprised, but we weren't. Not really. We knew. We always knew we were gone make it. We never doubted it, not for a minute."

"Especially Fluffy, huh?"

"*Especially* Fluffy. You got that right. So anyhow, we changed our clothes, went on out to the table, and met Chance and Lane.

"They were very excited about us, and once we told them we had a couple of original songs, they wasted no time settin up an appointment for us to come down to their offices.

"Within two weeks we were signed."

"Dayum! Guess you guys were on top of the world then, huh?"

"Oh, honey, you couldn't tell us nothin. Ruthie was struttin around, swearin she was gone be the next Dinah Washington. Fanny was already practicin signin her autograph. And me and Addie, we were just glad to be there."

"Signing her autograph? Get outta here!"

"I ain't lyin! I ain't lyin! Ask Ruthie and Ad. The girl was fillin up comp books, signin her name over and over. First, she would sign her real name, Fanny Lou Philpot. Then she took to signin as Fluffy. Next thing you know, she had renamed herself Fluffy LaTour."

"Go on, girl!"

"No lie! Don't even ask me where the LaTour part came from. Oh, and did I tell you about Ricky Starr, Tricky Ricky Starr?"

"Ricky Starr? You mean the guy with the monster bush, the uncoof one?"

"One and the same, chile. Well, Ricky was on the same bill with us that night. In fact, he had opened the show, and he was pissed off at us as usual. He felt he was the star of the show, and therefore, he should be the one to close the show. As usual, we ain't pay that no-talent hack no mind.

"Anyway, after we talked to Chance and Lane and they had left, we all went back into the dressing room. I mean, we were so excited, we were pinchin ourselves. All of us, that is, except for Fanny, who had pulled a disappearing act. And when Jimmy Dunn came back to tell us to get ready for the second set, of course, he noticed she wasn't there."

"Now, don't you tell me the girl snuck out with Chance? Or Lane? Or both of them?"

"Uh-uh. Jimmy went back out and found her sittin at a table with Tricky Ricky Starr, of all people, and some other guys Jimmy didn't know. When we asked her about it later, she just shrugged it off. Being as we were so excited about Chance and Lane, we didn't really pay it any mind at the time."

Venus was now rubbing her temples, shaking her head from side to side, her eyes closed.

"What? What's the matter?"

"Oh, nothin. I was just thinkin. You know, back in the real day, the sixties, our people had mystery. Now, it's true that if we had had the kind of media exposure these black singers get today, we would have made a whole lot more money, all of us.

"But back then, because nobody was writin about us in magazines and puttin our business out in the street on BET and *Entertainment Tonight* and the Internet and what all, we had a certain mystique workin for us. Nobody knew a damn thing about us except what we showed on stage.

"And that was a damn good thing, too. Especially for Fluff, after that shit she pulled with Tricky Ricky."

Addie

"Hmph! Shit-pullin is just one of Fanny's many talents!"

Addie Lights and I, side by side again, were pulling out from the front door of what Addie had referred to as Birdie's building, where, once again, the mysterious Hummingbird had eluded us.

"I swear, that girl told me she would be here. I told her I was bringin you down and we could all have dinner at my place. Sorry about that, Legs. I don't know what else to say to you."

"Hey, that's all right. I'm sure we'll meet, sooner or later."

"She's doing much better now, you know. She really has been taking care of the building for me, collecting the checks and money orders from the tenants and sending them to me on time. She'll be all right."

Addie sounded more like she was trying to convince herself than me. For my part, I didn't know what else to say. I had left another message for Birdie at Cleo's, along with another twenty bucks, but so far, I hadn't heard anything. I decided a change of subject was in order.

"Anyway, back to Miss Fluffy and Tricky Ricky Starr."

"Oh, yes, by all means. Back to Fluffy and Ricky Starr. You know, I shoulda known somethin was up when Jimmy Dunn said the two of them were out there sittin at a table puttin their heads together. I shoulda seen it comin. All the time we had known him, Fluffy couldn't stand the boy, called him backwards and brain-damaged all the time.

"And now, all of a sudden, here's her and Ricky sittin together, smilin and laughin? I shoulda known."

"So how long after that evening did you all have the confrontation with Fluffy and Ricky?"

"Oh, not that long afterwards, chile. Venus told you we were signed by Chance and Lane around two weeks after that night, right?"

I nodded.

"Well, what happened was, we went down to their office three, four days after the showcase. First, we ran through a few songs that we hadn't done at the show, and they seemed to like them. But what really put us over, I think, was the originals, two of the songs we had written ourselves: 'Change My Mind' and 'You May Not Know.'

"Girl, those two lil tunes knocked them out. You could almost see them cartoon dollar signs in their eyes. Chance jumped up outta his seat so fast, I thought the man had been stung by a bee!

"'*That's it, that's it! We're putting those on wax. How soon can we get these girls into the studio?'*

"Him, Lane, and Jimmy had a quick conference, and by the time we left that office, we were scheduled to record the two songs ten days from that night. So we went home in a daze. We rehearsed and rehearsed to the point where we could sing those two songs coming right out of our sleep. I mean we were tight! Then the shit hit the fan."

"How did it go down? Did Fluffy tell you all first herself, or did she go to Jimmy Dunn, or what?"

"Well, it was about three days before we were scheduled to record. Jimmy had taken the contracts offered to us by Chance and Lane to MuDear and PawPaw, and a lawyer from the church who was a friend of theirs.

"All of them had sat down at the kitchen table and had gone over them. Everything seemed legit, so we were supposed to go in with the signed contracts on the same night that we started to record.

"So on that night, we were all at Jimmy's studio, gettin

ready to rehearse yet one more time before we went down to the studio Chance and Lane had rented. We knew studio time was expensive, so we aimed to try our best and nail the tunes in one take when we got down there.

"Like I said, we were all there. That is, all of us except for Fluffy. When we had left home that evening, instead of gettin into Jimmy's van with the rest of us, she had told us she had to make a run and that she would meet us there.

"Anyway, we were all sittin around, waitin for her, fidgetin in our seats like skittish ponies at the starting gate, and I swear to God, I shoulda known somethin was up as soon as she came sashayin in there, wigglin and gigglin and flittin all over the place like her underpants was on fire.

"But to be honest, we were so shocked to see that jive-talkin, monster-wig-wearin, no-singin fool Ricky Starr come bigfootin his way up in there, chile, we was speechless.

"I mean, Fluffy couldn't *stand* this guy. At least that's what we had thought. So they come strollin in, Fluffy talkin all fast about being sorry she was late and all, while Ricky was struttin around in Jimmy's lil studio like he owned the joint or something. Finally, Ruthie couldn't stand it no more.

"*'All right, Fluff, what's the deal?'*

"Ruthie was speakin to Fluffy, but she was jerkin her head in Ricky's direction.

"*'What do you mean, what's the deal?'*

"Fluffy was actin like it was the most normal thing in the world for her to come two-steppin into Jimmy Dunn's studio with Ricky Starr on her arm. But before Ruth could say another word, here come Ricky all up in Ruthie's face.

"*'I understand yall is gettin ready to sign a record deal with Chance and Lane.'*

"By this time, even Jimmy Dunn had a surprised look on his face. I mean, after all, who was this backward, gold-chain-orange-shoe-wearin, monster-wighead plowboy, comin in here, gettin all up in our business?

"So Ruthie just narrowed her eyes, looked at him and nodded her head yes.

"*Well, looka here. There's gone be some changes round here. I'm Fluffy's man now, and bein as I am her man, I'm also gone be yall's manager.*'

"*You're gone what?*'

"I swear, Ruthie was so stunned her chewing gum fell out of her mouth. But that didn't faze Ricky one bit.

"*I'm gone be yall's manager, and right now, I'm workin on a much bigger deal for yall that will make you more money and give you more opportunities than Chance and Lane's lil pissant company ever could.*

"*We can all make some real money. I got it all set up. Come on, let's face it, ladies. Fluffy is the talent of the group, Fluffy is the voice of the group, Fluffy is the group. And with all due respect, without Fluffy, yall ain't shit.*'

"The three of us whirled around on Fluffy, all at once. And I swear, if looks could kill, that girl would have dropped dead on the spot."

"So what did she say?"

"Well, she got to hemmin and hawin, talkin about how she'd explain the whole story to us later on the way home. Well, as far as we was concerned, she ain't have to explain shit. I knew I wasn't gone be part of nothin that involved Tricky Ricky Starr. Ruth and Venus felt the same way, and they didn't hesitate to tell her so.

"Meanwhile, Jimmy Dunn slumped down in his seat and put his head down into his hands like he was havin a bad dream or somethin.

"*Fluffy, this lil tone-deaf gold-tooth wearin son of a jackal is not gone be our manager. Not ever. So yall might as*

*well get that straight right now. Now, I don't know what
kinda shit you got goin on with this boy, but you better
straighten that mess out tonight.'*

"Ruthie was turnin away when, all of a sudden, Fluffy
jumped up in her face, that killer flash bright in her eye.

"'*I don't better straighten out nothin. I am the lead singer.
This is my group. You the one that need to get that straight.
Come on, Ricky.'*

"With that, Fluffy grabbed Ricky by the arm and both of
them just strolled on out the door. Me, Ruthie, and Venus all
stood there with our mouths open. What were we gone do?

"We were three days away from a record contract and a
recording session, and here Miss Movie Star just gets it
into her head to pull some shit like this. Jimmy seemed to
recover first.

"'*Do you think you could pull off the songs with just the
three of you?'*

"The three of us groaned. We had always been a quartet, always a lead singer plus three in the background. All
of our harmonies were constructed around that model.
What could we do at this late date?"

"Birdie! Birdie!"

Every head in the place turned and looked at me. I
hadn't even realized that I was screaming.

"Damn right. Birdie! Birdie just might save the day.
Chile, I tell you, when we left Jimmy's that night, we felt
like the world had fallen down on us. We still couldn't
believe that that no-singin fool actually thought we would
let him manage our group, let alone Fluffy! You *know* she
should have known better.

"When we got home, we didn't even mention it to
MuDear and PawPaw. We wanted to see what Fluffy had to
say first. She had told them some tired old story about

havin cramps and havin to come home early. So we just went on upstairs. Once we got into the bedroom, we closed the door and cornered her, demanding to know if she had truly lost her mind.

"'*Ain't a damn thing wrong with me. It's yall that got the problem. If you guys would just listen and give me a chance to explain, instead of jumpin all over me, I think you'll see it my way.*

"'*Ricky has a hook-up with Music Man Productions. That's right, Music Man, the biggest Black-owned music company in the country. Those two guys Ricky and I were talking to were scouts from Music Man. And they were interested in us, the Sweethearts of Soul, and here yall are getting ready to sign away our futures with those little rinky-dinks, Chance and Lane.*

"'*Hmph! Chance and Lane ain't shit! And I'll be damned if I'm gone sign with them when I have an opportunity to go to Los Angeles and audition for the Music Man, Mr. Frank Flood himself.*

"'*Oh, come on, yall. All that stuff about Ricky managing us, that's just bullshit. I'm just shinin him on. I'll tell that fool anything he wants to hear to get that audition with Music Man. And once he signs us, and I just know he will, that will be the end of Ricky.*'

"We stood there tryin to digest what Fluffy was tellin us, and I must admit it was goin way too fast for me. Ruthie stepped over to Fluffy.

"'*So let me see if I got this right. You expect us to just walk out on a signed, legal contract with Chance and Lane, a sure deal, walk out on Jimmy Dunn, and just go runnin halfway across the country with that half-wit Ricky, who can't even read street signs, on the possibility of gettin a contract with Music Man. Is that it?*'

"Ruthie was talkin real slow, like she was talkin to a another half-wit, which, at that moment, we figured she was.

"'*Yes. That's exactly what I expect. Chance and Lane is just nickel-and-dime, while Music Man Productions is the top of the line.*'

"'*Um-hmn. That's what I thought you said. You know, Fluffy, you are so full of shit it's a wonder the three of us can stand the stink of bein in the same room with you. You do what you want. We're stayin right here.*'

"Fluffy looked over at me and Venus. Both of us walked over and stood with Ruth.

"'*Swear to God, you two are like sheep, followin behind everything Ruthie say. Well, suit yourselves, then. But don't say I didn't ask yall. And when I make the big time, don't yall come crawling to me for shit.*'

"And those were the last words Fluffy ever spoke to us. It's funny, but after all these years, I remember them like it was yesterday."

"So that was that? She just left that night?"

"Not that night. On the night we went down to the studio and recorded, when we got back home that night, Miss Fluffy was gone."

"So did any of you ever hear from her again, or was that it?"

"Oh, well, she called and talked to MuDear a few days later, tellin her how she missed her and loved her and she loved all of us, and sayin how she had to find her dream, you know, all that kind of bullshit.

"But from that day to this, none of us have ever spoken to Fanny Lou, or Fluffy LaTour, or Fanya Dance, or whatever the hell she callin herself these days."

"Dayum! But still, you all got your record deal. You all became stars."

"You damn right, we did. All thanks to Birdie. I swear I don't know what we would have done without her. On the night we recorded 'Change My Mind' and 'You May Not Know,' that girl stepped up to the microphone and sounded like she had been singin those songs for months and not just three days. You heard her. You heard how she sounds."

"Sure did," I agreed. "What a voice. Pure and sweet and clear as water."

"You got that right. But you don't know how close we came to not gettin her. At first, MuDear and PawPaw were dead set against it. Especially MuDear.

"'*I've already lost one daughter. Now, yall want to take my baby away, too. Uh-uh. No way. She's too young, too fragile. She doesn't have the experience you girls have. My hummingbird would be just like a lost sheep out there with them wolves.*'

"Girl, we begged like we never begged before, promisin to take care of her, to look out for her, to call home every night. MuDear still wasn't havin it.

"Ruthie pleaded—'*Well, MuDear, Fluff is gone. She ain't comin back. If we don't have a lead singer, we might as well forget about havin a group, and all our work will be for nothin.*'

"Finally, PawPaw spoke up.

"'*Come on, hon. The girl is right. What are they gone do without a lead singer? Fanny Lou is gone. Besides, you owe em.*'

"MuDear glanced over at PawPaw, and was suddenly very quiet. She dropped her eyes away from his. Then she spoke.

"'*Well, if yall promise to—*'

"'*Oooooo, thank you, thank you, thank you!*' We all swirled around her, huggin and kissin her, dancin around her, Birdie squealin and jumpin up and down with us."

"Wow," I said. "Close call. But what do you think made MuDear change her mind?"

"Oh, it was PawPaw. No doubt about it. Like I said, when he spoke, everybody listened. Although, lookin back on it, I sometimes think MuDear was right, that we should have let Bird stay home and found someone else."

Her voice had trailed off, a distant look clouded her eyes.

"Why do you say that?" I asked.

"Oh . . . nothing," she mumbled, brushing her hair away from her eyes.

"Yes, we did become stars. But I guess you already know that wasn't the end of it. Guess you know Miss Fluffy had even more shit to pull before she was through."

I knew, but I wanted to hear it straight from the horse's— well, straight from the songbird's mouth.

"Those two songs, with 'You May Not Know' on the A side, and 'Change My Mind' on the B, were supposed to be released in about six months. Meanwhile, we spent most of our time gettin ready for the road.

"We had new outfits made. Professionally, this time, by Miss Beale, who used to own the bridal shop Venus has now. Posters were made up displaying our pictures, eight-by-tens were sent out to radio stations and nightclubs all along the chitlin circuit, the whole bit. We couldn't wait.

"About two weeks before our single was scheduled to be released, we were comin home from a shoe-buying trip MuDear had treated us to. Since we were ridin in MuDear's big ole station wagon, we were listenin to gospel music, which was all she ever played on the radio.

"But when we got to the stoplight, we heard our song comin from the radio of a car in the lane next to us. We heard 'Change My Mind' loud and clear, and we could tell it was Fluffy singing. Well, the light changed, the car moved on ahead of us, but we sat frozen in shock.

"Even MuDear couldn't move. Our car just sat there until the people behind us started honkin their horns. All the way home, we tried to convince ourselves that it hadn't been 'Change My Mind' that we had heard, it hadn't been Fluffy we had heard singing, that it was some kind of mistake.

"But when we pulled up in front of our house, it seemed like half the kids on the block was standin out there on the sidewalk, waitin for us. They were so excited, most of them were actually jumpin up and down.

"'*We heard yall song! We heard yall song! Yall sounded great!*'

"People were huggin us, kissin us on the cheek, braggin about how they knew us when and everything. People had heard us practicing that tune over and over, so they were familiar with it. You would have thought we'd won a million dollars or somethin. There wasn't nothin we could do but smile and try to go along with it, but after we got inside, we were crushed.

"It hadn't been a nightmare. That *was* our song, a song written by the four of us, that we had heard. That *was* Fluffy we had heard singin it. For once, we stood up to MuDear's rule about no rock and roll in the house and turned the radio on to WDAS, the local black station.

"And then we heard it again."

"They played it one more time?"

"Oh, they played it all night long. Thing was, it wasn't 'Change My Mind' by the Sweethearts of Soul. It was 'Change My Mind' by Fluffy LaTour and the Fluffettes!

✳   ✳   ✳

Phone Message for Legs from Birdie

Hi. Brenda Wade here. Got your note. Thanks again for the cash. Hope everything is fine with you. The girls were buggin me to call you. I swear, sometimes they act like a bunch of old hens. I can take care of myself. I'm grown. It's true that sometimes I have good days and sometimes I have bad ones, but I'm hangin in there. I'm maintaining.

In your note you mentioned that I talked about everybody else but myself. You're probably right. I guess they told you about me and Butch. Yeah. Not much to say about that, except he's gone, and I'm still here.

See, my sisters all have rich, full lives, and they don't seem to know how blessed they are. They've all got nice homes, they're all doing work they love, they've all got beautiful kids, and two of them are about to be grandmamas.

Bet they didn't tell you about that, did they? Ha ha ha! Just ask them. And no matter what they say, neither one of them can hardly wait. They're tickled to death about it, regardless of the circumstances with the kids and everything. I keep reminding them that we made our share of mistakes when we were young, too, but they don't want to hear it. They've forgotten how it feels to be young, and in love.

As for me, there's no real story to tell you. No house, no kids, no real job to speak of, no grands on the way. It was just me and Butch, you know? Just me and Butch. And now he's gone. And I'm still here.

God bless you, Legs. Good night.

✳   ✳   ✳

Ruth

"Hell, yeah, she did. Addie ain't lyin. Fluffy LaTour and the mothafuckin Fluffettes, chile! And you know who the Fluffettes was, don't you?"

I shook my head.

"The Hoecakes! Them skanky, stank, no-sangin heifas!"

"Do you mean the Cupcakes?"

"I mean the *Hoecakes*, always was, always will be. Coco, Cherry, and Chocolate Hoecake. Ooo, chile, you really got me reminiscin now!"

Ruth Thomas and I were sitting in her big, messy, and comfortable living room, drinking, you guessed it, Miller's Draft beers. So this was the house that MuDear built. If I had expected prim, proper, little-old-lady starched doilies and overstuffed furnishings, I certainly would have lost that bet.

This house reflected Ruth Thomas and nobody but. Black, white, and red all over. I sat back in one corner of the long, white leather sofa, facing Ruthie, who occupied the other end. I could feel my boots settling down into the plush red pile carpeting.

Matching red velvet drapes adorned the windows, and large black lamps suspended by gold braided rope hung from the glittering white popcorn ceiling, dangling in midair over top stark black marble matching end tables. It was bold, it was dramatic, it was definitely Ruth, and that's the truth.

"Come on, let me give you a tour."

Ruth jumped up, slipping her feet into leopard-patterned slides, moving swiftly around the black marble coffee table. I followed, almost racing to keep up as Ruthie flung open the French doors leading to the dining room. All done up in blond, gilt-edged French provincial, with soft cream-colored walls and gold velvet drapes, it was in stark contrast to the almost nightclub-like decor of the living room.

"And now, ladies and gentlemen, for your viewing pleasure, just one of the famous, much-talked about, and now-legendary Kennedy-King-Kennedy clocks, bought and paid for with the blood, sweat, and tears of the singing Sherwood Sisters!"

Ruthie gestured dramatically toward the right wall, and there indeed, perched between the two windows, the brothers Kennedy and the solitary King seemed to blink in my direction.

"See? The eyes follow you wherever you go. If I come in here twisted late at night, girl, I don't even turn the lights on. I swear, they spook the hell out of me."

I had to admit, it did seem a bit eerie, especially knowing the circumstances behind the purchase of all those clocks.

"Why not just take it down?"

"Oh, no. I couldn't. It's MuDear's. I just couldn't. We all have one: me—Venus, Addie, even Bird."

We walked on through the dining room and into the large, cheery kitchen, painted a bright sun yellow, then doubled back up the stairs to the three bedrooms. Ruthie's was the largest, all red velvet and purple satin.

"This used to be MuDear and PawPaw's room. Lord, if they could see it now, it would probably shock em back to life."

Ruth giggled to herself as we swept past the middle room and walked straight to the back bedroom, once occupied by Birdie and Venus, now a sort of combo den/laundry station.

"This is where we snuck out the window to sing with the boys."

Ruthie's eyes lit up in devilish merriment as she described how the girls would climb out the back window onto the porch roof, shinny down the iron fire-escape stairs, and run through the narrow alley out to the streets.

Now, as a kid, I myself had been something of a tomboy, always the first to take up a dare. But these girls could have broken their necks, especially out there in the dark.

"Damn, you all must have really wanted to sing."

I looked at Ruth now with a whole new kind of respect. She didn't appear to notice.

"And that was me, Addie, and Fanny's room."

Ruth pointed toward the middle room. Unlike the others, this door was closed, and she made no move to open it.

"That's Sunni's room now," was all she offered, leading me back down the stairs.

"Sunni?"

"My daughter."

"Oh, that's right. You do have a daughter. Sunni, huh? Pretty name."

I jumped on that opening like a dog catching a Frisbee. Was Ruth one of the grandmothers-to-be?

We were back in the living room now, and I wasted no time moving toward the wall of framed photos flanking both sides of the oversized mantelpiece. There were still more pictures on the mantel itself.

Strangely, Ruthie hadn't directed my attention to these photos when we were in the living room earlier.

"So which one is Sunni?"

As if I didn't know. There was picture after picture of the girl, taken at what seemed to be every phase of her young life. She looked to be around the same age as Venus's daughter, maybe late teens, early twenties. But where Raven was certainly a pretty girl, Sunshine Divine Thomas was positively ravishing, a true natural-born beauty.

I found myself staring at the photos in open admiration. Ruthie smiled bashfully, almost succeeding in hiding that pride present in the mothers of all truly beautiful children. I know.

"She is a looker, ain't she? Everybody say so, from the day she was born. Named for the sun, my baby was."

"Simply gorgeous," I agreed, wondering aloud if the girl had any interest in modeling or acting, or maybe in following in her mother's footsteps with a singing career of her own.

"Yeah, she actin, all right. Every day and every night, actin up a storm. She keep it up, she gone act her lil fast ass into an early grave. And that's the truth."

Ruth's smile was gone, replaced by a scornful sneer. Something told me this was the wrong time to push it any further, but I did, anyway. I told her how much I missed and worried about my own son, now a college dropout, living some three thousand miles away somewhere in California, doing God knows what with God knows who.

"Ah, kids. What are you gonna do?"

I threw my hands up in true exasperation, trying to empathize with the now-distressed expression she clearly wore, but I got no response. Apparently, she wasn't willing to share.

"And here are MuDear and PawPaw."

Ruth's tone brightened, her grin suddenly back again, as she led me to the photos on the right side of the mantel, of a kindly looking elderly couple sitting at a table holding hands, a large white three-tiered cake on a table before them.

"Their fortieth wedding anniversary. We took them to the Latin Casino to see us when we played there."

"The Latin? You all played the Latin? Wow!"

New Jersey's famed Latin Casino was a little before my time, but I had heard the stories of the swank, upper-crust nightspot.

"Oh, yeah, quite a few times. The Latin was the top of the tops around here, the crème de la crème, don't you know. The food was lousy but the entertainment was great."

There were more photos of MuDear and PawPaw in church, at picnics, sitting together at the kitchen table. Always close and nearly always holding hands or touching in some way.

"Just look at em. They loved each other all their lives. And when he died, she just withered on the vine. If it wasn't for MuDear and PawPaw, I wouldn't believe a love like that could even exist. Not in real life. I have never seen anything like it, before or since, except in the movies."

"What? How can you sing love songs with such feeling and passion and not believe in them?"

"Hmph! Singin it is one thing, livin it is whole nother story. Come over here, I wanna show you something."

Ruth motioned me over to the right side of the mantel. And there they were, the Sherwood Sisters, snaggletoothed and precious, dressed in their Sunday best, posing on the front steps of a church.

And another, this time the little girls holding on to MuDear and PawPaw's hands, looking mighty serious for ones so young. And here, older and more poised, the Sherwood Sisters standing at the church pulpit, in starched white blouses, dark skirts, white lace tights, their thick natural hair bound up in white ribbon. Their eyes were closed, their mouths wide open, singing the praises of the Lord.

And, finally, the Sweethearts of Soul, at first wide-eyed,

fresh-scrubbed, and eager; later, sultry, slick, and sophisticated, all lipsticked pouty mouths and blue-black, heavily mascara'd, come-hither eyes staring out in bold, hand-
on-one-hip, full-grown-woman poses.

"Ha! Would you look at us? Womanish. That's what
MuDear called us. Said we looked like a quartet of dressed-
up racoons."

Ruth and I laughed heartily at that one, settling back
on the sofa and opening fresh beers while in the background Dinah Washington sang something nasty about
going to the dentist and getting drilled real good.

"Dinah, Dinah, Dinah. My idol. Did you know that Jimmy
Dunn, our manager, was her bandleader at one time?"

I nodded, simultaneously shaking my head to the music.

"Well, chile, I don't know what that woman laid on that
brother, but after all those years, the man still went cow-
eyed at the mention of her name."

"Well, they say Miss Dinah was a real piece of work,
you know."

"Um-hmn. And they also say she was one very independent woman who wanted to control her own life and her
own career, and you know that don't sit too well with the
boys in charge."

"What do you mean?"

"You see what happened to her."

"What happened to her?"

I sat up quickly.

"Died way before her time. That's what."

"Now, wait a minute. What are you saying, Ruth? I
remember something about her dying from mixing alcohol
with some kind of diet pills, or something like that."

"Um-hmn. Somethin like that. And Sam Cooke died

because he attacked some ole lady when he was butt naked in some ole rundown hoehouse hotel. Um-hmn. And Otis Redding was killed in a freak plane crash. Um-hmn. And I won't even talk about Ray Wright. Uh-uh, won't even go there. All I'm sayin is back in them days, if you was Black and you wanted to control your own destiny, bad things had a way of happenin to you. Know what I'm sayin?"

"Ray Wright?"

"Forget it. Leave it lay." Ruthie shook her head.

I nodded, pondering her words, and for a minute there, I don't know if it was the beer or the conversation or Dinah's playful, mocking voice, but for some reason, I almost felt like crying.

"Aw, lighten up, girl. Speaking of bad things, they told you what happened with Fluffy and Tricky Ricky, didn't they?"

"Well, I know Fluffy ended up recording without him."

"You damn right she did, just like she told us. As soon as Ricky introduced her to Music Man and Fanny got to winkin and grinnin at that ole fool, Fanny was in, and Ricky was out the door with a one-way ticket back to Philly. And I got that straight from the Hoecakes' mouths!"

Venus

"Yes indeedy, sweetie. Ruthie told you the God's honest truth. You know them skeezas couldn't resist rubbin it in."

Venus Jones and I sat in her peach-colored kitchen as she sorted clothes for the wash.

"Within a month of Fluffy going to L.A., they got a call from Music Man Productions, askin if they were available for some backup work, offerin to pay their transportation and lodging as well as payin them a flat rate. Naturally, they took the deal, thinkin this was their big break.

"It wasn't till they got down there that they found out Fanny had set up the whole thing. Now, it's true she didn't like em and everything, but business was business.

"Hell, she ain't like Ricky, neither, but look what happened there. Cherry Cake told us that right from the start, Music Man and Fluff had put their heads together and planned on dumpin Ricky."

"Jesus! So the Hoecakes—I mean, the Cupcakes—were in and you guys were out, huh?"

"Heck, no. The *Hoecakes* was out. As soon as they did that record and one little measly tour with Fluffy, she dumped their sorry asses, too.

"I don't know what made them think she was gone do them any better than she did Ricky—or, for that matter, any better than she did us.

"Now, as for the Sweethearts of Soul, we might have been down for a minute, but we was never ever out, baby. We still had 'You May Not Know.' For some reason, Fluffy had left that one alone for the time being, and we already had it in the can, with our little Hummingbird singing lead. So that was our trump card. We called Jimmy Dunn and told him what was up, he called Chance and Lane and told them. Next thing we knew, we're back down to the studio, puttin a lil sweetnin on 'You May Not Know,' and within a matter of—"

"Excuse me, did you say 'sweetening'?"

"Yeah. Sweetnin. I don't know what they call it nowadays, but back then you sometimes had to go back into the studio and lay a few more tracks, tweak the song a lil bit, make the record sound as good as it possibly could.

"Chance and Lane were already pissed. The first night we went down there, they told us that the reason they had never signed a girl group before us was because women had such a bad reputation in the music business, mainly on account of boyfriend and husband troubles. You know?"

"No. How so?"

"Well, their men would be jealous, seein em up there on that stage, lookin good, bein watched and hit on by all the other guys, even though most of the time that's where the girls were when them same men first met em. Standin on the stage, singin, or on their way someplace to sing, or on the way back from singin.

"Hell, that's what attracted them in the first place. But once they got you, everything changes real quick. All of a sudden, you some kind of hoe for bein up there. You thought you was cute. Uh-huh, you was a party girl, you was a loose woman, a floozy, whatever.

"Bottom line was, they wanted your ass off that damn stage and home in that kitchen where you belonged. And the sad thing about it was, Chance and Lane was right. Oh yeah, we knew all about that. Girl, I could tell you story after story of girls who had real talent but never even got started because they was tryin to please their men, the damn fools.

"But anyhow, the second Chance and Lane let that lil info drop, we was ready for em. And we came back at em with the swiftness: No, we wasn't like that. We was pros, we had been singin since we was babies, we would never even *think* of lettin some man get in the way of our careers. Oh, we swore up and down that we were the exception to the rule.

"And here we was, barely a month later, standin with

our heads hangin and our tails tucked between our legs, listenin to Fluffy LaTour and the goddamn Fluffettes singin *our* song on the radio."

"Wow. It never occurred to me that women singers would be having that kind of trouble with their men. I always thought that most guys would be thrilled to have some glamorous celebrities like you all were even give them the time of day, the same way girl groupies act over male singers."

"Ha! Girl, you is *so* trippin. But you do have a point. Well, half a point, anyway. It's a two-sided thing. Yeah. It's true. They love havin you on their arm, showin you off to their friends and all, but at the same time, they still jealous. Not just jealous of other men, neither. Jealous of *you*, what you stood for, of your independence. Jealous if you made more money than they did. It takes a very secure man to deal with a woman on the stage. Any stage.

"Oh, yeah. Let me tell you, girl. Any woman who is a singer, actress, whatever, who goes out on the road, who makes her own money and calls her own shots, she got man trouble. Any of em. Don't care who they is, or how much money they got. They got man trouble."

I nodded solemnly. This conversation was opening a whole new door for me.

"So, anyhow, back to the Sweethearts. Let me see, where was I?"

Venus was smiling again, the twinkle back in her eye.

"You guys ran down to the studio and did the sweetening, or whatever you call it."

"Oh, yeah, the sweetnin. Like I said, Chance and Lane were pissed, and Jimmy Dunn wasn't none too pleased, neither. But then they heard Birdie's voice. I swear, once they heard that chile sing, they pulled Fluffy's vocal off the track and replaced it with Birdie's so fast, you would have thought

Fluffy had never even been in the room. Two weeks later, "You May Not Know" was all over the radio, on all the juke-boxes, blaring out of the record stores. Everywhere.

"Chance and Lane were so mad about Music Man Productions runnin off with their singer and their song, they made sure our song got big play, and next thing you know, the Sweethearts of Soul were bona fide stars, baby! Stars!"

Venus laughed as she dragged the laundry baskets over to the basement door.

"Now, I just know you could stand a lil somethin to eat right about now, ain't that right?"

Moving quickly, Venus opened the refrigerator, extracted a large bowl, half a loaf of bread, and a covered roasting pan, and was now setting them down on the table in front of me.

"How about a roast beef sandwich and some potato salad?"

She didn't have to ask me twice. I sat happily sipping on a Pepsi with my tape recorder running as Venus spooned out the salad, all the while talking about the SOS.

She sighed, took the seat across from me, and continued her story.

"And no sooner did we have that record out, Jimmy Dunn had us booked on a tour. Man, those was some whirlwind days. Now, we were used to playin at all the local venues, but most of the time, we worked alone, or with maybe one or two other local acts.

"But this time, we had to go up against four, five, six other acts per night. This was the big time!

"I remember the first show we did like that. We were playin the old Adelphi Ballroom."

"The Adelphi? I don't believe I've ever heard of that one."

"Oh, yeah. Used to be in West Philly, on the corner of Fifty-second and Media streets. Let's see: it was us; Billy Harner, a blue-eyed soul brother; a group called Rico and the Ravens, who were Puerto Rican but looked white; and the Del Fonics. That's right."

"The Del Fonics? The Fonics were on that show?"

"Oh, yeah. Plus there was another blue-eyed soul group that called themselves the Temptones, modeled themselves after the Temptations. Used to dress like em, tried to sing and dance like em and everything. You know. They was pretty good, too. Later on, of course, they came to be known as Hall and Oates."

"Get outta here. Daryl Hall and John Oates?"

"The very same. And there was one more group on that show, but for the life of me, I can't think of what they called themselves. The only thing I can remember about em is the hairless lead singer."

"Hairless? You mean he was bald? He had thinning hair, like Tricky Ricky?"

"I mean he was *hairless*. He was probably somewhere in his late teens, early twenties. All of us were kids then."

"He must have really looked strange."

"Actually, he didn't. Not at first. It was really the wig what gave it away."

"The wig?"

Venus nodded her head slowly, chuckling through a mouthful of potato salad.

"The wig. Now, when we first met these dudes, this lead singer was wearin what looked like a process, and a pair of shades. Nice-looking guy, you know. Medium height, sunset and sand-colored complexion, nice body build. It was four of them, and we met em all at the same time in that nasty Adelphi dressing room, so we really didn't notice anything unusual about the guy.

"We were the first ones to get there that night. First thing we did was put up a clothesline on one side of the room, and then we draped sheets over it to give us some privacy."

"Sheets? You all had to dress in the same room as the guys?"

"Yes indeedy, sweetie. Where you think we was playin, the Latin? Ha! Not just yet.

"Anyway, the rest of the acts started showin up. By then, it was show time, and since we were opening the show, we really didn't have time to socialize.

"So we go on, do our lil three-song set, including 'You May Not Know,' our brand-new hit.

"The song was well received, the audience singing along with us. After our set, we went back upstairs to a balcony next to the dressing room. This little balcony was right above the stage, but out of the view of the audience. So we stood up there to watch the rest of the show.

"So the last act was the Del Fonics. They were the only ones with a big hit record out. Being as we had seen them perform many times, we went back to the dressing room and began changing into our street clothes. And, chile, that's when the shit hit the fan.

"'*Fire! Fire!*' That's all we could hear. People was screamin and hollerin, and the PA system went dead, shutting off the Fonics in midperformance.

"We was half in, half out of our clothes. I didn't have no blouse on, some of us didn't have our shoes on, and here's the manager up there tellin us to 'Come on, yall gotta get outta here.'

"The manager was directin us out to a little side exit. The other groups had gotten out ahead of us, and we was runnin out of the dressing room, still half-dressed, when we see the lead singer of that group whose name I can't remember rush past us and back into the dressing room.

"I don't know what made me do it, but for some reason, I turned around to see where that fool was goin."

"He ran back into the dressing room in a building that was on fire?"

"Sure did. So I went back and peeped in, and there he was, sittin in the mirror, doin somethin with his wig."

"Doing what with it?"

"I don't know. Adjusting it, puttin glue in it, somethin. I don't know. Now, we had watched their act onstage. Ruthie had said somethin about the back of his head lookin funny, about how the hair was risin up off the back of his neck, and I ain't pay it no mind then.

"But now I could see. It was definitely a wig. And then he took off his shades, and, girl, I swear to God, no eyebrows, no eyelashes, no hair at all. And his eyes! Good God Almighty! Eyes so light you could see through em. Looked like one of them Children of the Damned, or somebody.

"Well, that like to scared me even more than the fire. Girl, I took off."

"Dayum! Way weird. So, you all did get out safely?"

"Oh, yeah. It was really more smoke than anything else. I think somebody had been smokin in the men's room. Anyway, the fire department came and put it out. We went back in, collected our clothes and stuff, and left. And that was our first rock-and-roll show."

"You know, now that you mention it, I think I saw Daryl Hall on TV a while ago talking about playing some club in Philly back in the day and being caught in a fire."

"Well, now you know he was wasn't lyin. For days afterwards, people talked about how we had burned that motha down! It was a good show, you understand, but after the news spread about the fire, it became legendary! People who weren't even there pretended they had been there.

"It's a wonder MuDear and PawPaw let us go anywhere after that. And we never would have set foot outside of Philly without Magdelina Smart."

"Who?"

"Miss Mattie Smart. See, in those days, girls under the age of eighteen always had to travel with a female chaperone. It was the law. The trouble with us was we didn't know any chaperones. MuDear had always gone with us when we sang gospel, and when we switched to rock and roll, Jimmy Dunn took us everywhere.

"So here we were, gettin ready to go on this three-month, twenty-city tour which Jimmy Dunn set up for us without a chaperone. Enter Miss Mattie Smart and the Brown Bomber."

"Mom!"

I turned, following the sound of the voice, and there in the doorway stood a very pregnant Raven Jones. Aha! So Venus is one of the grandmamas-in-waiting.

"Where are your manners?"

"Oh. Hello. I didn't know anybody was back here with you."

"What, you thought I was back here talkin to myself? I ain't that crazy. Yet. This is Miss Legs Diamond, the reporter from *Black Music Magazine* that I told you about."

"Oh, yeah! You're the one doing the story on my mom and the group. Did they tell you any secrets yet, any dirt?"

The girl's eyes held the same merry twinkle as her mother's.

"Don't you be worryin about *my* secrets. You better be takin care of your own business, daughter."

Raven rolled her eyes in mock exasperation.

"Well, nice meeting you, Miss Diamond, and good luck. You're gonna need it. I'm goin upstairs to take a nap, Mom. I'm kinda tired."

The girl turned slowly and lumbered into the dining room.

"Oh. Looks like somebody's going to be a grandma."

I didn't let on about what Birdie had told me.

"Yeah. Lucky me."

Venus looked so dejected, I didn't quite know what to say next. After almost a full minute, she looked up at me, shrugging her shoulders.

"Listen, don't get me wrong. I would love to be a grandmother. Just not now. Not without a husband for my daughter. Not without a college education. She just don't know how hard it is tryin to raise a child alone. You'd think she would, growin up with no daddy around. But no matter what you say to these kids, you just can't make em understand."

"Raven isn't in touch with her father?"

"Raven never had a chance to know her father. By the time Raven was born, her father was dead. It's not like he left us on purpose, but still . . ."

I remembered Ruthie referring to Venus mockingly as "the virgin mother," making reference to some sort of shrine Venus kept in her bedroom in memory of Raven's father.

"So, who is the other grandmother-to-be? Birdie told me there were two of you. So it's you and—who? Ruthie?"

"Ruthie? It damn sure better *not* be. That's all I got to say."

I sat up straight in my seat, somewhat taken aback by the tone of venom in her voice.

"I'm sorry. I just thought that Sunni might be—"

"Listen. Please do not mention that chile's name in my house."

"Sunni?" I whispered.

"Right. Miss hot tamale, hoochie mama Sunni. Prancin up and down the Strip, wearin them whorish poom poom pants. She's the reason for all this mess in the first damn place."

"What mess? What are you—"

"I don't want to talk about it, all right? If you want to talk about the SOS, fine. If not, this conversation is over."

"Fair enough."

Seeing as she meant every word, I decided to drop it. For the moment. But I made a mental note to find out as soon as possible what the hell "poom poom pants" were.

"So when we last spoke a few minutes ago, you had mentioned something about a Miss Magdelina Smart and a Brown Bomber?"

I grinned over at Venus. She half-smiled back, in spite of herself, nodding her head.

"Yes indeedy, sweetie. Miss Mattie Smart and the Brown Bomber. What happened was, MuDear and PawPaw couldn't find anybody willin to go on the road and chaperone us, and Jimmy had been runnin all over town trying to to find somebody, too. So one afternoon, about a week before the tour was to begin, Jimmy comes over all excited, claimin he had finally found us a chaperone, a nice Christian lady who had traveled on the gospel circuit as a hairdresser some years ago.

"So he loads everybody up in his van, MuDear, PawPaw, and all of us girls, and takes us over to Johnson's Funeral Home, her current place of employment."

"She worked in a funeral home?"

"Yeah, chile. Jimmy explained to us on the way that

Miss Mattie Smart now worked part-time doing the hair and makeup of dead people for various funeral parlors around town. Well, we girls all cut our eyes at each other. We're thinkin like, oh, God, no.

"Well, when we get there, this prim but pleasant-lookin woman answers the door, introduces herself as Miss Magdelina Smart, and invites us in. She looked to be somewhere in her late forties, early fifties. She wasn't a bad-lookin woman, but she like to scared us to death when we first saw her. For some reason, she seemed to favor the same masklike pancake foundation that she used on her customers. I don't know. Maybe she had a deal with the suppliers or something. Look like that stuff was spackled onto her face.

"As MuDear bombarded her with questions, we were checkin her out on the sly. She didn't seem too bad.

"'What beautiful heads of hair your daughters have,' Miss Mattie exclaimed to MuDear, lookin us over as if she could hardly wait to get her hands on us. She was a widow, childless, and she supplemented the small pension her husband left her doing hair and makeup. She had never traveled with a 'worldly' music show, as she called it, but she didn't think she would have any problem adjusting. She had always loved the road, she said, seein new places, meetin new people.

"'I'm sure the girls and I will get along together just fine,' she said to MuDear and PawPaw, beaming at us.

"By the time we left the funeral home that afternoon, the deal had been struck. Miss Mattie Smart would be responsible for our hair, makeup, and clothing. She would also serve as our mother hen on the road, making sure to keep us decent. MuDear especially liked that part. Miss Mattie would also be serving as our chauffeur. The five of us would be travelin in her big ole dirt-brown, wood-sided station wagon, affectionately known as the Brown Bomber.

"So everything was set. The tour was to start in a week, and, lucky for us, the venue for the first ten days of the tour was Philadelphia's own Uptown Theater. Following the Uptown, we had ten days at the Royal in Baltimore, ten at the Howard in D.C., and ten at the Regal in Chicago, with about two or three days off between each gig. Then a bunch of two- and three-nighters.

"This was really great, by the way. Our four-piece band would be traveling on the bus with the musicians from the other acts. Each theater had its own house band in those days, so all we traveled with was a rhythm section.

"We spent our last week in final fittings for our very own custom-made gowns, ten apiece, which were done for us by Miss Beale, the lady who owned the shop that I own today, the one who taught me all I know about sewing. Our afternoons were sometimes spent with Miss Mattie Smart, who experimented on us with different blends and types of makeup.

"We were too excited to be nervous, too excited to even think about being away from home for three whole months, when we had hardly spent so much as a night away from MuDear and PawPaw since the day we had arrived at their home.

"Meanwhile, we had to contend with watchin Fluffy LaTour and the Fluffettes on *American Bandstand*, and seein their record shoot straight up to number three on the Top Ten. But that was all right, that only made us stronger. We worked harder on our routines than we ever had before. We couldn't wait to step onto that Uptown stage.

"Finally came the big day. It was a Friday, and in those days, you did five shows a day. That's right. Five. This was one of the first of those all-Philadelphia lineups, so every-body wanted to be on point. We knew we would be repre-senting Philly everywhere we went. We knew Motown had gone before us, and left giant footprints for us to fill."

"So how did it go?"

"Piece of cake, chile. Piece of cake. This time, Rico and the Ravens opened the show, as they were the only group without a record, followed by us, followed by the Intruders, followed by the Del Fonics, followed by Barbara Mason. We stood in the wings and did backup for Barbara. You know Barbara Mason?"

"No, never had the pleasure, but I know her work and I'm a big fan of hers."

"Oh, she's a real class act, that lady. You know, Barbara was one of the first true singer-songwriters back then, a stone supertalent. Her career should have gone much further."

"What do you think happened?"

"Hey, could have been anything. Hard to say."

"So you guys were on the road with the Del Fonics and the Intruders?"

"Oh, sure. We worked with them plenty of times. We had gone to school with the Fonics and knew the Intruders from workin at Chance's Under 21 Club, and I already told you about Rico and them. Oh, yeah. The headliner of this par-ticular tour was Billy Paul. I forget to tell you."

"Billy Paul? The 'Me and Mrs. Jones' Billy Paul?"

"That's right. Now, Billy is the one who taught us about pacing, how to hold back a little bit. Comin from a gospel background, we were used to comin out swingin, doin that straight, hard, wide-open singin. Now, that's all right for a one-night stand. But you try doin that five times a day for ten days, and it will kill you.

"Barbara taught us about the importance of fresh lemons, honey, and tea. We drank that every morning and every night, baby.

"One of the Intruders, Bird, the tenor, made sure we changed our clothes and dried our bodies off thoroughly and covered our throats before goin out into the night air. You do that enough times with your pores still open, you'll spend the rest of the tour in bed with pneumonia.

"Rico and the Ravens insisted that we gargle every morning and every evening with hot saltwater, claimed it kept your vocal chords nice and tight."

I nodded, taking in all this inside singer info. "How about the Del Fonics? Did you learn anything from them?"

Venus threw back her head, laughing loudly and lustily.

"Oh, the Fonics. The Fonics taught us about timing."

"Timing? You're talking about movement, musical cues, working with the band?"

"No, not quite. I'm talkin about money. I'm talkin about not settin foot on a stage anywhere until you were paid in full. I'm talkin about standin in the wings while the band is striking up your intro and not makin a move until you had that money in your hand.

"That's what I'm talkin about. Timing."

Addie

"Ooowee, the Uptown. And Miss Mattie Smart. Girl, you bringin back serious memories now. So Venus told you all about the Uptown, huh? Bet she didn't tell you about her skirt fallin down onstage, did she?"

"What?"

Addie Lights and I were seated together again on the sofa in what I had taken to referring to as the Halls of Adeline. On this particular afternoon, we were enjoying a pitcher of frozen daiquiris that the maid had whipped up and set before us.

Directly across the room, right above one of the double fireplaces, there sat perched a forty-inch-wide television screen that I had not noticed on my previous visits.

"Oh, honey, watch this."

Addie reached over, picked up the remote, and with a slight clicking sound, the TV screen actually slid back into the staircase, disappeared completely, and was immediately covered by one of the smoky mirrors that I had seen there before.

"Pretty cool, huh?"

She beamed. Jesus.

"Oh, wait a minute. You gotta see this."

Addie clicked the remote again, the television magically reappeared, snapped on, and suddenly, there was rap music blaring from somewhere behind the staircase. On the screen, dancing, bumping, and grinding, was a handsome young man, holding a microphone with one hand, the other loosely draped over the arm of one of the half-dozen dancers that surrounded him, moving to the beat.

"You know, you know, you know, you know, I'm the one you're looking for . . ." was all I managed to hear before my full attention was captured by Addie, who was now dancing across the room, shaking that thing, singing along word for word with the song.

"Whew! What cha think?"

The song had ended and Addie fell across the sofa in a slump, breathing heavily.

"Uh—what do I think about what?"

"My son, chile! Didn't I tell you my son was a rapper?"

She was pointing to the screen, at the young man, who was now being interviewed by the TV-show host.

"He really doesn't favor me at all, he's the spittin image of his daddy, but that's my boy, all right. That's my Bobby. Callin himself MC Flashlight now."

Addie beamed proudly, as I smiled up at the screen.

"MC Flashlight, huh? Handsome kid. Bet he's gonna break some hearts before it's all over."

"Hmph! He's already breakin some hearts. Too many, and it ain't even started yet. Nothin I can do about that, though. Takes after his daddy. That's all I can say."

"It's nice to see one of the Sweethearts of Soul's children following in their mother's footsteps."

"Yeah, guess so, though I don't know if the other Sweethearts would agree with you there."

"Oh? Why not?"

"Oh, nothing. Anyhow, back to the Uptown. Venus at the show."

"Oh, yeah. You say her skirt fell down? You mean completely down?"

"Yup. We were on stage doin this song, Birdie was on lead, and at a certain point, me, Ruthie, and Venus, who was in the middle, were all supposed to turn around and walk back toward the band. Well, Venus picks the wrong time to make the turn, so she's walkin to the back and Ruthie and I are still standin there. So when we turned on cue to walk to the back, Venus turned around and walked forward. We were wearin those long straight skirts with the splits up the side, you know. And when Venus got to the front of her mike, somehow, the button popped on her skirt and it fell straight down to the floor."

"Oh, no. What did she do?"

"That was just it. She didn't do nothin. She didn't realize the skirt was on the floor, lying around her feet, so she
just kept on singin and makin hand motions. Well, chile,
the audience got to whoopin and hollerin, the musicians
were laughin out loud, and me and Ruthie were nudging
her, tryin to give her a hint.

"Finally she caught on, bent down, pulled up the skirt,
and just went on with the act like nothin happened."

"Oh, God. I would have been so embarrassed, I would
have just left the stage."

"She said later on that she started to run off, but when we
kept on singin, somethin told her that if she ran off, we would
probably curse her out, which we would have. Anyway, when
we finished that song, we got a standing ovation.

"It wasn't so much for us. It was for her, for hangin on
in there.

"Of course, after we left the stage, she didn't want to
come out of the dressing room. But all the other acts, every
one of them, came back and congratulated her for being so
professional. It really made her feel good.

"The only reason it happened in the first place was
because she had stuffed herself before the show. Not a
good idea."

"Stuffed herself?"

"Yeah. See, there was this lady everybody called 'Mom'
who lived across the street from the back of the Uptown,
and every time the Uptown had a rock-and-roll show, she
would sell home-cooked meals to the artists and the musicians. Everybody warned Venus to wait until after the
show to eat, but nooo.

"Me, Ruthie, and Birdie each had a sandwich. Venus
sat down there and ate smothered chicken, mashed pota-

toes and gravy, greens and biscuits, and candied sweet potatoes. Bet she learned her lesson that night."

I chuckled, thinking of how Venus had steadfastly refused to have the chicken and dumplings on our two occasions at Miss Tootsie's restaurant.

"Yeah, that was some show. And you better believe Venus never made that mistake again. Now, that was the first night, that Friday. Everything was good. But, then again, we were playin in front of a hometown crowd. Everybody's friends and family were there, people we had gone to school with, even some people who had snuck up there from the church.

"Would you believe MuDear and PawPaw even had the nerve to come to the Sunday matinee? Sure did. Them, Jimmy Dunn, and Miss Mattie, wearin what looked like some kind of Egyptian funeral mask.

"They came backstage after the show, and MuDear seemed greatly relieved to see that there was no hanky-panky goin on. Well, of course, there wasn't. We were all Philly acts. We were all home. Just like Miss Mattie used to say, 'You don't shit where you eat.' We saved our devilment for the road, honey.

"And you know what? No matter where you went, there was always a woman called Mom on the road, don't care where it was. Usually, she would live right behind the theater, or across the street, or sometimes, even right next door. In every single city, in every town, and let me tell you, *those* ladies was the ones that kept the trains on that chitlin circuit runnin on time. I don't know what we woulda done without em.

"Sometimes they ran what they used to call tourist hotels, or guest houses, or boardinghouses. Other times, it

didn't have no name at all. It was just Mom's, and it was
home for all us orphan children on the road. Now, don't get
me wrong, the road was fun and all that. But it was still
hard on you, especially on the women. I don't even wanna
think about what it must have been like for the real pioneers, like Billie, and Sarah, and Ella and them, back in
the forties and the fifties.

"Can you imagine travelin round the country in old cars
and broke-down buses with no air-conditioning in the summer, and sometimes even no heat in the dead of winter?
Especially down south, where you had to wait till you got to
the 'cullid' part of town just to get something to eat or take
a pee? And that was in the early sixties. Some of the old-
heads we used to travel with would tell us how good we had
it, compared to when they first started out, and after
hearin some of them horror stories, we learned not to complain a whole lot.

"Women would be talkin bout ridin in them cars and
buses wit all them men, and havin your period come on!
Your period! Lord Jesus! Where were you gonna go, what
were you gonna do but sit tight, stuff yourself, and pray
there was nothing showin on the back of your skirt. And
that's where all them moms in all them lil towns came to
the rescue, opened up their homes to them pioneer girls,
filled em up with good homemade, solid food, let em take a
bath, and sleep in a comfortable bed with clean sheets.

"Chile, you can't begin to know how good that must
have felt to them girls, comin off them dusty, dirt roads. So
while we're grateful to all the great singers who got out
there and paved the way for us, we're also grateful to all
them moms who fed us and took good care of us out there.
If anybody ought to be getting an award, it oughta be them.

"And you know Miss Mattie knew em all. Good ole Miss Mattie. Wonder how she's doin these days?"

"She's still alive?"

"Oh, yes, very much so. Last time I went out lookin for Birdie, let me see now, about three, four weeks ago, I ran into her at the bingo parlor. She must be somewhere in her mid-seventies by now, still spry as ever. Must be something to what she always says about liquor and young boys bein good for you."

"Young boys?"

"She swears they're better than vitamins for what ails you.

"And she told me she still takes a lil taste every day."

"A taste? You talkin about a seventy-something-year-old woman takin a taste of liquor? Every day? I thought she was supposed to be such a fine Christian lady."

"Oh, that she is, that she is. I know we used to make fun of Miss Mattie all the time with her death-mask makeup and bullet curls, but—"

"Bullet curls?"

"Bullet curls. Girl, she used to curl your hair so tight, and those lil rows in your head would be so straight, I swear, it looked like lined-up bullets. Rat-tat-tat-tat-tat-tat! Rat-tat-tat-tat-tat-tat tat! Rat-tat-tat-tat-tat!"

Addie ran her hands back and forth across her head, demonstrating how the bullet curls were set. I giggled, remembering my grandmother wearing those same tight curls.

"Oh, yeah! And did she used to put that pink stuff on it to keep it from 'going back'?

"Honey—pink, green, blue, and everything else. And I ain't nevah lied.

"I swear, that woman could put such a hard press on your hair, somebody could throw a full bucket of water on your head, and it would just bounce right back off. Boing! Boing! Boing!"

Addie, of course, was acting out the whole scenario, and I of course was helpless with laughter.

"And she's still wearin that same makeup, still wearin them bullet curls. I think she got a bullet curl wig now, though.

"And you cannot tell her she ain't the hottest thing in the hood. And I ain't nevah lied!

"Bless her poor ole soul. Miss Mattie was one of those, what we call around the neighborhood, 'outside wives.' You know the kind of woman that will go with a married man for years and years and pretend to be married to him?

"That was Miss Mattie. She had told MuDear and PawPaw that she used to travel with gospel groups doin their hair and makeup. Well. She wasn't lyin about that. She just wasn't tellin the whole truth. What it was, she was the long-time mistress of—you got that tape on?"

I nodded.

"Well, turn it off. This is strictly off the record."

I turned off my machine, leaned forward, and when I heard Addie whisper the name of the man and the extremely popular gospel group that he was a member of, I almost fell off the sofa.

"And I ain't nevah lied!"

"Long-time mistress? Like, about how long are we talking?"

"Like, from back in the forties till the day he died, and the man just passed about five, six years ago."

"Wow! How did she get herself caught up in something like that?"

"Caught up is right. She told me one time when she was in her gin and I caught her in one of her confessin moods that her and this guy grew up together, were sweethearts since the sixth grade, or somethin like that. They went to the same church and everything, you know. As a matter of fact, he and his gospel group started off singin in that very same church.

"Anyhow, they got engaged and everything and was supposed to get married as soon as they finished high school.

"But then he got drafted and went into the war. She waited for him and everything, and as soon as he got out, he was back singin with his old group again.

"Now, he still wanted to marry her, but he also wanted to sing and to travel. She wasn't for it, told him she didn't want no travelin man, told him he either had to pick the group or her.

"Well, you see who he picked, don't you? Of course, he picked the group. So that was the end of that, or so she thought.

"So about four, five years down the line, I think she said, his group came back to Philly to do a benefit to raise money for their old church. She went to see him. Now, I ain't got to tell you what happened, do I?"

"They got back together."

"You know they did, girl. He was married, had a couple kids, but he still wanted her. He wouldn't leave his wife because if he did, she wasn't gone let him see the kids, or so he claimed."

"And Miss Mattie bought that?"

"Sure, she bought it. Hell, it probably was the truth. Back then, all that woman had to do was go to court and claim desertion.

"Besides that, his singing career would have been destroyed. Just think of it: Renowned gospel singer leavin his wife and two children for his other woman. Uh-uh. No way was that gone fly, especially not in the Baptist church.

"So he did what I guess he thought was the next best thing. He made her his outside wife. That lil house she live in now? That's the same lil house he bought her way back then. Took her all over the world, and when he couldn't take her, always brought her something back. Perfumes from Paris, tea sets from Japan, dresses from Italy, sculpture and paintings from Africa, Persian carpets. A picture of the two of them, hand in hand, standing in front of the Sphinx. The man gave her everything, everything except his name.

"I always felt sorry for her, though. When the man died, she wasn't even allowed into the funeral. Oh, yeah, the wife knew all about her. They always do, you know. The wife got the big house, the Cadillac car, the bankbooks. And Miss Mattie, well, she got a lil house full of faded photos and memories.

"I don't know who's the sorriest, her or Venus. Well, at least Vee got Raven to remind her of Ray."

"Ray?"

"Ray, chile, the love of her life. Next time you go to her house, you take a peep in that bedroom. Same thing as Miss Mattie, pictures all over the wall, all over the place, Venus and Ray, Ray and Venus. Her first, last, and only love."

"The last? So Ray was Raven's father."

"Of course he was. Who else? Didn't you just hear me say the woman ain't never had another man in her life? Guess she figures if she prays hard enough, she can bring him back from the dead."

"Yes, she mentioned that Raven's dad was dead."

"You don't—oh, my. You don't know about Ray?"

I shook my head.

"Oh, Lordy. Well, once again, let's go off the record."

Reluctantly, I clicked off the recorder.

"Ray—Raymond Wright—was one of the members of the Heartbreakers. I don't know if you remember them, but—"

"Of course I remember the Heartbreakers. They were one of the biggest groups of the sixties. Wasn't he the one who drank himself to death or something?"

"Or something. That's the official story. Then there's the real story. Oh, no. Uh-uh. Don't look at me. I've already said too much. You want to know the whole truth about Ray Wright, you got to get it from Venus, or one of the others. I ain't sayin another word, except it's really time for that girl to get herself a new man.

"Damn, it's been twenty years now. Girl probably got cobwebs up in there."

"Addie, you need to stop."

"All right, all right. I'm not even goin there. Now, we were talkin about Miss Mattie Smart, right?"

"Right."

"So, anyway, like I said, Miss Mattie made a very good impression on MuDear and PawPaw, and we was thinkin we wasn't gone have no fun at all with her on the road. She seemed just as strict as Jimmy Dunn.

"True, she had come with MuDear and PawPaw to see us perform at the Uptown Sunday matinee, but at that time, she wasn't workin for us officially yet.

"Jimmy Dunn was still our caretaker at the Uptown, and you know he was there every day and every night, treatin us like prison inmates, as usual.

"So we didn't find out the real deal on Miss Magdelina Smart until we got ready to actually go on the road."

"What real deal?"

"Like I said, the first leg of the tour was the Uptown, in Philly, and that was for ten days. After that, we had a couple days off, and then we were off to the Royal Theater in Baltimore for another ten days.

"The Baltimore show started on a Friday, just like the Uptown, so we were to leave that Thursday evening, get to Baltimore, and check into our hotel. We were so excited, we hardly got any sleep the night before.

"Well, Miss Mattie came to pick us up at about five, five-thirty that Thursday evening. She had one of those lil U-Haul kinda things attached to the back of the Brown Bomber that we loaded our suitcases into. The whole neighborhood must have been out there, all our friends, people from the church.

"MuDear was cryin like we were goin off to war, and I think PawPaw was, too, though he tried to be all cool about it and everything. You know men. Anyhow, after we had all hugged and kissed and taken pictures and everything, we started off.

"Before we hit the road, we had to go by Jimmy Dunn's. He wanted us to do one last run-through of our lil fifteen-minute act. But instead of drivin us to Jimmy's, we found ourselves back in front of Johnson's Funeral Parlor.

"*'Yall go on ahead. Ruthie, you take the wheel. I got to stop in here and take care of some business. You all just come on back for me when you're ready.'*

"PawPaw had taught Ruthie to drive and she had her driver's license, so we didn't think nothin of it. We went on down to Jimmy's. Well, by the time he had given us his lecture and taken us through the run-through fifty million times, about two hours had passed. Finally, he let us go.

"By now, it was about seven-thirty or so, dark outside. So we go back to the funeral home, Ruthie parks, and I run to the door. Well, I rang and rang that doorbell, but nobody answered.

"'*Try the door, try the door. See if it's open.*' You know how impatient Ruthie can get. So I tried the door, and it was unlocked. Now, I wasn't hardly gone walk in no funeral parlor by myself, so I called Venus, asked her to come with me. Well, the two of us walked in, didn't *see* nobody, didn't *hear* nobody.

"We're yellin '*Hello, hello,*' and gettin no answer at all. Venus was ready to split. So was I. Then we heard the snoring."

"Snoring, did you say?"

"Snoring. We followed the sound all the way to the back of the funeral home as it got louder and louder. We could hear it comin from a lil side room, so we opened the door and tiptoed in. And there she was."

"Miss Mattie?"

"Miss Magdelina Smart. Girl, she was stretched out on her back in a coffin, alongside some other people. Newly dead people. I guess they was dead. They wasn't makin no noises, and I wasn't tryin to look. She was the only one snoring."

"Let me get this straight: The woman was lying in a coffin in a room full of dead people, snoring?"

"Not only was she snoring, she was drunk as a skunk. Shit-faced! We dragged her out of the funeral parlor and were just about to load her into the backseat of the Brown Bomber when the cops pulled up."

✳ ✳ ✳

Letter for Legs from Birdie

Hi, Legs. Birdie here. How are your interviews coming along? I hope the girls are cooperating.

I'm writing to you this time because I'm a little concerned about Venus and how you're goin to treat her in your story. I want you to go a little easy on her if you can. I'm sure Ruthie and Addie have filled you in that Venus has only had one man in her whole life, Ray, that she's a professional virgin, and all about that.

They tend to laugh at her and make fun of her. I used to also. I don't anymore.

See, what happened with them is, for Venus and Ray, it was love at first sight. No doubt about it. Only thing was they met at the best part of her life and the worst part of his. True, Ray was a member of the fabulous Heartbreakers, and I don't have to tell you just how fabulous they were. I mean, they were it! Right?

Well, on the night we met the Heartbreakers, Ray was drunk, sick, and about to be skinned alive by two human barracudas. I ain't kiddin. For real. What happened was, we were appearing on a rock-and-roll show at the Howard Theater in Washington, and the Heartbreakers were working across town at this ritzy private corporate function at one of the big hotels there.

So that night while we were at the Howard, word got around that it was one of the Heartbreakers' birthday and there would be a late-night party for him at their hotel, and we were all invited. What the young folks call an afterparty nowadays. We just called it a party.

Well, honey, we could not wait. We adored them. We thought they were the sharpest things since sliced bread. So, after the show, we all piles up on the band bus and go on over there with the rest of the folks in the show. Miss Mattie had already conked out earlier that night, thank God.

So we get to the suite, and everybody's partying hearty. We got to meet all the guys in the group, who seemed really nice and glad to see us.

"Where's Ray? Where's Ray?" Venus wanted to know. She always did have a lil crush on the guy, even before they met. He was tall, handsome, and a fabulous dancer, and if there was anything that girl liked to do, it was dance. We looked around for him, but no Ray in sight.

Well, anyhow, we danced and ate and drank and had a good time, and then Ruthie ran out of cigarettes. At the time, she was busy gigglin and flirtin with one of the Heartbreakers, and, trust me, she did not want to leave that man. So I volunteered to go down to the lobby and get her a pack. I asked Venus to go with me. So we go downstairs, get the cigarettes, and were on our way back to the elevator when we see this guy in front of us half staggering, and half being dragged to the elevator by these two women. We get up close and realize that the guy is Ray Wright.

"Well, Hellooo, ladieeees!"

He slurred his words slightly when he spoke and was clearly feelin no pain, but even so, that sexy baritone voice had us swooning. He was smiling that awesome smile, and when he looked at Venus, his eyes stayed right there on her. Well, the two women with him didn't like that one bit. They rolled their eyes at us and grabbed Ray even tighter.

"What's your room number again, baby?" one of them asked him as we all stepped into the open doors of the elevator. Ray fished his hotel key out of his pocket.

"Seven-oh-seven. But they're giving a party in here somewhere for Jack tonight. I just can't remember the room number."

"Don't you worry bout no party, baby. We gone make our own party."

This was the other one talking.

Girl, you should have seen these chicks. Cheap fake-fox coats, fishnet stockings with holes all up and down the sides, scuffed patent-leather spike heels, way-too-tight dresses. Venus and I stared, wondering where Ray could have found these skeezas. They stared back at us, still rolling their eyes around.

When we got to the seventh floor, they stepped out, and that would have been that, except for Ray. He stopped, held the door open and turned around.

"Hey. You pretty ladies have got to come along to my room with us and have a nightcap with me."

He was speaking to both of us, but again, he was only looking at Venus. She was blushing and ducking her head like a schoolgirl. I started to say no, but she nudged me in my side so hard, I thought she would break one of my ribs.

"Well, okay, if it's not too much trouble," she answered, flashing him one of her charm smiles.

Next thing I know, Venus had pulled me out of the elevator along with her, and we were following the three of them down the hall, the two women once again supporting Ray on either side.

Well, we got into his room. Venus and I introduced ourselves and sat down on the bed.

"The Sweethearts of Soul! Oh, yeah. I've heard your record. You girls sound good, real good," Ray said, nodding his head appreciatively.

There was a sofa there, and the two women lost no time

seating Ray down in the middle with the two of them on either side of him. From somewhere, I don't know where to this day, somebody pulled out a fifth of vodka.

One of the man-eaters jumped up, raced down the hall, and returned with a bucket of ice. The other one ran into the bathroom and reappeared with plastic glasses. Three plastic glasses. She poured drinks for Ray, herself, and her girlfriend. It was as though me and Venus weren't even in the room.

"Oh, no, oh, no. Don't you ladies care for anything?" Ray asked, as soon as he noticed me and Venus sitting there twiddling our thumbs.

"Oh, we'll just have some soda," I said, scurrying out of the room and down the hall to the vending machines, where I bought Cokes for me and Venus.

So I come back and we're sitting there, drinking Cokes while they sat and had vodka rocks. It was just as well. We didn't know nothin about no vodka in those days, nohow.

Ray, by this time, was holding his stomach, complaining that he didn't feel good. We could see beads of perspiration breaking out on his forehead, and he had removed his jacket and tie.

"Hold up just a minute, ladies."

He got up and staggered into the bathroom. As soon as he closed the door, the two barracudas glared at us.

"Why don't you lil young bitches beat it?" said one.

"Yeah. Why don't yall get the fuck outta here?" snarled the other.

I was scared.

"No. Ray invited us for a drink, and we're not goin nowhere until we finish our drink," Venus said, standing up and putting one hand on her hip. The four of us had a staring contest until Ray returned from the bathroom.

When he came back, he carried a gigantic bottle of milk of magnesia with him. He sat back down between the man-killers, opened the bottle, and took a large swig, followed by a large gulp from his glass of vodka.

The barracudas looked like they were actually trying to climb him like a tree by now, legs all wrapped around his legs, hands all in his hair, whispering and sticking their tongues in his ear and everything. He didn't look well at all. I was giving Venus the signal that we should go, but she was so busy looking at Ray, she acted like she didn't hear me. Finally, I stood up.

"Well, thank you for the drink. We really have to get back to the party now, or the rest of the girls will be worried about us." I grabbed Venus and forced her to stand up with me.

"Oh, no, girls. You can't go. We haven't even gotten acquainted yet."

Ray stood quickly as me and Venus headed for the door. We could see he wanted us to stay, but Ray wasn't really in no shape that night to get acquainted with us or anybody else. Actually, he looked a little scared of those women, and we were both scared to leave him alone with them.

Still he managed to get up and stagger over to where we were. The two women were shooting daggers at us, and I'm steady pulling Venus toward the door.

"Tell you what. We got to check in with the other girls now, but we'll be back," she whispered into Ray's ear, flashed that smile, and you know that smile Venus got.

I pulled her out the door. So what we did was, we went back to the party and told the other guys in the Heart-breakers about Ray's condition, especially about the barra-cudas, and they sent somebody down to rescue him.

By then, the party was breaking up anyway, and we thanked the guys, collected all our people, and left.

I thought that was the end of it, but the next day when we woke up, there were two big boxes of chocolates, the fancy, expensive ones, and two giant bouquets of long-stemmed roses for Venus and me, from you-know-who. About an hour later, he called to thank us and insisted we all be his guests at an early dinner.

Well, we all went, but me, Addie, and Ruthie might as well have been wallpaper. He only had eyes for Vee.

And that's how it began. She met him at the best part of her life, and the worst part of his. She was coming up, and he was going down.

And now, here I am trying to dig myself out of the same dark hole that she fell into when he died. If it hadn't been for Raven, I think Venus would have refused to go on living. She's lucky she had someone to live for. See, Vee got past Ray's death because of her child, but she never got over it. I didn't understand that till I lost my Butch. I do now. See, Venus doesn't want to let Ray go, doesn't want to move on. Neither do I. Good night.

*   *   *

Addie

"That's all she wrote."

Addie was quiet for a long time after listening to my report of Birdie's letter to me. I could see her weighing it in her mind, whether to tell me any more or not. Finally, she spoke.

"Well, since Bird told you that much, I guess it ain't no harm in me fillin you in on the rest. Actually, it ain't that much more to tell.

"The bottom line was Ray suffered from sickle-cell anemia. Back then, it was a big secret. He was afraid if the record company found out, they would get rid of him, and for Ray, not being a Heartbreaker was like not being alive. So he stayed in the group, sang like a deacon, and danced like a demon, drinkin for the pain.

"He managed to hang in there for a few more years, too, but eventually, the combination of the sickle-cell, the wear and tear on his body from constant traveling and performing, not to mention the drinkin, finally got the best of him. When we met him, he had already lost his wife and family. Then the Heartbreakers kicked him to the curb, he lost the hair salon and the barbershop he had bought during the good times, and he owed the IRS big time.

"The next time we ran into him, he was tryin to go it alone, doin a one-night stand at some toilet in Cleveland.

"Venus, of course, fell for him hard. She did everything she could to rehab him and nurse him back to health, but it was too late, too much damage was done. They spent the last year of his life together, where she was more like his nurse than his lover.

"When he died, though, you would have thought he was still a Heartbreaker. Oh, yeah. They gave him this big, elaborate funeral, where all the old friends came back, people he couldn't even get on the telephone during the last year of his life.

"Venus had his body flown back to New York, as his family had requested. We rented a limo and rode up there to the funeral, and Venus, pregnant with Raven, was not allowed into the church. We were told at the door that the Sweethearts of Soul were not welcome. Just like Miss Mattie. It was true then, and it's still true today. Outside wives just don't get no respect."

Legs and Roe

What's up, Roe?

Well, let me see: when last we spoke, you were, on the one hand, raving about Ruth Thomas's bowling-alley performance, and on the other hand, trying to get at some mystery as to why the SOS, as you call them, aren't speaking.

Yeah, well, guess what? I still haven't figured that one out. Yet. So far, they each seem to live their own lives independent of the other. Each of them has one kid apiece, except for Birdie—

Ah, the mythical Birdie. And have you met her yet?

You mean, in person?

No, by carrier pigeon. Of course I mean in person.

Welllll, not exactly.

But you have *spoken with her on the telephone?*

Uh—no, I haven't, but the awards ceremony is only about three weeks away. I'm sure we'll meet by then.

Um-hmn. So she says she's going to the ceremony?

Well, not exactly. But the others are all committed, so I'm sure they'll be able to talk her into attending.

You sound mighty sure of yourself for somebody who hasn't even met the woman face-to-face.

What can I say? But guess what? Guess who's going to be interviewing Frank Flood next week?

Frank Flood? The Music Man?

The man himself. Now, you know how long I've been trying to get either him or Fluffy to talk to me. Well, his secretary called me yesterday, and said Mr. Flood could spare a few minutes with me on the fourteenth. Deal done.

Watch yourself, girl. And, Legs?

Yeah?

Make sure you ask the Music Man what Fanya Dance is really like.

Ruthie

"See? She got it all ass-backwards, as usual. We played the Regal in Chicago first, not the Royal. And I ought to know. I was the one doin the drivin. But, yeah, she right about Miss Mattie. Man, we had to do some fast-talkin that night."

I am sitting on the round bed in Ruthie's red, purple, and leopard-covered bedroom. Ruthie is trying to finish the story Addie started of the shit-faced Miss Mattie, but she is clearly preoccupied, searching through dresser drawers, peering into envelopes, looking under various bottles of perfumes and toiletries on her dresser.

"I just know my motherfuckin money better be here, and it better be here tonight. That girl don't know who she playin with. Let her keep it up, and I swear, she gone be the youngest chile in Philadelphia with a full set of false teeth."

"Beg pardon?"

"Oh, nothin. Nothin. Just talkin bout my daughter."

"Do you want me to help you with anything?"

"No, nothin you can do."

I gathered that there was money missing, and clearly, Sunni was the leading suspect. Ruthie stood in the middle of the room, looking around for a few minutes more, then finally shook her head and gave up, motioning me to follow her back downstairs.

"Yeah, chile. Here we are loadin Miss Mattie's drunk ass into the backseat of the Bomber and up pulls The Man."

Ruthie and I were now back downstairs in her living room, sharing beers. She seemed a little more relaxed now, but I could tell that missing-money thing was still bothering her.

"'Get them promo records and some pictures,' I whispered to the girls while I stepped out of the car, tryin to act like it was the most normal thing in the world for four teenaged girls and a middle-aged drunk lady to be parked in the driveway of a dark funeral parlor on a Friday night.

"'Uh, good evening, officers.'

"Girl, you talking bout a Chiclet smile? I was grinning so hard, my teeth hurt.

"'Anything the matter, girls?'

"One cop had stepped out of the police car and was flashing a light on us, while the other still sat in the passenger seat.

"'Oh, nothing we can't handle, Officer. See, our Aunt Mattie here just lost a dear friend, and I think the shock of seeing him in the casket was just too much for her. She just passed right out cold. We came to take her home.'

"I tried shaking my head and looking down, all sorrowful-like and everything. Then Venus stepped in.

"'Hi, Officer. We're the Sweethearts of Soul. I'm sure you've heard our new record, "You May Not Know."'

"Venus was smiling that megawatt smile on the two young white men. By then, the girls had gotten Miss Mattie into the backseat and were all standing beside me. The cops looked at us, from one to the other, especially at Birdie, who seemed terrified.

"'Would yall like some free copies of our record?'

"Before they could even think to answer, Addie was handing out the merchandise.

"'And here, here's some eight-by-ten glossies for you to take home to your families.'

"Venus was right behind her, handing out the photos.

"One thing I learned about people, no matter where you go: they love the idea of meetin celebrities, and they love getting something for free. I don't think those cops knew the Sweethearts of Soul from a can of paint. But seein those glossies and records was more than enough to convince them that we must be something hot.

"They both grinned, ooohed and ahhed over our pictures, while the girls filled them in on our recent Uptown Theater appearance as well as our upcoming tour.

"I had the motor idling and had turned up the radio so they couldn't hear Miss Mattie's loud snoring. Finally, after what seemed like forever, they left."

Ruth sat back, putting her feet up on the sofa.

"And that was just the first of many close calls with Miss Mattie. Honey, that woman was a real piece of work."

"Surely Jimmy Dunn didn't know that she was a, uh, that she had a drinking problem?"

"Guess not. See, Miss Mattie was one of them ole-school chicks. Sober as a judge by day, drunk as a skunk by night. Now, when she was sober, she handled her business. But when she got looped, hey, that was a whole nother story."

"Whew. So what happened when he found out?"

"When who found out?"

"When Jimmy Dunn found out?"

"Found out what?"

"When he found out about Miss Mattie?"

Ruthie cocked her eye at me, a slow smirk stealing across her face.

"Oh, Jesus! You all never told him about Miss Mattie?"

"Now, what you think? Put yourself in our places."

"Well, that would be difficult, because I can't even imagine a bunch of teenaged girls being on the road for the first time in your lives with only a drunk, passed-out chaperone in the first place."

"Hmph! That was just the beginning. Not only had we never really been on the road before by ourselves, here we were tryin to find our way to Chicago, in the middle of the night, fussin over a map, and scared as hell. But we were determined we were gone make it.

"If we had called back home and told about Miss Mattie, that would have been the end of it. MuDear would have pulled us back in so fast, we never would have gone nowhere. We woulda been through before we started.

"So here we were, flyin down Route 13, on our way to Chicago. You know what? I'm wrong. Addie's right. We *was* goin to the Howard, in Washington, cause now I remember we had to get on 95 and damn near got lost out there by the airport, tryin to find the damn thing."

"But you guys did make it to D.C. all right?"

"Oh, we made it eventually. It was pretty much a straight run as long as you followed the signs and all that. So from Philly to D.C., that was the easy part. The trouble started after we got off of 95.

"We got off 95 somewhere in the heart of D.C., and none of us had a clue where the Howard Theater was, or the hotel we had been booked into. By now, it was really late, and the section of town we were in looked pretty rough. Besides, I had to pee real bad.

"So we take this turn and we end up outside of the city and it looked like we were back in the country somewhere. Since we were in the damn woods, anyway, I decided to pull over and go to the bathroom before I had an accident. So we pulls over on the road beside this tree, jumps out, and all of us stepped back into the woods and go to the bathroom.

"Well, honey, we back there squattin, drawers down to our ankles, dresses hiked up to our waists, when we hear this noise. Sounded like some kind of wounded animal or somethin.

"'What's that? What was that?' Birdie whispered. Now, I'm tryin to pull up my panties and finish peein at the same time.

"'I don't know. I can't stop peein,' I said, and I really couldn't. Vee was startin to mumble the Lord's Prayer, as usual.

"Then we heard it again, only this time, it was closer.

"'Ahhhh! Ahhh! It's somethin movin over there behind that bush! Let's go, let's go!' Birdie was screamin like a crazy person. But for once, nobody told her to shut up. We had all seen those bushes move, so this time it wasn't just her imagination. We pulled our panties up and took off outta those woods, you hear me?

"We jumped in the Brown Bomber, I turned that ignition, and we pulled off so fast we burned rubber on the road. Girl, I was drivin that car like I stole it! We flew down the road for about a mile till we saw a sign saying D.C., turn left. I hung a quick left, and we were about two or three miles down that road before we realized Miss Mattie wasn't in the car."

"What? You mean you all left that poor woman back in the woods peeing?"

"Hell, no. She never got outta the car in the first damn place. She had been in the backseat, snorin. What happened was, when we took off, she had been leanin on the door of the car and fell out."

"Get the hell outta here!"

"Swear to God, swear to God. That's the truth, or my name ain't Ruth. Girl, we were scared to death. We didn't know whether the woman was dead or what.

"So at the first exit we came to, we doubled back and drove down the road real slow, lookin for that same spot. And when we found it, sure enough, there was Miss Mattie, lyin on the side of the road, all curled up in a ball, still snorin. You would have thought the woman was home in bed or somethin."

"Oh, girl, go ahead. You've got to be lying now."

"No lie. Right hand to God. You ask the girls. They'll tell you."

Ruthie was roaring at the memory. I'm shaking my head, trying to imagine this little old lady lying on the road, snoring.

"Well, we pulled over and parked. We picked her up and put her back in the backseat of the car. And I swear, she never woke up, not once. Now, you know we was movin fast, cause we had already seen them bushes movin.

"But finally, we got back on the road again, and you can believe when we got into D.C. the second time, we stopped at the nearest gas station and asked for directions to the hotel, like we shoulda done in the first damn place.

"Oh, yeah. I'm tellin you, you could probably fill a book with just the stories on Miss Mattie."

"Sounds like it."

"But, you know, it turned out good for all of us. Miss Mattie made quite a bit of money on the side, doing men's hair as well as women's."

"Men's hair? What? She did processes, too?"

"No. Press and curl only. She used to brag to everybody about doin the dead people's hair.

"'Strictly press and curl, darlin, strictly press and curl. And when I burn em, they don't complain.'

"Well, she burned us quite a bit, and everybody else, and we *did* complain. But who else were we gone find who could be bribed every night with a pint of whiskey? Chile, before it was all over, Miss Mattie was one of the reasons we all started wearin wigs. And that's the truth.

"But anyhow, back to that night. Have you ever heard of Torchy Tucker?"

"Who?"

"Torchy Tucker and her Powderpuff Revue."

I shook my head.

"Well, when we finally got to the hotel, the first person we met in the lobby was Torchy Tucker. They were female impersonators. Real good. One of them used to dance with an eight-foot snake, and some of them danced with twirling fire batons and hoops on fire and stuff. And all the while, they'd be singin and dancing, all dressed like women."

"No kidding?"

I was trying to draw a visual, but having a little trouble seeing it.

"Oh, yeah. Well, anyway, we introduced ourselves to Torchy and told her about our predicament with Miss Mattie.

"Well, Torchy and her girls must have felt sorry for us. We probably looked so pitiful, standin there, tryin to figure out how to check into the hotel by ourselves.

"So her and her girls helped us to get Miss Mattie up into our rooms, while Torchy got us checked in. We didn't know nothin about how to check into no hotel, even though the rooms had already been reserved and paid for.

"The Powderpuffs looked out for us the whole time we were there. Taught us a few makeup tricks, too. They even baby-sat Miss Mattie for us a few times when we wanted to sneak out."

"What? You mean the Sweethearts of Soul actually snuck out?"

Ruthie grinned, lighting a cigarette.

"Hey. It was our first time outta town on our own. What did you think we was gone do? How do you think Venus met Ray? How do you think Birdie got together with Butch? Girl, for the first time in our lives, we were free, free, free at last."

I told her about the letter and phone messages from Birdie. I was a little concerned. She had sounded kind of down to me, and I told Ruth so.

"Yeah, well, what are you gone do? You ever seen Butch Taylor?"

I nodded.

"No. I mean, did you ever see him in person?"

"No. I saw him a few times on TV, though, back when he was still making records."

Ruthie nodded slowly.

"Yeah. I know he looked good on TV, but, seriously, Butch was one of those people, you really had to be there. You really had to see him up close and personal. Pretty enough to be a girl, swear to God.

"He was a friend of ours from way back when we first started playin the clubs in Philly. Super nice guy. That was the thing about Butch. As fine as he was, he didn't even seem to know it. He was about ten, eleven years older than we were when we first met him, so he kinda looked after us, treated us like little sisters.

"But, trust me, that's not the way I was lookin at him at all."

"What about Birdie? Was it love at first sight, or anything like that, for her?"

"Oh, no, chile. I mean, we all thought he was a cutie and everything, but way too old for us. Especially Birdie. I guess that's one of the reasons we all became friends first. Anyhow, we used to run interference for him sometimes, keep the women off of him, and I *do* mean women.

"Chile, they were all over the place. Backstage, at the stage door, standin around his car, leavin all kinds of notes and things on his windshield and shit. We even heard there was some woman who when she had sex with him had punched holes in the condom, just tryin to get pregnant by him so she could have a pretty baby. That kinda mess.

"I'm tellin you, he had em comin and goin and comin again."

"I can dig it. If I had been around, I probably would have been one of them, too."

Ruthie laughed.

"Funny thing, though. All the women loved Butch, except the one he married."

"Married? Oh yeah, I seem to remember him being in and out of court for alimony, or something like that."

"I'm sure you do. That woman picked everything but the gold outta the man's teeth."

"You say she didn't love him?"

"Hell no. I think she was in love with the *idea* of being Mrs. Butch Taylor, the star's wife. But as for Butch Taylor, the man, that bitch couldn't have cared less."

"What did she do? Run around on him or something?"

"Hmph! What didn't she do? But I can remember the first time we ever heard about her.

"Butch came to see us at a club one night, claimin he was throwin away his little black book, he had found the girl of his dreams. We were happy for him, so we asked him to bring her around to see us.

"The next night he did. They caught our show, then we went out to meet her. Very beautiful girl, seemed nice enough, but Addie said whenever Butch wasn't lookin she was sizin us up, like we was the competition or somethin.

"I dug it, too. She was all sweetness and light unless she thought you weren't lookin at her. Then them eyes got narrow as laser beams.

"Well, we figured the chile had a right to be paranoid. After all, just about every other woman in the room was slidin her eyes over at Butch. He wasn't only hot-lookin, his career was pretty hot at that time. He already had about four or five hits under his belt.

"Then one afternoon, we ran into them downtown at Wanamaker's department store.

"After makin a lil small talk, Butch decided to go over to the men's department and left her with us. We was standin at the cash register together, and when they went to total her things up, they noticed that her charge card, which, was in his name, had expired.

"'*Butch! Butch! Get over here! Now!*' The girl was yellin like somebody had pulled her wig off or somethin. '*He's so fuckin stupid!*'

"Butch came runnin over. The store had sent him a new card but he forgot to bring it along. No big deal.

"Once she realized we were starin at her, she became Lil Miss Sweetness again. But it was too late. We had peeped her card. That girl didn't give a damn about Butch. Bad enough he was bein cheated by his record company, he was also bein cheated on by his wife, and when the hits ran out, and the money ran out, she ran out, too. Nearly destroyed the guy."

"I don't get it. Any man that good-looking wouldn't seem to have any problem at all finding somebody new."

Ruthie was quiet for a minute, her face a blank. "Somethin most people didn't know about Butch was, well, he wasn't the brightest star in the night sky."

Ruthie was speaking quietly now, her head bowed. I said nothing.

"He was what you might even call slow, mildly retarded."

I looked at her, astonished.

"You must be joking."

"No, I'm not joking. Wish I was. Fact of the matter was, Butch was almost totally illiterate. Read on about maybe a second-grade level. Could hardly spell much more than his name. Oh, he managed to hide it pretty well. Learned to memorize street signs, simple directions, what he would say at interviews, and stuff like that.

"But anybody who knew him really, really well could tell you that Butch's movie-star looks and that fantastic voice were probably God's way of compensatin him for makin him so slow. He was a great showman, could tear up any stage anywhere, anytime. Offstage, he was just the opposite. Quiet, shy. And that was one of the reasons why."

Oh, no. First Simon Hall was gay, now Butch Taylor was retarded. My idols were crumbling before my eyes.

"It didn't take that bitch long to find that out, neither. Hmph! That's why she married him in the first place. Claimin to be pregnant and all. Couple of months later, she suppose to have lost the baby. Sheeit! Wasn't no baby in the first damn place, if you ask me. You know she left him for his sleazy manager, don't you?"

I shook my head.

"Hell, yeah. The same manager who cheated him out of all of his money. Left him lookin like a first-rate chump. When he was makin all those hit records in the sixties, they were callin him the man with the golden touch. Well, by the seventies everything he touched seemed to turn to shit.

"Boy couldn't get arrested. He was gettin a benefit here and there, a one-nighter every once in a while. But by then, most of the artists gettin signed were self-contained bands—you know, bands who could sing *and* play. There wasn't much call for solo crooners like Butch.

"Same with us. People ask me all the time what happened to the Sweethearts of Soul, why we broke up, and I tell em the same thing I'm tellin you now. Disco killed the Sweethearts.

"That's right. See, you gotta put yourself in the club owner's shoes. From the mid-sixties straight through the early seventies, we was workin four, five, sometimes even six nights a week. Hit record or no hit record.

"That's a four-member singing group with a four-piece, sometimes six-piece backup band that club owners had to pay out.

"Well, along come disco, and suddenly the club owner could pay some guy with a stack of records one-third of that payout, stick one of them glass balls up on the ceilin, put in a few colored lights and a killer amp, turn the volume up, and call it a disco. Hey. You do the math. Same thing that happened to Butch happened to all of us. We just didn't get swindled like he did, thanks to God and Jimmy Dunn."

"And that's when he met up with Birdie again?"

"Met up with? They never lost touch in the first place. They ran into each other on the Strip one night, got to talkin about old times, just hangin out, you know.

"Butch was doin pretty bad by then, and Birdie, well, by then, Birdie, who dragged home every stray cat, one-eyed dog, or broken-wing bird she ever saw, Birdie had been through some hard times of her own by then.

"Oh, Lord, the two of them. You should have seen em. Holdin on to each other like two wounded birds, backs against the wall."

Ruthie was shaking her head again, looking down at the floor. Hmn. Something wasn't adding up quite right here.

"So the two of them hooked up?"

Ruthie nodded, eyes closed, a slight smile on her face.

"Stayed together until his death, about a year and a half ago."

I looked at her again. I didn't know what it was, but I could feel it. There was something she was leaving out.

"Well, the rest of you approved of that, didn't you? I mean, you say Butch was a nice guy and all, even though he was slow."

"Oh, we definitely approved. We loved Butch like a brother. We were happy for both of em. They were even talkin about gettin married at one point. We were delighted."

"Okay. Then why didn't they get married?"

"Well, they decided—hell, we all decided it was better financially for them to stay single. There was a situation where one of them's checks probably would have been cut, or reduced, or somethin like that. Better to leave things as they were."

"Checks? What kind of checks?"

"You know. Their disability checks."

"What kind of disability?"

Ruth bit her lip for almost a full minute. I waited.

"They were *wounded*. Like I said, they were *wounded*. Excuse me, gotta make a phone call."

With that, Ruthie was up and gone into the kitchen, leaving me to wonder what in the hell she had been talking about. I could hear her yelling something over the phone, but she had turned the radio up back in the kitchen, so I couldn't hear what was being said.

A couple of minutes later, she came rushing back into the living room, slipping into her leather jacket.

"Look, we'll have to pick this up some time later. I gotta go get my daughter."

I had no choice but to follow her out the door and into the street, where I stood watching as she jumped into her big old red Caddy and took off.

Disability checks? Wounded? What the hell?

Venus

Venus Jones and I sat in her cozy living room, finishing off the last of her homemade peach cobbler, which was so good it made you want to cry, washing it down with lemonade. It was the evening after my meeting with Ruthie.

As usual, Venus was her cheery self. I decided to take a chance on bringing up the interrupted conversation I had had with Ruthie the night before.

"Ruthie had been telling me a little bit about Butch and Birdie."

Venus kept busy, but a cloud fell over her voice.

"'Death of a Song-and-Dance Man.' That was the headline, you know, the headline announcing his obituary.

'Death of a Song-and-Dance Man.' It was a damn shame. Do you know there were only about twenty, twenty-five people at his funeral, including the four of us?"

Venus went on as if talking to herself.

"Where were all those big-time friends of his? Where were all those beautiful people who had swilled that champagne and scarfed down that caviar at all those famous, legendary three-day penthouse parties him and that money-grubbing skeeza used to have? Where was *she*, for that matter? Not even a card, not even a flower.

"It's an old sayin, but it's true. Nobody knows you when you're down and out."

Venus sighed as she brought a fresh pot of tea over to the coffee table and sat down on the love seat beside me.

"Ruthie mentioned something about them getting disability checks."

Venus stirred her tea slowly, took a sip.

"Well, you know he hadn't been a well person for quite some time, going all the way back to the seventies. When that woman left him and they took all his money, he had sunk into this deep depression. Wouldn't eat, couldn't sleep. You know. A bad case of the blues.

"From what I understand, a few of his real friends went by his apartment one day—well, it was really just a room— and found him unconscious. When they got him to the hospital, the doctors found that he had had a brain tumor all his life."

"A brain tumor? About how old was he by then?"

"About thirty-five, thirty-six. Seemed nobody had noticed it all those years, and by then, the way it was positioned, the doctors felt it was too risky to remove it."

"So was that the reason for his—uh, slowness?"

"So Ruthie told you, huh? Yes. That's what the doctors felt. That's why he qualified for the disability check. He seemed to be doin all right, though, as long as he took his medication, which Birdie made sure of. It wasn't until about the last year or so that he started really actin strange."

"Acting strange? How do you mean?"

"Took to walkin around talkin to himself, yellin at people on the street for no reason. You know, that kind of thing. Birdie was constantly callin one of us to go with her and pick him up and bring him back home."

"What did the doctors say?"

"They found the tumor was pressing against his brain and growing. They gave him stronger medication, trying to dissolve it, but he didn't like to take it. Birdie said it made him drowsy and weak, made him drool all the time, and sometimes lose control of his bladder. Made him so he couldn't have an erection. Well, you know men. You can understand why he didn't want to take it."

"So that's what killed him, huh? The tumor?"

"That's what did it. One morning Birdie went out to the market to get some groceries, and when she came back she found him still lyin in bed, dead."

"Damn. Tough break."

"Tell me about it."

"Do you know they had been together for almost fifteen years? Longer than a lot of folks stay married?"

I nodded.

"Ruthie said that Birdie was also receiving some kind of check."

"Birdie had her own problems. But Butch took care of her for as long as he could. And she did her best to take care of Butch, and she did a damn good job, too."

Venus was busying her hands with the tea things again.

"What problems? What kinds of problems did she have? How was she disabled?"

"Well, after the incident. Uh, you know . . ."

Venus stopped what she was doing, looked at me slowly, warily.

"Uh-uh. I don't wanna talk about Butch and Birdie no more. You said you wanted some road stories. Do you still want some road stories?"

"Sure. I'm always up for road stories." By now, I knew when I was licked.

"Oh, honey, we had so much fun on the road. All these people talkin about how the road was so hard, so draining, so rough. Don't you believe a word of it. We had a ball playin the chitlin circuit.

"But you really had to watch out for yourself, and we learned the ropes. You better believe we did. I was always known as the Miss Goody Two-Shoes of the group, and they can tell you, I would be ready to go in a minute if things didn't look right.

"On one tour we played—I think we were in Richmond, but it might have been Norfolk, Virginia. Well, after the show, there was a lil first-night party in the band director's room. So we're sittin up there drinkin our lil beer—beer was really mostly all we drank back then—and meetin some of the locals. Well, these guys come in and invite us to what they called the juke joint."

I nodded. "Yeah, I know what a juke joint is. They have them all over the South."

"Well, I know what one is, too, *now*. But at the time, we had never heard of a juke joint. We didn't know what the hell the guy was talkin about. Anyhow, we all piled up in cars and goes to the juke joint, which is really nothin but this big ole white square building way back in the woods.

"Well, we walked in single file behind the men, and chile, it was dark as the devil in there. All we could see was a few blue lights around the place and flames from lighters whenever somebody lit up a cigarette.

"We could hear voices, though, and we could tell we were in a room full of people. We just couldn't see nobody. Next thing I know, I'm feelin somebody grab my butt. *'Hey, baby. Looking for papa?'*

"Well, that was it. I was red ta go. Ruthie told me to stop actin like an idiot, but I ain't care. I was red ta go! By this time, the guys had found a table for us. I had no choice but to stay, since nobody else wasn't goin nowhere, and I certainly didn't have no ride.

"Anyway, after a while, I learned to take those kinds of things in stride. After all, wasn't too much I could do about somebody grabbin my butt in the dark. But you really had to stay sharp on that road."

"Did you ever have any really bad experiences?"

"Not us, personally. But a few other women did. I think we did all right because when we went out on that first tour, we were with all Philly groups, and those guys kind of watched out for us, schooled us, you know. We'd all sung together at so many places, we were really like family.

"I'm talkin about people like the Del Fonics, the Intruders, the Trammps, Rico and the Ravens, Billy, the Blue Notes, the Vibrations, the Volcanoes, and plenty of others.

"Just about everybody knew everybody. We really lucked out that way.

"But it wasn't like that for *all* the women out there.

There was some real horror stories. There was one show we worked in Chicago, the Regal again, ten-day gig. It was us, some of our Philly guys, and a couple other acts. One of the acts was—"

Venus leaned over and whispered the name of a female singer who had been quite popular at the time.

"Now, that's not for publication, okay? Strictly off the record."

I nodded.

"She was a nice girl, you know. Sheltered, had come from a church background like us. She was all alone except for her three-piece rhythm section, so she took to hangin out with us. This was her first time out of town. She was from down south, and we were tryin to show her the ropes.

"Well, like I said, this show ran ten days. And from day one, she had developed this instant crush on a certain bass player who I will not name. I mean, this girl just drooled over this guy night after night. He was playin for another group and acted like he didn't know the chile was alive. Well, the more he ignored her, the more she wanted him. We'd worked with the guy before, and he'd always seemed kinda stuck-up to us, so we didn't really say much to him besides hi and bye. He was real handsome, true, but so what? There was lots of handsome guys around.

"Anyhow, on the last night of the show, we were invited to a party by a local musician. We weren't even plannin to go, since we knew we had to be up bright and early the next morning and on the road, on to the next town.

"So after the show, we were gettin on the bus to go back to the hotel and here comes this girl, runnin and wavin her arms. '*Sweethearts of Soul!*'

"We froze, thinkin somethin horrible must have happened. But no, seems this bass player had invited her to meet him at the party after the show.

"Well, now. Like I say, we really didn't want to go, but we knew she really liked this guy, this would probably be her last night to see him, and she really didn't want to go alone. So we agreed to go with her.

"Well, as soon as we stepped up on the porch and they opened the door and I seen that hay on the floor, I was red ta go."

"Hay? You mean hay, h-a-y, like horses eat?"

"Yes indeedy, sweetie. See, from the door, you could look right inside to the living room. Now, they ain't have nothin on but blue lights, but I could see hay on the floor, and people's feet. Look to me like people were layin in the hay on the floor. Chile, you know I was red ta go.

"I had already started my lil speech when one of the guys offered to go in and check the place out first. So we wait on the porch, and after a few minutes he comes back out and offers to lead us past the hay room back into some other rooms where there were sofas and chairs and tables and things like that.

"I was still skeptical, but this girl asked if the bass player was inside. Hearing that he was, there was just no stoppin her. So all of us went on in, went to the back, and, like the guy said, people were sittin around on sofas and chairs, talkin, eatin, dancin, just like a regular party. I relaxed a lil bit.

"Now, this was one of those huge apartments where you go down a long hallway and the rooms are off to the side. Well, from what they told me later, there was somethin goin on in just about every one of those rooms, and we must have passed five or six of them to get to the back.

"Anyhow, we get seats at the kitchen table. Somebody

had just got us some beers when this bass player comes strollin back into the kitchen. He slides over to the table, speaks to all of us like all of a sudden we're his best friends. Then he gives this singer one of those looks. You know what I mean.

"This girl is so happy, she's about to burst. And we're happy for her. Finally, she's gone get with this guy. So we're all sittin around talkin to other people at the party, and the singer and the bass player seem to be doing just fine.

"After a while, she waves at us, then disappears into another room with the bass player. Cool. We figure when we're ready to go, we'll just call her and that will be that.

"Well, when we were ready to go, we called her. No answer. We had the guys go from room to room, lookin for her. No luck. She had just disappeared. And so had the bass player. I'm tellin you, we walked back and forth in that place, made the people turn the lights on and everything.

"The girl had vanished. We went outside, callin her name. Down to the corner, around the corner. Nothin.

"Finally, we decided to go on back to the hotel, thinkin she might have gone back there, you know, taken him with her to her room. A few of the guys were goin to stay anyway, so we asked them to be on the lookout for her. You know, make sure she got back to the hotel all right.

"It wasn't until the next morning that we found out what happened."

"And what happened?"

"You ever heard of Spanish fly?"

"Spanish what?"

Riiiiiinnnnngggg! Riiiiiinnnnngggg!

"Hold up, let me get that."

Venus reached over to the end table, picked up the telephone.

"Hello. Oh, hi, Gladys. What? Wait a minute, hold on."

Venus laid the receiver down on the table, picked up the TV remote, which lay on the coffee table in front of us, and flicked it on, activating the floor-model television that sat across the room from us. She picked the receiver up again.

"Okay, it's on. What channel did you say?"

Venus punched a few numbers on the remote in one hand, the other still holding the telephone receiver.

"Oh, my God! Oh, my God!"

Venus stood up, screaming, as she watched what looked like a teenage music program on the television. Just then the front door opened and in walked Raven.

"Mom? What's the matter, Mommy?"

The girl was at Venus's side in a heartbeat, fear coloring her voice.

"Gladys," Venus spoke into the receiver, "thanks for callin. Uh-huh. I gotta hang up now. Bye."

Venus grabbed Raven roughly by the arm, pointing at the TV.

"Look at him! See! The damn CD is number five on the charts! He's a star, a goddamn star! And look at you, standin up here, big belly, poor as a church mouse!"

Raven glanced at the screen, then slumped heavily into an armchair. There on the set was Bobby Lights, a.k.a. MC Flashlight, a.k.a. son of Addie Lights, rapping and dancing up a storm on the BET *Weekly Hip-Hop Countdown* show.

Raven sighed.

"Oh, my God!" Venus repeated, gawking in amazement at the very sight of Bobby, now grinding his pelvis against the backside of a slim, pretty, underdressed young dancer, who was shaking it for all she was worth.

"Wait a minute! Is that—oh, hell, yeah, that's her!

That's that lil hot tamale hoochie mama Sunni, pushin her lil narrow butt all up in the boy's stuff!"

Venus's eyes were bulging, her mouth wide open. I sat staring at the screen. It was Bobby and Sunni, all right, going at it, doing everything but the wild thing.

Bobby Lights and Sunni Thomas? Raven Jones, daughter of Venus, pregnant by Bobby Lights, son of Adeline, dancing on TV with Sunshine Thomas, daughter of Ruth? Oh, Shiiit!

"Well, don't just sit there. What you got to say about *that*?"

Venus was pacing the floor, pointing dramatically, first at Raven, then at the TV. She seemed to forget that I was even in the room.

"Aw, Mommy, get a grip. It's just a video." Raven's tone was nonchalant, but I could see how tightly her hands gripped the arms of the chair.

"I don't care what it is. He's on the TV, and I just had to hear it from that nosy-ass Gladys down the street that 'I'm the One You're Looking For' just posted number five on that countdown thing they do every week. What you mean, *just a video*?"

Raven sighed again, realizing her mother was just not going to let it go.

"Mommy," the girl said slowly, as if speaking to a backward child, "This is the first week they've even played the video on the air. Nobody expected it to take off like that. This is a *good* thing."

"I know damn well it's a good thing. I ain't so old that I don't remember how to read countdown charts. So where's the money at?"

"What money, Mommy?" Raven sounded irritated.

"Raven, the boy got a number-five record nationwide, the boy in videos, *somebody's* buyin the boy's record. Where's the money at?"

Raven flinched each time her mother referred to Bobby as "the boy."

"Oh, Mom, it's way too early for that. Bobby won't be getting any money from the CD sales for at least three or four months. That's the way they do it. They don't just pay you every day for every CD you sell."

Venus thought that one over for a few moments, her almond eyes slanting into slits.

"All right, then. This is Friday night, right? The boy performed right downtown Tuesday night, right?"

"Right." Raven sighed, rolling her eyes.

"And the place was sold out, right?"

"Right, but—"

"And here's this big write-up in yesterday's *Globe*, all about his big show. Here's a big picture of them signin autographs and everything out in front of the Showtime. Here's another picture of him and his group goin into the Luxe for dinner after the show. Right?"

Venus had picked up a newspaper from the coffee table and was showing it to Raven.

"Okay, Mom, I see where you're going with—"

"No, no, just answer my question. That's him goin in the Luxe, ain't it? And after that, it says here they all went to some kind of afterparty at the Shim Sham Lounge, and—"

Venus literally shoved the *Globe* under Raven's nose.

"Just stop it, Mom, stop it!"

The girl flung the paper angrily to the floor.

Venus sighed, sitting down on the sofa next to her daughter.

"Raven. Honey. I'm sorry. I don't mean to upset you. It's just—girl, you got to open your eyes and see what's goin down here."

She tried to take hold of Raven's hand, but the girl pulled away from her.

"So how long is he gone be away this time?"

I could tell by her tone that Venus was trying her best to calm down.

"Six weeks."

"Six weeks. Did he leave you any money?"

"Well, he only gave me two hundred dollars this time, but he's going to send—"

"Two hundred dollars! Do you know it costs more than two hundred dollars just to order drinks and appetizers in that place? Do you know the Luxe is the most expensive restaurant in Philly? Two hundred goddamn dollars?"

Venus was back on her feet now, pacing the floor, one hand on her hip, the other pointing an accusatory finger at her daughter.

"And what about *you*, Raven? I don't see *you* in any of these pictures. I don't see *you* at the Luxe. I don't see your name nowhere in this story. Nothin bout no fiancée, nothin bout no baby on the way. Not a word about you. Just Bobby. No, excuse me. Just MC Flashlight, and *his* crew, and *his* music, his—what it say here in the paper?—his '*wonderfully lyrical spoken-word music.*'"

Venus was reading the quote directly from the *Globe*, which she had retrieved from the floor.

"See? That's why I don't tell you nothin. All you see is the worst in Bobby. I was going to say he's going to be sending me money every week from now on, before you cut me off."

Raven folded her arms over her big belly, poking her mouth out defiantly.

"I thought yall was supposed to be partners in this music thing."

"We *are* partners."

"Oh, yeah? Well, somebody ought to remind Mr. Flashbulb, or whatever the hell he callin hisself these days that he got a partner. Cause the only name I see in here is Bobby's, and *you* the one wrote the damn song in the first place. Two hundred dollars! Sheeit!

"And speakin of partners, what's that slutty lil Sunni doin all up on the TV with him? Look to me like she's more a partner with him than you are!"

That tore it. Raven raised her swollen body up from the armchair with amazing swiftness and stalked out of the room without another word. But I saw her face as she passed me, and I could see she was crying.

"Oh, Lordy, Venus. That child is really hurtin."

Venus turned in my direction, as if seeing me for the first time, and I could see tears standing in her eyes, also. She sat back down, head bent, shoulders slumping.

"Girl, you don't know the half of it. That's *my* chile's song that boy's singin all over the country, *my* chile's words comin outta his mouth. Bobby ain't wrote shit. Raven's been writin poetry all her life. And you should hear her sing! If I could just get her to stand up for herself. But she's so shy."

I told her about how excited Addie had been about Bobby's upcoming tour when I interviewed her, showing me the tape of his last television appearance, and filling me in on his itinerary.

"Um-hmn. I bet she didn't mention anything about my Raven, did she?"

I had to shake my head.

"Well, ain't that a bitch! Bobby goin on tour, Bobby on

TV, singin Raven's songs, Sunni on TV, dancin to Raven's songs, and Raven sittin up here with nothin but a big belly to show for it. She's bein played, and she just won't see it.

"Not again. Please, God, not again. One fool in the family is enough."

Uh-oh. Looks like the proverbial shit has really hit the fan now. Bobby Lights, Addie's son, and Ruthie's daughter, Sunni, together on TV? Raven, Venus's daughter, pregnant by Bobby? Engaged? Songs? Rap? Money? Dayum!

Addie

"Oh! So now, it's all *my* fault, huh? Hmph! If they think they gone put all the blame on me for this mess, they got another thought comin! I can't help it if that lil hot twat Sunni keep followin my boy around everywhere he go.

"She just tryin to get some of that money, and I told him so, too. And what do Venus expect me to do about Raven? I don't know why she callin me. I can't make that boy do nothin! He's a grown man. He may not be actin like one, but he is a grown man.

"If it's really anybody's fault, it's Ruthie's, anyway. Ole Ruthless Ruth! She done raised that girl up to be just like her. Just like her! Tell me something. Has Ruthie ever said anything to you about Sunni's daddy? Ever shown you any pictures of him? I know damn well she ain't, and you know why?

"Cause she don't *know* who the girl's father is, that's why. See, Ruthie really is ruthless, you know. That ain't just no nickname. That ain't just somethin we call her to be cute.

"See, Ruthie's the one who lived the highest on the hog. That's right. You wouldn't think so today, would you? Aside from some good times, the Sweethearts of Soul don't really have a hell of a lot to show for what I call our 'star days.' But we did manage to make a lil bit of money.

"As you know, I bought some real estate, Venus got the shop and the triplex, Birdie, well, Birdie was Birdie, and Ruthie spent every dime on high livin in downtown penthouse apartments, designer clothes, cooks, Cadillacs, maids, and fancy men.

"Oh, yeah, she had the men, all right. Comin and goin, each one better lookin than the one before.

"But the truth is, not one of em meant a damn thing to her. Not a one. Ruthie does not trust men. Never has. Well, there *was* one. But Friday Brown was a real man. He wasn't no lil soft-hand pretty boy that she could order around like the rest of em. He wasn't gone stand for none of her shit. He wasn't gone let her treat him like she did the rest. So he had to go. Why you think none of us ever stayed with Ruthie? Too much wild, crazy shit goin on alla time. That's why.

"Every man became Sunni's new daddy. *'That's your daddy, girl. Say hi to your daddy. Go to your father, girl.'* And that's what he was. Till the next one came along. Then it started all over again. Every hustle Ruthie ever pulled on every man, every scheme she worked to snatch that cash from out his pockets, Sunni was right there watchin and learnin from her.

"Now, what kind of way is that to raise a child? You can't blame the girl for growin up the same way.

"Ruthie's livin in MuDear's house right now because she pulled one scheme too many and had nowhere else to go. All those years and all that money that's gone through her hands, you'd think she'd have put a lil change aside and gone to beauty school, or took up dressmaking like Venus did, or some real estate courses like I did, or somethin. But noooo. Every nickel she gets goes into her new act, her so-called showbiz.

"And she's *still* usin the men for whatever she can get outta em. Then she throws em away like a used Kotex and moves on to the next one. You'd think she woulda run outta fools by now, but nooo. There's always a new one waitin in the wings.

"Ruthie aside, though, the truth is, I'm too shamed to face Venus. I can't get Bobby to leave that Sunni alone. She got him whipped, all right. Hypnotized. I seen her mother do the same thing to so many men, it's not funny.

"And the worst thing about it is, I know what he goin through. I've been there myself, with his daddy. Oh, yeah, chile. Back when I was a young girl, Bobby's father had me goin the same way. Had *me* hypnotized. I woulda done anything the man said, chile! Anything.

"You shoulda seen Robert. Tall, fine, built, black as night, and clean as a city-dressed chitlin! God, he was gorgeous! And the sex! We had that hot, wild, monkey sex, the kind that made your eyes roll back in your head, girl, the kind you get addicted to. You know what I'm talkin bout.

"I could never get enough of him. *Had* to have him, day and night. And he knew it, too. And if it wasn't for the Spirit Woman, I woulda lost everything I had."

"The Spirit Woman?"

Ruth

"The Spirit Woman? Oh, yeah. Miss Gustine. Gustine Blue. Owns the diner down there on Locust Street. Well, at least Miss High and Mighty tellin the truth about that part. I know she tryin to blame my girl for all this mess, but Bobby's just as much at fault as Sunni.

"That boy's so much like his father, it's scary. And *we* the ones that rescued Addie's simple ass from that man in the first damn place—*us*, the Sweethearts of Soul. And that's the truth, or my name ain't Ruth! She can talk that hocus-pocus shit all she want. But *we* the ones who did it.

"I don't know how much she told you, but Addie really was under the spell of that man. It was like she was rooted or somethin, and some say she was.

"We was doin all right then, workin all the time, livin large. Addie was stayin in MuDear's house then. I had an apartment downtown, Venus had the triplex, and Birdie was stayin with her.

"On one of those rare weekend nights when we weren't giggin, we went around to Mr. Silk's, a nightclub on the Strip. Well, we was sittin at a large banquette talkin with Gus, the owner, when this guy walks in—and, girl, he was so fine he looked like wine, do you hear me?

"Drop-dead, catch-your-breath, and hold-your-drawers fine. So he sits at the bar across from our banquette, sends us a magnum of champagne, along with a note askin to meet us. We're, like, *whoa!* Classy move. We look over at him and we're, like, in a contest, tryin to outsmile, out-wink, outflirt each other.

"So the band strikes up an intro, the guy walks over to us, holds out his hand, looks directly at Addie, and asks her to dance. We're, like, dayum! Go head, Ad! So while they're dancin, me, Venus, and Birdie call Gus over and ask for the downlow on the dude.

"So, according to Gus, the guy's supposed to be in real estate, buyin properties, fixin em up and reselling em.

Always clean, always flashin money. A real stylish gent, you know? So, anyhow, him and Addie dance together a few more times, and next thing you know, Addie done moved her seat over to the bar with the dude.

"That's how it started. They got tighter and tighter. Dude might as well have moved in. This went on for about two, three months, and one night, Venus gets a call from Maryland. Addie and this guy done eloped! That's right, got married!

"Well, my antenna shot up over that shit. Why would they have to elope? Addie wasn't married. Robert claimed not to be married. And I know Addie. I *know* that girl woulda wanted a big ole church weddin, with a real preacher, bridesmaids, reception, wedding cake, the whole nine.

"But when I suggested we, ah, check the guy out, she went off on me, told me I was just jealous cause he picked her over me and I was tryin to ruin her happiness and all that ole bullshit. So I said fine, I'm through wit it.

"Anyhow, by the time I finally got good ole Robert checked out, Miss Married Lady had already put his name on MuDear's house along with *hers.* Um-hmn!

"Oh, yeah! Man took to havin wild parties, people layin up in there night and day, stuff missin, stuff gettin stolen. What he was doin was systematically drivin Addie outta her own house!

"By the time we called in Bad Friday Brown, it was almost too late. Addie, pregnant, broke-down, and broken-hearted, had moved in with Venus, too. You *know* she ain't wanna move in with *me*!

"Anyhow, Friday finds out that Robert does this kinda stuff all the time, goes from city to city, sweet-talkin and marryin women, then bullyin them out of their property.

"That's why he went for Addie in the first place. He

already had us checked out, and knew she had the title to MuDear's place.

"Anyhow, we had heard about Miss Gustine Blue, the Spirit Woman, all our lives. People came from far and wide to see her, and more than a few swear by her. Myself, I don't go in for all that ole mumbo-jumbo mess, but when Venus suggested takin Addie down there, I was all for it. Anything to pull her outta the slump she was in.

"She was so down and out, she wasn't even arguin back at me, wasn't even callin me names or cluckin bout my wild and sinful ways. So you *know* the girl was in a bad way. So Venus made an appointment, and they went to see Gustine Blue.

"Now, you know how we always tease her bout that left eye puttin a hex on you, right? Well, from what I hear, Gustine Blue told her to do some chantin with some feathers and powders and candles and some other mess she had to mix up, then she had to fix her left eye on Robert's picture for nine minutes every day for nine days, and at the end of them nine days, he was supposed to be outta the house.

"So Addie did it, and just like Miss Gustine say, Robert packed up his shit and split on the ninth day. And from that day to this, Adeline *swear* she got the power, or the evil eye, or the hoodoo or some mess. Addie ain't got shit but a bad left eye.

"What that fool don't know is while she was hoppin round the room on one foot, speakin in tongues, and throwin Oxydol and colored talcum powder around, I made Venus and Birdie chip in and we hired Bad Friday Brown and some of his boys. They pulled that Negro off the street one night, took him to Cobbs Creek Park, beat the shit outta him, made him sign away any and all rights to MuDear's house, and ran his sorry ass outta town.

"Told him if he came back, he'd be a dead man. Evil eye, my ass! It cost us plenty, but we saved MuDear's house! Again! Later on we heard he was murdered, somewhere in Chicago.

"No, it wasn't us. What? Don't look at me like that!"

Venus

"You think I don't know what they think about me? And I know what they say about me, too, Ruthie and Addie. Treat me like I'm some kinda backward child. Poor Venus, livin in the past, lost in the sixties. Yeah? Well, not no more. Cause I have fuckin had it! No more Miss Nice Guy. Not this time.

"The worst thing about it is, in a way, I believe I'm partly to blame for what's happenin to Raven now. I know they told you all about me still being married to a dead man and my shrine to Raven's dad and everything. Well, all that's true. So what?

"I really *am* still in love with Raymond Wright. I've never even considered anybody else. Now, if that makes me crazy, then I'm fine with that. I'll just have to be crazy, that's all.

"But what I never really thought about in all these years was the effect my craziness would have on Raven. I think now that maybe I kept her a little too close to me, you know? See, me and Ray's thing was private. It had to be. He was married. And before you put me down as some kind of heartless home wrecker, let me tell you the only reason I ended up with Ray in the first place was because his wife didn't want him no more.

"As his sickle-cell symptoms grew worse and worse, he began to drink more and more, to kill the pain.

"But he wasn't no good to the Heartbreakers like that, fallin-down drunk, too looped to step up on a stage. So they let him go. He wasn't no good to his wife, constantly arguin about bills and taxes that he couldn't pay. So she let him go. Ray wasn't no good to nobody.

"Nobody but me. I fell in love with him when I was fourteen years old and saw him perform with the group on the old *Right On* television show.

"I was still in love with him the night when me and Birdie ran into him and these trashy women on a hotel elevator. It might have started as a schoolgirl crush. But it grew into the real thing. For both of us.

"When the Heartbreakers turned him away, when his wife turned him away, he turned to me. I wanted him. And I was more than willin and prepared to take him any way I could get him, rich or poor, drunk or sober, in sickness and in health. And that's exactly what I did. So I don't have no regrets, don't make no apologies to nobody.

"I have only wanted one man in my whole life. And I got him. Our time together was short, only three years. And it certainly wasn't no crystal stair. There were times when Ray's legs hurt him so bad he would scream and cry all night long, chewin aspirins and pain pills like they was candy. Back and forth, in and out of the hospital, gettin worse and worse. Drinkin himself into a stupor.

"But we had our good times, too. There were times when just wakin up in the morning and findin him next to me made me happier than I ever expected I would ever be, when just the sound of his voice, that deep, husky baritone, callin my name, whisperin in my ear, tellin me he loved me, thrilled me down to my toes. It was like I was put here on earth for no other reason than to love Raymond Wright. Just to love him.

"And I'd do it again in a minute, in a heartbeat, tomorrow, today. It was no sacrifice at all. And just look what I got! I got my darlin baby girl. See, I always raised Raven to honor her father, always talked him up, kept pictures of him, kept his name alive. I wanted her to think of Ray as a good and honorable man.

"You know, to this day, nobody really knows how he died. There are no witnesses of record. All we really know for a fact is his body was found lyin on the El tracks at Fifty-second and Market, with the back of his skull cracked open. His death certificate lists the cause of death as accidental fall. But right from the start, the rumors started flyin. Some said he was pushed. Nobody says who pushed him, or who would have reason to. Some say he fell. And then there were those who swear he jumped."

"Wow. Did you guys ever look into it? I mean, did he have any gambling debts, or anything like that? Drugs? Other women?"

Venus looked at me like I had just hauled off and smacked her across the mouth, then quickly jerked her head away. A few seconds of uncomfortable silence filled the room before she turned her now-brimming almond eyes back to mine.

"I don't know what the truth is. But I always praised his name around my daughter, because I didn't want him to look like a loser in her eyes. Even though that was the way he started to feel about himself, especially toward the end of his life.

"Now, my Raven, who I believe has inherited her daddy's talent, and I already know has his same big ole heart, also has the sickle-cell trait. Not the disease, but the trait. So we've got to watch her health, and especially the baby's. But it's her life that I'm really worried about.

"Like I say, my life is what it is. I'm too old to change now, and I really don't even want to. But I don't want the same thing for my girl. I don't want her sittin up here with me, givin away her talent, takin whatever crumbs she thinks she can get. Especially not from the likes of Addie's boy, who hasn't got the talent in his whole body that my chile has in one little finger. I can see it comin, just by the way she actin already, and I tell you, my chile is *not* gonna let life pass her by, while she sits on the sidelines, like I did.

"Oh, no. Addie claim *she* can't do nothin bout it? Oookayy. That's all right. Cause *I'm* gone fix *this* mess. Yes indeedy, sweetie! I'm gone change this outcome, I'm gone flip this script, don't care what it takes. My girl's gone have a life. Tonight, we start. Tonight, we go see Miss Gustine Blue."

Addie

"If I thought talkin to Ruthie would do any good, don't you think I woulda done it by now? She can't do nothin with that girl, no more than I can talk any sense into Bobby. And poor Venus is probably down at that shop right now, makin a weddin gown for Raven for a weddin that may not ever happen. Just like she made one for herself, all those years ago, for her own weddin that never happened. Talk about your déjà vu! Damn!

"And I've already rented Memorial Hall for the reception, and hired the caterers and the band. If there's no weddin, no way can I get my money back. So she ain't the only one with problems.

"That Sunshine Divine's been travelin down this road for years now, usin this one, scammin offa that one. Ruthie used to think that shit was cute, till she started pullin the same thing on her. Sunni has maxed out Ruthie's ATM cards, stolen her checkbooks and sold em to them boosters over in the projects, sold her mink coat, her jewelry, all kinds of stuff.

"One time, some ole guy about seventy-somethin years old came to Ruthie's house with the cops, talkin bout Sunni and some other girl stole his car! No lie! The ole man call hisself givin them a ride, and they pulled out a pistol and put that sucka outta his own car! Stole it! And I ain't nevah lied!

"Sunni, Raven, and my son been doin this same lil dance since they was babies. The thing is, all of them used to be so tight, especially Sunni and Raven. Whenever you saw one of em, you looked for the other one. It wasn't till they got in their teens that they drifted apart. Sunni started to go wild then, hangin out with them hoochies that be down at the playground till all hours of the night and all.

"Raven, well, she'd always been one of them bookish kinda kids, anyway, always goin to the library, writin poetry and stuff, what the kids call a nerd nowadays. We used to call em squares. And she always was a mama's girl, too, all stuck up under Vee's butt alla time like a baby chick or somethin.

"Bobby went from one to the other. First, he went with Sunni, who always seemed to have a boyfriend for every day of the week, just like you-know-who. Don't let Ruthie fool you. She's slowed her roll a step since she's gotten older, but back in the day, she was a pistol.

"Anyway, Bobby went with Sunni first. Then they would get into it, usually over some other boy Sunni was a lil too friendly with, then he would go with Raven, who's been in love with that boy since the day she learned to walk. She's been chasin him ever since. Like they say, you always want the one you can't have, huh?

"Anyhow, this back-and-forth shit went on with Bobby for years. First Sunni, then Raven, then Sunni again, then Raven, and so forth. Then Bobby started rappin, and when he took a look at all that poetry Raven's been writin for years, well, the rest was history.

"Now, Venus is yellin bout my son's just usin her chile for her words, her talent. Maybe it's true, maybe not. He told me he has feelings for the girl. But *feelings* don't sound like love to me. And he *still* can't seem to stay away from Sunni. And he don't have *nothing* to say about that. Truth is, I don't think Bobby know what he want.

"But one thing I do know. I know Bobby ain't put no gun to Raven's head and steal her stuff. She wanted him to have it. She *gave* it to him! Now, what am I suppose to do about that?"

Chapter 10

＊

The Music Man

"So you want to talk about the Sweethearts of Soul? I don't really know much to tell you."

"I understand that, Mr. Flood. I just wanted to meet you in person. If you'll just give me a bit of your time, we can wrap this up quickly, and I'll be out of your hair."

Frank Flood grinned, rubbing his hand across his bald-as-a-billiard-ball pate.

"Out of my hair, huh? That wouldn't be much of a problem, would it?"

"I, uh, what I meant to say is, I'll be on my way," I stammered. Ouch. Talk about yer poor choices of words. Geez.

He was right, of course. There wasn't really that much he could tell me. He didn't even know the Sweethearts. But there was no way in hell I was going to pass up a chance to meet Frank Flood, up close and personal. And I figured there must be something he wanted to tell me, or he wouldn't have agreed to see me in the first place.

I had been let into Flood's suite by a tall, handsome, well-built, mahogany-hued man with snow-white hair and a dazzling smile. The Music Man had simply introduced him to me as "Mr. Brown," and after a quick conference between the two, the man had left.

The Music Man, a cocoa-brown, slender, intense fellow, had moved across the room with the grace of a dancer, first filling my glass, champagne, his, Chivas, before returning to his seat across from me in the spacious, elegant sitting room. This was my first time in a suite at the world-famous Plaza Hotel, and though I was desperately trying to act cool and blasé, something in the twinkle in his eye and the slight smile playing at the corners of his handlebar-mustached mouth told me he damn well knew it.

So this was the Plaza! And this was the Music Man! I was absolutely bowled over by both, the former for its old-time, movie-star glamour, the latter for his near-miraculous accomplishments in the worlds of business and music.

A black man going up against the white men who controlled music in America, with nothing more going for him than killer charm, a set of brass balls, and a musical ear so keen, so acute, it was said among many in the music biz that the man could actually hear dog whistles.

And winning! Dayum!

"Did you know that Fanya and I are getting ready to celebrate our twenty-fifth wedding anniversary in June? Yep, the big twenty-five. And the only reason I agreed to meet with you is because you said you were doing a story on the Sweethearts of Soul, and there's not a day that's gone by in all these twenty-five years that my wife doesn't regret not reaching out to them again way back then.

"So the next time you see them, would you give them a message from me? Would you please tell them that none of us are getting any younger, and that she still considers them her family, and still misses them terribly?"

"Well, no disrespect, sir, but—"

"Call me Frank."

"Well, no disrespect, uh, Frank, but all those years ago,

she knew where they were, she knew they were just a telephone call away. She didn't even show up to MuDear's or
PawPaw's funeral, or send flowers, or no—"

"Hold up, hold up!" Music Man sat forward, glaring at
me. Oh, hell. What now?

"You tell me how she was gonna show up when nobody
even *informed* her about their deaths? How was she gonna
keep in touch when they had gotten their phone number
changed to an unlisted one? When her letters were sent
back to her unopened?"

What? I had to admit to the man that this was all news
to me.

"Damn right, it is. For every major event in her life,
she's sent letters to them. Her first record contract, our
marriage, every birth of every child, and we have three, her
first film deal, our grandchild—oh, yes, we're grandparents
now! I finally made her stop sending those letters because
I hated to see her so torn up and miserable each time the
damn thing was returned.

"See, that's one of the reasons Fanya won't talk about
her family in interviews no more. She's been burned too
many times in the past. Any story about her and the
Sweethearts, she always comes out looking like the bad
guy. And that's just not true.

"Now, I don't know any of those ladies personally. But
from what I do know about what went down, even if Fanya
had stayed with them, she would probably have broken
away from them. Eventually, anyway."

"Why do you say that?"

"Cause Fanya was different. See, she was just like me.
I could see it in her eyes the first time I met her. She had
that hunger, that fire in the belly, that killer will to do anything it takes to get to the top. And that's what it takes in

this business, make no mistake. See, talent is a gift from God. Can't buy it, can't sell it, can't lend it, can't give it away. The world didn't give it, the world can't take it away. Either you've got it or you haven't.

"But killer ambition and drive are something else. And she had all three. Just like me. We two were kindred spirits from the moment we met. Now, the Sweethearts had talent, I'll give you that. And I'm sure they wanted to be successful, to be stars and all that. But not like Fanya. Uh-uh. Not as much as she wanted it. If they did, they would have come right along with her from the jump."

Frank Flood and I talked for about a half an hour more, me telling him some things about what was going on with the Sweethearts, him filling me in on some other things concerning Fanya, before Mr. Brown reappeared and the interview was over. We shook hands and parted on good terms.

I left the Plaza Hotel that afternoon with my head spinning, trying to digest and absorb this new information and fit it into what I already knew about the SOS.

"Fanya dreams big," Frank Flood had whispered to me, just before I walked out the door, "even bigger than me. I never would have even *thought* of making films, let alone actually do it, if it hadn't been for her, pushing me on. Hell, I never would have done a lot of things. My baby dreams big, and I—well, I make it happen."

Spoken like a man in love, even after twenty-five years.

"Spinnin," Addie had said. "When Fluffy was spinnin, Fluffy was gone."

Chapter 11

✳

The Rock and Soul Foundation Awards

"Get out! I said get the fuck outta this goddamn car now, or we'll *throw* your sorry monkey ass out!"

Oh, shit. Here we were in the dark, on the shoulder of I-95, and Ruthie has jumped out of the limo, opened the driver's door, and is trying to kick out the damn chauffeur.

"Ruthie, get your butt back in this car. Who gone drive if you put the man out? Stop actin crazy." Addie sounded nervous. She wasn't the only one.

"Our Father, who art in heaven . . ." Venus whispered.

"Hmph! *I'll* drive this mothafucka! Think I can't? Just help me get this asshole outta here and I'll show you."

"Why you wanna be callin me names, lady? Ain't no call for you to be goin off on me like that. Now, if I said the wrong thing to yall, I apologize. But there's no way I'm leavin my limo out here on 95 with yall," Madison ("Call me Mad Dog"), the driver, said, refusing to budge from the car.

"Listen, everybody," I said, "let's just calm down here. Ruth, the man said he's sorry, he didn't mean any harm, so let's just leave it at that, okay? We came out to have a good time tonight."

"Yeah. Come on, Ruth. Get back in the car. Please?" Venus was begging now.

Ruthie stood there on the road for a few minutes, cursing at no one in particular, then walked to the back door of the limo and got in again. The window separating the back-seat from the front shot up quickly.

"Hmph! That's what he shoulda done in the first place. All in our business, gettin into our conversation and everything. He don't know us," said Venus.

"I'll let it go this time, because we got someplace we've really got to be, but if he say anything nasty about my sister again, that's it. He gotta go. I mean it."

"I believe the man's drunk, anyhow. Drunk, or high, one. He was almost an hour late pickin us up in the first place," Addie said, sucking her teeth loudly.

I agreed with Addie. The guy did seem a little looped, and he had been way too familiar. Like Venus said, "He don't know us." I made a mental note to file a complaint with the limo service next week.

As the car rolled out onto the highway, the Sweethearts of Soul and I settled back into the plush leather seats and relaxed to the rhythm of the road and the sound of the oldies tape emitting from the speakers. Rather, I should say, the Sweethearts of Soul, minus one. And that one was the reason the chauffeur had narrowly escaped having his way-over-the-line ass thrown out on the highway. It all started with the Spanish fly.

In fact it had begun the evening before, at the surprise party given for the SOS at Cleo Knight's place. Miss Cleo had called me about a week ago and suggested the idea.

"Hey, they're Philadelphia's own, they're our girls, let's do this thing up right," she said. The more I thought about it, the more excited I got. So I called my magazine and arranged to have the Sweethearts picked up by limo and taken to Cleo's. Cleo agreed to provide the food.

I called my reporter friends from the daily and weekly publications in Philly and promised them that this would be a great human-interest story to cover; and, besides, there would be plenty of free good soul food. Hint: if you want reporters to cover your next event, promise them plenty of free food. Trust me on this one; they'll be there with bells on. Meanwhile, I hit the phones, calling any and all of the local singers, groups, and musicians who had ever worked with the SOS.

And I hit up all my local radio-station contacts, who promised to come through for me. And did they ever!

Since this was a surprise affair, I made up some bull-shit story for the Sweethearts, calling them all the evening before, telling them it was imperative that they come down to the magazine on the next evening for a photo shoot.

"Wear anything you like, but something nice, you know. Presentable. You all know how to do it. Don't worry about transportation. The magazine wants a picture of you all stepping out of a limosine, so we'll be picking you up."

I gave them no time to even think about it. The next evening, as I pulled up in the limo to each woman's residence, I will admit to you that I was nervous as a long-tailed cat in a roomful of rocking chairs. Suppose they didn't speak to each other the whole night? Worse yet, suppose they got into an actual fistfight? I was plenty worried.

Turned out I needn't have been. The Sweethearts of Soul were, if nothing else, seasoned professionals who knew how to act in public. And they must have at least spoken on the phone to each other, because they were all dressed in black. Venus, her auburn hair rising in an elegant upsweep, was wearing a simple velvet pantsuit, set off by pearl earrings, a matching choker, and dangerously high-ho silver heels. Simply stunning.

Ruth, dolled up in her black satin "shimmy dress," sparkled as brightly as her large, dangling rhinestone earrings, matching drop necklace, and black satin heels, also accentuated with rhinestones. Sexy, yet elegant. Both women wore floor-length black dusters, Venus in velvet, Ruth in satin.

And Addie—well, Addie also wore a floor-length coat, only hers was Blackglama mink. Under that, she was draped in a head-to-toe black silk Chinese-style gown, set off by gold earrings, necklace, and shimmering golden high-heeled slippers. On her blond head perched what I guess you would call a tiara, and her nails were painted a gleaming gold. That Adeline. She definitely had "a way."

The ladies greeted each other politely, if a bit coolly, and we were on our way. No one mentioned Birdie.

It was only a short ride from Ruthie's, the last of the SOS to be picked up, to Cleo's, and when the car turned onto Fifty-second Street, I was almost as unprepared for the sight as they were.

Talk about yer glamour! Talk about yer excess! Talk about yer over-the-top! Cleo Knight had gone all out, off the hook, off the chain! There were strobe lights lighting up almost the entire block, there were velvet ropes holding back the photographers and other curious onlookers. There was a red carpet extending from the curb to the front door of the club. The girls went off! Went off, I tell you.

"Oh, my God!" whispered Venus, eyes practically bugging out of her head.

"This is for *us*?" Addie squealed, as the limo pulled into the reserved parking space directly in front of the club. They all turned and looked at me. I nodded, pointing to the sign in the club's front picture window.

"Cleo's welcomes Rock and Soul Hall of Fame Honorees, the *SWEETHEARTS OF SOUL!*"

"Oh, my," was all Ruthie could manage. They tried to act blasé, but I could tell they were all near tears.

And when the Sweethearts of Soul (and me, of course, swearing for all the world that I, too, was a Sweetheart) stepped out of that limo and onto the red carpet, there were so many cameras popping their flashes, we were all temporarily blinded. As we proceeded into Cleo's, bumping into each other and stepping on each other's heels, I saw the Sweethearts grab each other's hands without even looking, something so instinctive, so pure and full of love, I myself was now blinking back tears.

Once inside, it was wall-to-wall people: friends, neighbors, people from Fire-Baptized Pentecostal Church. And the celebrities! I tried to get everybody's names, but after a while, and more than a few splits of champagne, I just said the hell with it. The whole affair was being taped, and I could find out who was who later on.

Of the ones I do recall, there were two of the Blue Notes (Harold and Bernard), Carl of the Vibrations, Doc Wade and Earl Young from the Trammps, Big Sonny of the Intruders, Rico of the Ravens, Roland and Karl Chambers, Ronnie Baker and Larry Washington, all from MFSB, the Sound of Philadelphia Orchestra.

Even Jack, one of the Heartbreakers, who just happened to be in town on business, came through. Venus began to cry at the very sight of him. And Wilbert and Poogie Hart, from the Del Fonics. The Fonics! Ooowee, chile!

And the music! Stone Philly sounds, all night long. "Bad Luck," by the Blue Notes, bopped through the air. "I Wanna Know Your Name," the Intruders' hit followed. Somewhere in the night, I heard "Didn't I Blow Your Mind This Time" by the Fonics, and commenced to swooning, simultaneously peeping over at the so-fine Hart brothers.

Billy Paul's "Me and Mrs. Jones" was there, as was Billy himself, looking good as ever. And the songs kept on coming. "Disco Inferno," the Trammps' song that first stoked the Saturday Night Fever fire, "Love Train," by the Ojays, recorded and produced right here in Philly; even "Hang On, Sloopy," the Vibrations' claim to fame. And, of course, the Sweethearts' own "You May Not Know" and "Change My Mind."

Oh, we had a grand time. It was one of those nights when everything goes right, everything. Some of these performers and musicians hadn't been in the same room together for years, and everybody was making up for lost time.

The highlight of the evening was the surprise appearance of Chance and Lane. I had been unable to contact either of them, so when they walked through the door, I was stunned, gawking like a teenybopper at these two men who had put Philadelphia on the musical map.

"This is one of the few times I've been together with the old gang when it isn't at somebody's funeral," Carl Chance said. "It's good to see everybody having fun for a change."

"Party hearty, Sweethearts," Lane said, smiling. "Then go up there to Harlem tomorrow night and *represent*!"

The Sweethearts and I *were* partying hearty, swilling down that 'pagne and acting like we didn't have to be at the awards in New York the very next night.

"Wonder if Fluffy will be there," Venus said, as we all sat watching the crowd.

"Be where?" Ruth asked, her up-to-now relaxed tone going tight.

"At the awards, fool. Where you think I'm talking bout?"

"Why should she? The Foundation is supposed to be honoring us, not that skank."

"Yeah, I know. But still . . ." Addie sighed, her voice dropping off.

"Still what, Ad? She's a big star nowadays. She ain't got time for no lil small potatoes like us no more." Ruthie was clearly irritated now.

"Maybe not. But Larry Washington, the percussionist, just told me that he worked with her on her last tour, and . . ." Adeline trailed off again.

"And?" Ruth, tight as a drum.

"And he said she was askin him all kinds of questions about us, how we were doin and everything. He said she seemed concerned."

"Yeah, right. She just telling him that shit to make herself look good."

"Oh, come on, Ruthie. You gotta give the girl some credit. She went for the gold, just like she always said she would. And she got it."

"Yeah, she got it. Got her movies, her gold records, her rich husband, her fine mansion, and shit. So why in the hell would she be concerned about us, especially after all this time?"

"All right, all right, that's it," Venus said, waving her hands around the table. "Let's just change the damn subject right now. We came out here tonight to have a good time, all these folks turned out just to see us, and we gone have us a good time tonight, dammit!"

"Best suggestion I heard all night! Hot Rod, we need more 'pagne over here, right now." Ruthie stood up, dancing and waving her glass around.

"You got it, baby," Hot Rod yelled from behind the bar.

Then I remembered the Spanish fly.

"Venus," I said, feeling no pain, "weren't you telling me a story about a girl and some Spanish fly? Or was it you, Addie?"

The Sweethearts of Soul suddenly went into freeze-frame silent mode. They looked from one to the other.

"What about Spanish fly?" Ruthie said, one eye cocked at me suspiciously.

Uh-oh. I had obviously said the wrong thing, but what?

"Well, either Venus or Addie was telling me a road story about some bass player putting Spanish fly into a singer's drink one night, and I never heard the ending to the story."

"Oh! You talkin bout that time we were on the road and that poor chile—oh, yeah, I remember. What happened was, the—

"SOS! Calling the SOS! Picture-taking time!"

Next thing I knew, the Sweethearts were being ushered over to the small band platform and were being posed for a photo shoot. They must have taken at least one picture with everyone there. By the time they returned to their seats, I had forgotten all about it. Then.

But here we were, the next night, heading up I-95, on the way to Harlem for the Sweethearts of Soul to be inducted into the Rock and Soul Hall of Fame. Everybody was in a good mood tonight, though we were all feeling the effects of the night before.

"But did you see them damn Hoecakes, honey?" Addie was laughing.

"Yes indeedy, sweetie!" Venus said, giggling. "Come struttin through like it was *their* party."

"What? You mean the Hoecakes were there and you guys didn't even tell me?"

"Well, I tried to call you over, Legs, but look like you was too busy with them Del Fonics," Ruthie said, smirking.

"I was not. I was just talking to them about doing a possible story, that's all."

"Um-hmn. Just a *story*," Addie piped in, smiling devilishly. "That's all."

"Speaking of stories," I said, simply to change the subject, "whatever happened to the girl with the Spanish fly. You know, the singer you started to tell me about?"

"Oh, okay," said Venus. "This is what went down. Remember I told you that her and this bass player had disappeared, and after we couldn't find them, we went back to the hotel?"

"Yeah. That's the part where you stopped," I said.

"Hey, do you realize that very same bass player had the nerve to be at our party last night?" asked Ruthie.

"Sure enough was," said Addie, "Strollin all round the place, striking poses, like he *GQ* cool or something. I can't stand that punk. He is one nasty piece of work."

"Sure is. Still handsome as hell, though," observed Venus. "Got to give him that."

"Yeah, and probably still pullin that same old shit, too." Ruthie sneered.

"He was there? Why didn't you point him out to me? I swear, you all don't tell me anything. Suppose I had given him my phone number or something, not knowing who he was?" I complained mockingly.

"Oh, don't worry. If we had seen you even talkin to him, we would definitely have pulled your coat. Uh—*did* you give your phone number out last night?" Ruthie was actually cackling.

"No, I did not. Hmph!"

"Okay, okay, here's the downlow. The girl disappeared with that guy, and early the next morning we get a call from the hospital, asking if we could come down and get her. Seems this punk-ass mothafucka had taken her out to the bus and slipped some Spanish fly into her beer. The girl went wild, started havin some kinda fit or convulsions, ran all out in the streets, rubbin herself up against cars and everything.

"Somebody called the cops, and they took her to the hospital. When she woke up the next morning, the last thing she remembered was sitting in the bus with him, drinkin a beer." Ruthie looked disgusted.

"And where was the dude, the bass player?"

"Gone, chile. The cops say, when they arrived on the scene it wasn't nobody there but her, runnin around like a crazy person, pullin off her clothes and stuff. Later on, one of the guys in the band said this bass player was famous for usin drugs like Spanish fly on girls, so he could take advantage of them. By that morning, that dude was already in the next town."

"Spanish fly? Man, that's some whack stuff."

We all looked toward the front of the car, where Madison, the limo driver, all of a sudden had inserted himself into the conversation. We exchanged irritated glances, and I was just about to tell him to please raise the partition window so we could have some privacy, when he started up again.

"Yeah, I member one night in Philly, way back in the seventies, somebody was supposed to have put some Spanish fly in this girl's drink at the old Tornado Club. I was livin right across the street from Cobbs Creek Park then, and my buddy come bangin on my door, tellin me to come on over to the park.

"'*You ain't gone believe this, man. Come on.*' So I runs over there with him, and all these dudes, musta been nine or ten of em, was takin turns pullin a train on this girl. The girl was out of it. She ain't know what was goin on. One by one, all of em had her."

"And how about you? Did you have her, too?" Addie asked, her voice low and soft.

"Me? Hell, no. Man, I wasn't gone touch that bitch with a ten-foot pole."

"So what did you and your buddy do? Did you call the police?" asked Venus, in a trembling voice.

"Hell, no. Hey, nobody likes a squealer. We just watched, that's all. We wasn't gettin involved in no shit like that. Besides, I heard she wasn't nothin but a hoe, noway, hangin out up there on the Strip. Supposed to be some kinda half-ass singer, from what I—"

"Pull over! Pull this car the fuck over now!" Ruth, sitting right behind the guy, grabbed him around his neck.

"Okay, lady, hold on, hold on. I'm pullin over."

As soon as the car pulled over to the shoulder of the road and came to a stop, Ruthie popped out of the back-seat, opened the driver's door, and was yelling for him to get the fuck out.

After I had managed to get everything calmed down, we proceeded the rest of the way to New York without incident.

And it wasn't until some time later, well after that evening, that I learned that the girl who had been drugged at the Tornado Club and left for dead in Cobbs Creek Park, the girl who had been gang-raped, beaten, and so brutally violated that she was unable to ever bear children, the girl who did not speak for nearly a full year following that incident, was Brenda "Birdie" Wade.

❋ ❋ ❋

Following the big party for the Sweethearts at Cleo's the night before—not to mention almost losing our driver on the way up to New York—the Rock and Soul Foundation's Awards Night seemed almost like an afterthought. I was just happy to be there in one piece, especially after the red panties incident. Yes. Red panties.

We had made it to Harlem and were about four or five blocks away from the famed Apollo Theater, where the event was taking place, when Ruth let out a blood-draining scream.

"Oh, no! Oh, God, no! I forgot to wear my red panties!"

"What? Now, I just *know* you not tryin to tell me we're all the way up here in New York, gettin ready to get the only award we've ever gotten in our lives, and you're not wearin your red panties." Addie's tone had an edge to it.

"See, what happened was, I washed them out this morning, and left them on the towel rack to dry, meanin to put them on after I took my bath," Ruthie explained apologetically.

"But after that, I had to run out for stockings, and the panties was still wet, so I put on another pair. I don't *think* I'm wearin the red ones. I think they're still on the towel rack."

"Aw, hell. Driver!" Venus banged on the partition window. "Driver, you've got to find us a store around here that sells women's clothes. And step to it. This is serious business!"

Mad Dog only lowered the partition to half-mast, and even with that, he sat with his shoulders hunched, as if he expected Ruthie to grab him by the neck again at any minute.

"Ma'am, I swear to God, I don't know where you gone find no kinda store like that. It's eight-thirty. These stores round here don't be stayin open late, not no clothing stores."

"Well, just drive around a while, and we'll see if we can find one," Addie told him.

"But ma'am, the show start at nine, and the dinner was at eight, so yall already missed that."

"And we wouldn't have missed it if you hadn't been almost an hour late pickin us up. Drive around a while."

I was worried. We were cutting it close. The SOS had already lectured me about the importance of wearing red panties, so I was definitely wearing mine. In fact, all of us were dressed in red that night. But apparently, that wasn't good enough.

"You know you gotta be wearin red panties. You gotta have that red right up close to the source of your power," Addie declared, as if it were the law.

"What source? What power?" I asked, lamely.

"The power of your womanhood, chile. Have mercy," Venus exclaimed, rolling her eyes at me.

"The power of—oh! I get it, I get it!" I yelled, clapping my hands.

"Dayum! About time," Ruth said.

So we rode around Harlem until nine before we gave up. Ruthie would just have to go on without them.

By the time we literally ran into the Apollo, the show was almost ready to begin, but what we did see was wonderful, almost like the party had been, only on a much larger scale. The Sweethearts seemed to know everybody in the business. They introduced me to everybody they knew, and everyone asked about Birdie. Seems they were the queen bees on this night, the only girl group being honored. Was I starstruck? A jaded, cynical, been-there, done-that, seen-it-all-and-moved-on music reporter like me? You bet your ass, I was.

A lot of the people present, as well as many of those

being honored, were just a little before my time, so they were rock-and-roll royalty to me. I had danced to some of these people's songs when I was a little girl, and I could remember my father playing a lot of their records.

I knew that most of them had seen better days, and many of them had fallen on hard times, but to a one, they displayed such grace and style, such finesse, you could have easily thought you were in the presence of kings and queens. The SOS were a part of this rich musical heritage, this African-American legacy of talent, and being with them made me feel just a tiny bit like I was a part of it, too. Like Ruthie said, "*We* made rock and roll. Couldn't nobody else have done it."

We were too late for dinner, but we did get to do a bit of table-hopping as the Sweethearts caught up on the news with their old friends. They made toasts to the ones now gone, and celebrated the ones still here.

Just before the awards presentation, Ruth nudged Venus, Venus nudged Addie, and Addie nudged me.

"Look who just came in the door, all late, makin her dramatic entrance," Ruthie stage-whispered.

The lights were going down, and I turned just in time to see Fanya Dance, the legendary superstar, being escorted to a ringside table by her equally legendary husband, Frank Flood, the Music Man. Fanya looked divine, as usual, wrapped in white ermine worn over a full-length backless dress. You had to give it to her. The woman was fabulous.

Just before they took their seats, Fanya and Frank looked around the room, nodding, smiling, and waving to people. When Fanya's gaze first met the Sweethearts of Soul, she hesitated for a few seconds, smile frozen in place. Then she waved excitedly. The Sweethearts stared back at her with Sphinx-like expressions. Fanya sat down.

"Aw, yall, come on," I said, "Be civil. It's you they're honoring tonight, not her."

The SOS pretended they hadn't heard me.

"You *know* she's had work done," a woman at the next table leaned over and whispered to the Sweethearts.

"Work? What kinda work?" Ruthie asked.

"Cosmetic work. You know. Plastic," the woman said, gesturing toward her face.

"Hell, she was plastic *waaay* before she had any goddamn work done!" Ruthie laughed out loud.

It was at this point that I realized I had to deliver the rest of the message Frank Flood had given me. I had already told them about Fanya missing them, about her not being informed of their parents' deaths, and so forth.

"If that's true, why didn't she tell you herself," they harrumphed.

"Why would she get her husband, a man we don't even know, to tell you?"

"Well," I continued, "she said every time she tried to reach out to you, you all wouldn't even talk to her." I shrugged my shoulders.

"Reach out to us? When the fuck did she ever reach out to us?" Ruthie sputtered.

"Frank Flood says many times. He says she asked for you all when she called MuDear that first time, as soon as she got the deal with him, and the only reason she used the Hoecakes—I mean, the Cupcakes—in the first place on that record was because MuDear said you all didn't want to speak to her."

"MuDear never told us about that," Venus whispered.

"He also said she called when she was getting married, sent you all invitations, and never heard a word from any of you."

The Sweethearts looked at each other, dumbfounded.

"This is the first I'm hearin about any of this," Ruthie mumbled.

"Same here," said Addie.

"He said when their three children were born, she sent pictures, and when she called, you all had an unlisted number. Every card and every letter she sent for five straight years was returned unopened, and she's still got them all. Finally, he said he made her stop sending them, because he couldn't stand to see her crying about it every time one of those letters came back.

"He said she wrote again, eight months ago, when their grandchild was born, but that he had intercepted the letter and thrown it in the trash."

"Grandchild! Fluffy's a grandma?" Venus asked.

The Sweethearts of Soul were looking at me now as if I had just smacked them all across the face, as I nodded in the affirmative. Then they each glanced furtively in Fanya's direction.

There was a bit of commotion on the stage, then the house lights went up. The band—rather, the orchestra—went into a slammin rendition of "Honky Tonk" that had the crowd jammin right from the start. A young man in his twenties came over to our table.

"Sweethearts of Soul?"

"Yes." All four of us answered in unison.

"They want you backstage as soon as the film is over. You're going on first."

"What? What film? Nobody told us we were first."

"Ruthie, it says so right here in the program. We just got here too late to read it," said Venus, with a hint of what sounded like panic in her voice.

"Oh, Lordy," Addie whispered.

Suddenly this thing was not just some abstract idea. It was here and now. These women who had not appeared or sung together on a stage in well over twenty years would be going on in just a few moments. Their nervousness was so thick, so palpable, you could almost smell it.

"Good evening, ladies and gentlemen. My name is Carl Chance." The sound of applause roared through the building as the audience recognized Mr. Sound of Philadelphia standing at the podium.

"Carl Chance!" The Sweethearts blurted in unison.

"He never said a word last night about he was going to be here!" Ruth was gasping for air.

"When they asked me to present this honor to the Sweethearts of Soul, how could I say no? These are my girls, always have been."

Suddenly, a large video screen lit up behind Carl Chance, and there were the Sweethearts of Soul, four teenaged girls in a studio, all wearing their hair in big bangs and what looked like large Afro-puffs. The next shot showed the girls onstage in an outdoor arena, looking Philly slick in British mod-look style (patent-leather boots, miniskirts, giant plastic earrings, fishnet stockings, and strange pageboy-type wigs).

In the next shot, here they were, captured in performance again in what looked like a nightclub, decked out like the real Foxy Brown, Pam Grier, at her baddest—gigantic Afros, tight low-cut hip-hugger jeans that exposed their navels, fringed vests with peace and Black Power signs, and so forth. Still another featured them, regal as queens, this time bedecked from head to toe in full African dress.

As the still images and performance clips were displayed

on the screen, Carl Chance provided a running commentary on the SOS. The girls, meanwhile, sat staring at the larger-than-life images of themselves like they were in shock.

"Time and again, people have heard me say the Sweethearts of Soul were ahead of their time. Let me tell you why. Here you had these females doing this church-based, men's-quartet-style harmony, with these high sopranos in there at the same time.

"They had a kind of churchy-blues-based foundation mixed with the kind of soprano singing you would hear in a Catholic church. That sound was pure magic!

"And don't let that name fool you. We used to call them the bad girls of rock and roll, the anti-Supremes, because of their strong, muscular voices, not to mention their down-to-earth, round-the-way girl attitudes. And they took that as the ultimate compliment, just as we meant it to be. In a business full of BS artists and no-talent wannabes, they were the real thing. If you will—"

Chance's speech was interrupted numerous times by loud applause and shouts of "Amens" and "That's rights" from the audience. I peeped over at the SOS. They were beaming!

"If you will look at some of these clips, you will see that at certain times, the Sweethearts of Soul even had an all-girl band. Unheard of in the sixties! Unheard of even today—remember, this is 1966, 1967, 1968. It was downright shocking!

"The Sweethearts were also unique in that they were the first girl group to wear Afro hairstyles and African jewelry onstage. They were the first girl group to wear individual, color-coordinated outfits onstage instead of cookie-cutter uniforms, the first to dance as the spirit moved them, rather than use the lockstep choreography that was popular at the time. It wasn't until sometime in the mid- to late seventies that we saw that again.

"The Sweethearts were something new, something different, something else, and, I must admit, we didn't know quite what to do with them. They blew us away."

"Damn! I didn't know we was all that. All we was doin was singin!" Addie said, blushing.

"Chile, we was *somethin*, wasn't we?" Ruthie was grinning from ear to ear.

"I wish I had brought Raven to hear this, so she'd know just what her mama was all about," said Venus.

The Sweethearts had made it a point not to bring their children tonight, to avoid any bad feelings.

While Chance was making his presentation, I had been slyly watching the Sweethearts of Soul, and I could see the shy, aw-shucks smiles slowly creeping across their faces, the pride swelling below their breastbones, straightening their backbones, tilting their faces upward, their chins forward. Carl Chance's well-chosen and heartfelt words had turned these ebony beauties into solid-gold majesties right before my eyes! I felt the same way they must have felt the night they had watched Simon transform into an angel on that high school stage. I wouldn't have traded this night for anything.

The video screen went dark, and the young man returned, beckoning the SOS backstage, as Chance cleared his throat.

"Ladies and gentlemen, it gives me great pleasure tonight to present the Rock and Soul Foundation's Pioneer Award to *my* girls, the *Sweethearts of Soul!*"

The Sweethearts were pumped, and when they stepped out on that stage to receive that award, with the big-band sound of "You May Not Know" playing in the background, they were absolutely radiant! Smiling, laughing, hugging each other, acting just like the excitable schoolgirls they had once been.

After each woman said her thank-yous, and after Ruth apologized for Birdie's absence, they turned to exit the stage. Krazy Kelly, a New York DJ the girls had worked with years ago, ran out on the stage and grabbed a mike.

"Oh, no, oh, no. We can't let the Sweethearts leave this stage without a song, can we?"

"Nooooooo!" shouted the audience.

The SOS froze on the spot, panicked, trying to whisper to Krazy that they hadn't been told they would be expected to sing, that they had not rehearsed, that they didn't have Birdie with them to sing lead.

"You say you don't have a lead singer? Well, I think I can remedy that little problem. I have a lil girl backstage here, claims she's some kinda singer, that she's a big fan of the Sweethearts and she would just love to sing with you all."

Ruth, Addie, and Venus looked like they wanted to be swallowed up by the floor. I was worried. No one had mentioned anything like this to my magazine. As far as we knew, the SOS were only supposed to show up, claim their award, smile, say a few words, and sit down.

"Let's see if we can get this lil girl to come on out here. Fellows, strike up the band. Give me 'You May Not Know,' key of C."

But the SOS turned and glared at the band, shaking their heads. My eyes were glued to them, and so closely was I concentrating on their dilemma that I failed to notice the woman in white, who was now stepping across the stage tentatively, a nervous, uncertain look on her face.

There was a smattering of polite applause as the crowd

recognized Fanya Dance, who now stood stiffly on the right side of the stage, looking over at Ruth, Venus, and Addie, who stared back at her. The entire room went silent for what felt like forever. Then it started, softly at first, the boos, the hisses, then it picked up in volume. Then two things happened.

Fanya Dance turned and began to walk off the stage, and Ruth Thomas stepped up to the mike.

"Ladies and gentlemen, we weren't planning on singing tonight because Birdie, our lead singer, could not be here. However, Fanya Dance was with us in the very beginning. She's here tonight, and she will be joining us for this number.

"And for those of you who booed, you can just get over that with the swiftness. Cause don't *nobody* mess with *my* sister!"

With that, Ruth turned to Fluffy, extended her hand, and Fluffy stepped forward and grabbed it. Ruth then turned to Addie and Venus, extended her other hand, and Addie and Venus stepped forward, Addie grabbing Ruth's hand, Venus grabbing Addie's. The four of them then embraced, holding on to each other and hugging long and hard. The band again struck up the intro to "You May Not Know," and now the Sweethearts of Soul stepped up to the microphones.

I don't have to tell you that they turned that motha out, do I? Killed! Left blood on the floor! You better know they did! Their voices soared over the crowd like bright yellow-gold and scarlet fireworks, like silver ribbons in a star-filled sky, sounding as if they had never missed a day of song together. Still strong, still forceful. Still beautiful.

I swear to God, if I hadn't seen it for myself, I never would have believed it. The Sweethearts of Soul, together again!

* * *

"Whoa! Where my boy toys at? Ice up the prune juice! Break out the Viagra! We gone git down tonight!" Ruthie stage-whispered, nodding her head in the direction of Frank Flood.

"I don't have no problem with gettin down tonight. It's gettin up tomorrow that I'm worried about," Addie said. "And don't talk so loud. You don't want to hurt Fluffy's old man's feelings, now, do you?"

"*Old* man is right. But you know what they say. Old in the hips, young in the lips. But you would know all about that now, wouldn't you, Addie?"

Addie glared at Ruthie, trying to look angry, but breaking out in giggles in spite of herself.

"Whoa! Let's do some Nyquil shooters. I'm buyin!"

"Girl, you better stop. Them young boys is gone be the death of your old ass yet."

This back and forth went on until the hostess led us to our table.

The afterparty was even trippier than the Awards had been. Held at New York's fabled Cotton Club, this bash was more like a combination house party/family reunion. There were so many celebrities there, I lost count. The food and liquor flowed through the club as freely as the music, and the band was smokin! Don't even ask me *what* they were smokin, cause I ain't talkin!

When the SOS weren't trying to make up for lost time with Fanya Dance, whom they refused to call anything but Fluffy, comparing photos of their children, teasing each other about weight gain, they were being pulled out onto the dance floor, or posing for photos. My magazine had sent up Malik, a twenty-something staff photographer, and he was just as starstruck as I was, taking pictures of everybody who walked by.

"Who dat? Who dat?" he would ask me every time he took a candid of someone. When I or one of the SOS would identify the person, he would go completely off.

"Oh, wow! Just wait till I tell my moms and pops that I got a shot of so and so. They played their records for me when I was a boy! So did Grandmom! Just wait till I show em these shots!"

At one point in the evening, I was sitting at the bar and trying to get the barmaid's attention. But she was so busy running down her line and slipping her telephone number to a grinning Frank Flood, I might as well have been invisible. Spotting me, he laughed, came over, and sat down beside me. The barmaid followed, sullenly asking for my order.

"I'll say this for you, Mr. Flood. You sure have got a way with the women."

"Baby, I've got several ways with the women. You have no idea," he said, still laughing. Then he had the nerve to cut his eye at *me*. First, I'm sitting there thinking, what does this lil skinny, no-neck troll think he's doing? Then I looked at the eyes again, really looked, and saw that twinkle, that thing. Animal magnetism, sex appeal, whatever you want to call it, I saw it, and for a second or two, I was like a deer in the headlights. Caught up. I turned away.

"Fanya and the Sweethearts look like they're doin all right, huh?"

He nodded in the direction of the Sweethearts' table, where Fluffy, Addie, and Ruthie were happily chattering away.

"Looks that way. I'm glad," I said, nodding my head. "Thanks for convincing her to come."

"I'm glad to see you here tonight. You know that little matter we discussed the last time I saw you?"

"Now, which matter would that be, Mr. Flood?"

"Oh, you remember you had mentioned something about the young one, Birdie, the baby? The one you said wasn't doing too good these days?"

"Yes, I remember," I nodded, leaning in closer.

"Hey, Legs, get over here." I turned, and Addie was motioning me over to a nearby table. "Somebody here I want you to meet."

Excusing myself from the Music Man, I went over and took a seat. Addie sat there with a pretty young lady and a very attractive man, whom I didn't recognize. At first. Then my mouth dropped open, and I'm sure my eyes were popping out of my head.

"Yes. It's him. The one and only—" Addie mentioned this prominent singer's name, and that's the name I addressed him by, but I knew who he really was. Simon Hall, with the wicked-witch grandmother. Simon Hall, who had turned into an angel in full view of everyone at the Christmas Pageant. Gorgeous Simon Hall, who was still built like Hercules.

I glanced at his companion, who was looking at him like he was a giant bowl of chocolate ice cream.

We made polite chitchat for a while, Simon and I exchanging numbers with regard to me possibly doing a piece on him, and he and Addie goofed around a bit. But the woman with him seemed to be in such a hurry to get him out of there and all to herself, that he soon made a polite apology, promised to stay in touch with Addie and the Sweethearts, and left with the lady.

"Ooo, she is *so* wasting her time," Addie snickered. "I hope she plans on takin a few good books along, cause ain't nothin happenin there."

"Well, maybe he's changed."

"Bullshit. He's just still in the closet, that's all. Always takes women out to public places where he knows he'll be seen. Didn't you notice him eye-ballin some of the men? Trust me. He ain't changed. And why should he? He is who he is."

Before I could say anything else, Venus rushed over and plopped herself into a chair, totally winded from dancing. And like Birdie had said, Venus could dance her ass off.

"Ad! Ad! Did you see Ruthie? She's sittin over there at the bar with Bad Friday Brown!"

"What? Friday Brown? Get outta here!" Addie turned all the way around in her seat.

"Well, I'll be damned. It *is* Friday! What do you think he's doin here?"

"I guess he just came to see old friends. And we *are* old friends. Especially Ruthie." Venus smiled, waving over at Ruth and Friday, who seemed deeply engrossed in conversation.

"That's Ruthie's old flame, Legs," explained Addie. "That's the one she let get away, the one she shoulda stayed with all along."

"You ain't lyin, girl. Bad Friday had her number."

I glanced over, did a double take, and . . . yes! It was the same "Mr. Brown" Frank Flood had introduced me to that afternoon at the Plaza.

"What kinda name is Bad Friday Brown?" I wondered aloud, saying nothing about having already met the man.

"I don't know, but that's what he's been called since we met him, and that was back in '65, '66," Venus answered. "In fact, Friday was the road manager on one of our first road tours. Was that Baltimore, Addie?"

"I think so. It was so long ago, chile, I can't remember."

Then I recalled the name, something Ruthie had said

about getting Bad Friday Brown and his boys to run Addie's so-called husband out of town.

"Well, what does he do? Is he a cop? A gangster? A bodyguard?"

"Yes," said Venus and Addie in unison.

"Yes, what? Which one?"

"Well, Friday does a lil bit of everything, so don't too many people go around askin for his job description. That wouldn't be polite. Know what I'm sayin?" said Addie, laughing.

"Still lookin good, though. And would you look at that hair? Used to be jet black." Venus nodded, appreciatively.

The hair that used to be jet black was now snow white, the skin mahogany brown, the smile, killer. Bad Friday Brown looked like a man who was more than capable of doing a little bit of everything.

Once again, we closed the joint down. Once we were all outside in the parking lot, Bad Friday and Ruth lingered a while at the front door of the club, while Venus and Addie exchanged phone numbers with Fluffy, promising they would all stay in touch.

We wandered around the huge lot, looking for Madison, who was supposed to be at the front door waiting for us at three A.M. sharp, closing time. We split up, each going in a separate direction. I'm thinking, Boy, just wait till I call that limo service Monday.

"Here! Over here, yall!"

We followed the sound of Ruthie's voice. When we reached the car, she was standing by the driver's door of our limo, banging on the window.

"Wake up! I said wake up, you sorry mothafucka! Would yall believe this fool is out cold? With the keys in the ignition?"

"Oh, Lordy. What are we gone do now?" Venus moaned.

* * *

Ruth Thomas was barreling down 95 South like some-body had tied fire to the rear of the limo and run us out of town at gunpoint. We were in northern New Jersey now, getting ready to hit the Turnpike, and I was just settling down from our little drama back in the parking lot. The four of us had banged loudly on the car—actually rocked it back and forth for the better part of ten minutes—before Mad Dog finally woke up. Seeing us all standing around the car, he wore an expression resembling a frightened squirrel.

"Roll down the window!" Ruthie yelled.

Madison slowly complied.

"What? What yall want?" he said in a sleepy, slurred voice.

The man was drunk, or high, but whichever, he was in no condition to be behind the wheel of a car.

"Just get the fuck out, and get in the backseat," Ruthie said.

"I ain't gettin in no back—" he started, but before he could finish, Ruthie had reached into the car, unlocked the door, and with our help dragged the man out of the vehicle. The four of us then jumped in, Ruthie in the driver's seat this time.

"Look, you got two choices. You can either get in the backseat, or you can stay your drunken ass right here in New York in this parking lot. It don't matter to me, one way or the other."

"Ruth, are you sure you can drive this thing?" I was kind of worried now.

"Girl, I can drive anything that moves," she answered.

I looked at Addie and Venus. Both nodded.

"She can drive it," Addie said.

"Yes indeedy, sweetie," Venus said, nodding.

"Come on, now, we ain't got all night. Make up your mind." Ruthie was gunning the motor. Mad Dog grumpily opened the rear door, climbed into the back, and promptly went back to sleep.

So here we were, on the road again, Ruthie and Addie in the front seat, Mad Dog, Venus, and I in the back. Vintage Miles Davis was playing on the stereo, and we were sharing a bucket of chicken we had just picked up at a service stop, and washing it down with one of the bottles of champagne Bad Friday had given Ruthie just before we left him. All but Ruth, who was reluctantly drinking the bottled water Addie had bought her at the service stop.

The SOS were already doing a play-by-play of the night's events, especially as concerned Fanya Dance. The animosity they had exhibited for her earlier had vanished, the same as the hostility they had felt for each other. Just like it was never there. Just like they had been speaking all along. Amazing.

"That's why MuDear let Birdie join the group," Addie said.

"Yep. And that's why PawPaw told her she owed us," Ruth said, nodding. "Damn."

Fluffy had invited them all to come out to her place in California for her wedding anniversary in June, and they were really high on that.

"Hollywood, here we come. From the hood to the Wood! Again," chuckled Ruthie.

"So what's up with you and Friday, Ruth?" Addie prodded. "You all seemed to be spendin a lot of time together at the party."

"Yeah, Ruthie. Catching up on old times, huh?" Venus put in her two cents.

"Somethin like that," Ruthie answered, her voice gone soft and dreamy, a voice totally new to me.

"He's gettin ready to do some work for Music Man, some kinda missin-persons case. But you know Friday. He wasn't gone say no more than that."

Missing persons? Oh, shit. This was rich. I decided to keep my mouth shut.

"Yeah, yeah, yeah, but what's that got to do with him spendin almost the whole night talkin to *you*? *You* ain't missin," Addie said, smirking.

We all laughed at that one. In fact, we were laughing so hard, none of us saw the northbound-traveling SUV jump the median strip. By the time Ruthie screamed, it was too late. We were hit.

$$* \quad * \quad *$$

It was four o'clock in the morning, and I was nervously working on my fourth cup of coffee. Good Samaritan Hospital's emergency ward was only half full, which the nurses informed me was unusual for a Saturday night. We had been brought to the hospital by ambulance. I was the only one who walked in under my own power.

Everyone else had been brought in by stretcher.

Everyone was conscious except Ruthie and Madison. Addie had a possible concussion from hitting her head against the car's side window. Venus suffered from a dislocated shoulder and neck sprain. Mad Dog had sustained no injuries, and had not lost consciousness at all. In fact, he had never regained consciousness. He had slept through the whole thing. Babies, fools, and drunks. Shades of Miss Mattie.

Venus's and Addie's injuries weren't serious, though they would be kept overnight for observation. Madison could go home as soon as he woke up, I imagined.

But Ruthie had suffered internal injuries. The force of the hit had been so severe, the wheel had been pushed into her chest and stomach. She was still unconscious, she had already lost a lot of blood and needed a transfusion.

At about five in the morning, when the doctor asked for next of kin who could possibly donate blood, I gave a blood sample, as well as Venus and Addie. Presently, the nurse who had taken the sample returned.

"I don't understand it. Ms. Lights and Ms. Jones are listed on this form as being Ms. Thomas's sisters. Is that correct?"

I nodded.

"Then why do all three of them have completely different blood types, and neither of the other two is compatible with Ms. Thomas's?"

She looked at me. I shrugged. Some things go even deeper than blood. Besides, nobody likes a squealer.

Addie and Venus had given me some telephone numbers where they thought I might reach Sunni.

I had called them all, and nobody knew where Sunshine Thomas was. I didn't hesitate. I couldn't afford to. There wasn't much time. I placed one more call.

At roughly six o'clock the next morning, Bad Friday Brown walked into Good Samaritan Hospital, saw Ruthie, went into the back and checked with the staff as to her condition, talked with me for a few minutes, made a call, then told me he'd be back in a few hours. I had already been treated and discharged. There was nothing more for me to do, really, but pray, wait, and hope for the best. A feeling of déjà vu washed over me like rain.

At approximately ten o'clock in the morning, Bad Friday Brown walked back into Good Samaritan Hospital, accompanied by a sobbing and distraught Sunshine Thomas.

At a quarter after eleven on April 7th, Ruth Thomas underwent serious abdominal surgery. The four-hour operation was successful, Ruthie survived, and she is alive and well and probably somewhere raising hell right this minute, God willing, thanks to receiving the most precious blood of her only child.

All I could think about when Adeline, Venus, and myself finally left the hospital was that Ruth Thomas had been the only one of us not wearing her red panties that night.

✳ ✳ ✳

Ruthie had fully regained regained consciousness when we left her that evening after Friday Brown took us to the train station. He was going right back to the hospital, and he had promised to bring Ruthie home as soon as the hospital released her.

"He still likes her," Venus had whispered to us from the backseat. We nodded.

The three of us marveled at how lucky we had been. The limo was completely totaled, the police officer who wrote up the report had told us, and what with the speed the SUV had been traveling at the point of impact, we all could easily have been killed. The teenage kid who had been driving the SUV had suffered a serious head injury.

I said nothing. I, like Madison, had walked away from this one without a scratch, just as I had the last one,

almost two years ago. On that rainy Philly night, I had per-
suaded Roe to hang out with me at a new downtown club
opening. The accident had been eerily similar to this one.

Roe and I had been laughing and gossiping, me driving
down Chestnut Street like a madwoman, as usual, Roe,
cautioning me to slow down, slow down. I didn't even see
the truck coming up the street the wrong way. All I saw
were the headlights. My car was totaled.

I had walked away from *that* one without a scratch, too.
And Roe, who hadn't even wanted to come out that night,
Roe, who had always done everything right, who had worn
her seat belt even before it was the law, who had never gotten so much as a parking ticket or bounced a check in her
entire life, Roe had been instantly killed.

Roberta Johnson Willis is *still* my best friend in the
whole wide world, and the fact that she's been dead going
on two years now doesn't have a damn thing to do with
anything.

* * *

Phone Message for Legs from Birdie

Hi, Legs. Brenda Wade here. I know you all are mad at me for not being there tonight. I know I should at least have come to the party at Cleo's. I wanted to make it. I really did. But it's no use. It just won't work, no matter how hard I try. I'm not as tough as Ruthie, or as single-minded as Addie. And I'm not as strong as Venus, I never will be. And I miss Butch so much, the touch of him, the beauty of him, the sound of his voice, that I don't want to wake up in the morning no more and not find him here beside me. He's crept inside my skin. He's so close to me now, I can smell him, I can almost reach out and touch him. He's just a few heartbeats away. And I cannot live without him. I just can't. Good night, Legs. God bless.

* * *

The Hummingbird

After the third man, she lost count. She held her body still and unresistant, and forced her mind out of real time to someplace else, someplace happy and safe, just as she had done when it happened to her all those years ago.

So she couldn't know that there had been seven of them, couldn't know that she now had new bruises to match the old ones, wouldn't even remember what they had done to her with the wine bottle.

She was now somewhere far away from here, somewhere being rocked in MuDear's arms, listening and humming along to the lullaby as MuDear sang it to her.

"Yes, Jesus Loves Me, for the Bible tells me so."
She would not talk.

Chapter 12

*

"It was Butch Taylor who walked by the park that night. Said he heard what sounded like a little girl hummin or moanin, and went in to take a look. It was Butch Taylor who saved her life."

Ruthie leaned back into the bed pillows, sighing.

"And it shoulda been us, and we all damn well know it."

Ruthie had been released from the hospital and brought home by Bad Friday the day before. Venus, Addie, and I sat around her bedside, wondering where Birdie was.

It was the same old drill for these girls—they were used to it—but new to me. As soon as I had returned home from the hospital and discovered her message on my machine, I immediately notified Addie and Venus. As always, they had gone out on a mission to find her, neck braces and shoulder slings be damned. Only this time, standing in for the incapacitated Ruthie, I had gone along with them. Just as before, Birdie had occasionally been spotted here, there, all around the town. But this time it was different. This time, almost a month had gone by since the Rock and Soul Foundation Awards, almost a month with no word from her to anyone. And then that message—well, you know.

"I don't know how you can blame yourselves for what happened to her that night. I mean, you guys had no way of knowing—"

"Bullshit," spat Addie. "We knew she was up on that Strip alone. We had always traveled together, or at least in pairs. She had called me earlier that night, said she felt like hangin, but I didn't feel like goin out. Venus was workin with Miss Beale, makin us some new outfits. And Ruthie—"

Addie fell silent.

"Go on and say it, Ad. Ruthless Ruth was out somewhere livin large, partyin hearty, as usual," Ruth finished, and from the look on her face, it was hard to tell which of her pains was worse, the physical or the emotional.

"Still," I pressed on, "there was no way you could know."

"Listen, Legs. Back in the day, there were a lot of guys doin that Spanish fly thing, especially at the Tornado. We all knew about it. Birdie must have somehow been distracted, maybe by the band. The Black Rebellion were playin that night, and she had been called up to the stage to sing. While she was up there, somebody must have slipped it into her beer."

Addie was telling the story slowly, haltingly.

"And you guys never found out who she left the club with?"

"Never. And anytime anybody—them doctors at that damn Byberry, or any of us—asked her, she would get so upset, her blood pressure would actually rise, and she would stop speakin again. So we finally stopped askin her," Addie answered, shaking her head.

"Byberry?"

"Yeah, Byberry, the old state mental hospital. Kept her in there for almost a year," Ruthie nodded, reaching over to the bedside table for a Kool, the hell with what her doctors said.

"The shrinks said until she was ready to talk about it,

we just had to be patient. And she was never ready to talk about it," Venus offered.

"And that's a damn lucky thing for whoever did it, because whoever it was, they better hope we never find out," Addie said, waving Ruthie's smoke out of her face disdainfully.

"Well, ladies," I said, rising from Ruthie's bed, "what part of town are we going to be searching tonight?"

"I figure we might do South Philly," Addie answered. "We haven't been down there since last week, and she sometimes likes to hang out around Point Breeze Avenue. Sure you don't mind doin the drivin, Legs?"

"Absolutely not," I answered. Truth be told, I was really enjoying gliding up and down the streets of Philadelphia behind the wheel of Addie's big silver Lincoln. I had been pressed into service because her dislocated shoulder was still giving her some problems, and nobody felt like crawling up into Venus's van.

"Damn! Sure wish I could go wit yall," Ruth said, puffing furiously on her cigarette. Well, then, of course, we spent a good five minutes talking Ruthie out of trying to crawl out of that bed, before she finally gave up and settled down.

The three of us had said our good-byes and were almost in the hallway when Adeline suddenly stopped, turned back.

"Wait a minute. Hey, Ruth?"

"Yeah?" Ruthie was already putting her cigarette out, preparing to go back to sleep.

"Friday Brown was lookin into what happened to Bird that night at the Tornado, wasn't he?"

"Yeah, he did do some checkin around. You know he always did have a soft spot for the baby, as he calls her."

"And didn't he say that the bass player was in there earlier that same night?"

Venus and I did an about-face, and the three of us walked back into Ruthie's bedroom.

"You know what, Ad? I believe he did. In all the excitement, I forgot all about it."

"So did I, Ruthie," Venus said slowly. "Yall know that's how the lil fucker used to operate."

"You know, I thought about it when I saw him at our party at Cleo's, then forgot about it. It's just comin back to me now," said Ruthie.

"The bass player? You mean the one—the girl in Baltimore?"

I glanced quickly from one to the other. All three were slowly nodding their heads, almost like they were keeping time to some distant beat that only they could hear. I could almost see the wheels turning around in their individual minds, which now seemed to be functioning as one.

"Aw, come on, yall," I said, in what I hoped was a light, joking manner.

Silence.

"Aw, now, look. Birdie knew the guy, knew him as well as the rest of you did, and you said you all had peeped his card way back then. Why would he take that kind of risk with somebody he knew?"

The Sweethearts had me frightened now, as they threw the same glance back and forth at each other, like they were having a game of virtual dodge ball.

"Yeah, why would he?" Ruth Thomas finally said, lighting up another Kool.

"Guess we just gone have to find out."

Aw, hell.

* * *

Philadelphia Globe—May 12, 1990

SWEETHEARTS OF SOUL MEMBER
FOUND DEAD IN COBBS CREEK PARK

By Nicole Brown, Staff Writer

The body of Brenda Wade was discovered early this morning in West Philadelphia's Cobbs Creek Park. At this time, the police have not cited a cause of death, nor ruled out foul play.

Miss Wade, once a member of the Sweethearts of Soul, the Philadelphia sixties rock-and-roll girl group responsible for such hits as "You May Not Know" and "Change My Mind," had been expected to attend an awards ceremony sponsored by the Rock and Soul Foundation to receive the organization's Pioneer Award on April 7th of this year.

The ceremony, held at New York's famed Apollo Theater, with the other members of the group present, proceeded as scheduled with legendary rhythm-and-blues recording artist and actress Fanya Dance filling in for Ms. Wade.

The Sweethearts of Soul have declined to comment.

* * *

Chapter 13

*

The Funeral

It was standing-room-only at Fire-Baptized Pentecostal Church, a beautiful old brick gothic building, covered in ivy, filled with Bibles and hymnbooks, dark, rich mahogany pews, blood-red carpeting, alabaster-white walls, deep stained-glass windows, a huge organ with tall golden pipes, and people: young, old, black, white, red, yellow, and brown.

High up on the back wall, overlooking the pulpit, the pews, and all who entered therein, hung a large stunning painting of the Crucifixion, featuring a Black Jesus Christ nailed to the cross, an expression of agony and ecstasy on his handsome face. An awesome sight.

There were so many people there, loudspeakers had been set up outdoors to accommodate the ones who couldn't manage to squeeze inside.

And the media! Radio, television, and newspaper reporters from all over the country—hell, from all over the world, as far away as Japan. Small children, yet unborn when the Sweethearts of Soul had their heyday, snaked around, between, and through the long legs of their elders, positioning themlselves to get the best possible view. Toddlers sat up high on the shoulders of their fathers and uncles, waving and chattering as if they were on parade.

Old ladies wearing their best broken-brim Sunday straws and Evening in Paris perfume stood fanning themselves and gossiping in the heat of a surprisingly warm and humid May morning, while cotton-toped old gents dressed in too-many-times-pressed brown suits swept their foreheads with stark white handkerchiefs.

"Did you see the mayor walk in up there, girl?"

"You know I did, honey. Still wearin that same ole Afro hairstyle since 1966."

"Git on outta here. You know they say he used to have a thang for Fanya."

"A thang? What kinda thang?"

"A thang. That's all I heard. I don't know how far it went, but it was definitely a thang."

"Ha! Yeah, right. Like she gone pick his tired ass ovah Music Man."

"Shhh! It's them. Here they come, here they come!"

The crowd fell silent and still, all eyes suddenly trained like lasers as a procession of limousines came to a stop directly in front of the church. Moving slowly and with superhuman effort, the first woman stepped out of the car. A young usher reached into the limo, extracted a hospital walker, and gave it to a grateful Ruth Thomas.

"Okay, that's Ruthie, the oldest," someone whispered.

"And that one's Addie, that rapper's mother," another informed the crowd as Addie grabbed Ruth's hand and exited the car.

"And the lil thick one is Venus," murmured somebody else as Venus Jones, a black-lace-gloved hand covering her eyes, took her place between Ruth and Addie.

"There she is! There she is!"

The noise level, which had until this moment been subdued and respectful, took on the tones of a rock-and-roll concert as people suddenly rushed forward, elbowing each other out of their way, shouting and waving.

"Fanya! Hey, Fanya! Over here!" a woman squealed, tripping over the curbside, nearly losing her balance.

Security people suddenly materialize from out of nowhere as Fanya, draped from head to toe in ermine (despite the warm May weather) gracefully emerged from the car and joined Ruth, struggling with the aid of the walker, Addie, and Venus as they slowly climbed the steps of the old brick building and entered through its bright red doors.

Inside, flowers of seemingly every variety and description filled the entire church. A glorious riot of roses, chrysanthemums, peonies, African violets, sunflowers, lining either side of the casket, overhanging the stage, decorating the pulpit, snaking up the aisles. Fanya had spared no expense.

The casket itself, all white with gold trim, featuring a dropped-down front side with a thick white quilted satin lining which fell all the way to the floor, gave it the appearance of a grand sofa, where Birdie was simply lying on her back, sleeping.

Her hair and makeup had been done by none other than Miss Magdelina Smart, closely overseen by the Sweethearts, of course. Her gown, white silk threaded with gold, had been hand-sewn by Venus; a crown of baby's breath and lily of the valley, designed by Ruth, covered her hair, which fell around her face in soft ringlets, and golden, rhinestone-emblazoned slippers, ordered custom-made by Fanya, covered her slender feet.

Clutched loosely in her well-manicured hands was Addie's favorite traveling Bible. Small, slight, elegant, and peaceful at last, *the baby* rested on her down-filled white satin pillow in full and loving splendor.

And, of course, you'll want to know if she was wearing red panties. *Absolutely.* Birdie was on a most important mission. She was going home.

And there to wish her well on her final journey was a stunning array of people who loved her.

Philadelphia's music community was present and represented in full force. Just about everybody who had attended the party at Cleo's, as well as some of the folks from the Rock and Soul Foundation were there. It seemed as if the entire congregation of Fire-Baptized was present, as well as childhood friends and neighbors of the Sweethearts. Simon Hall, Al and Ty Chestnut, even the Cupcakes came through. *And* the Bonner sisters!

"One thing I can say today is Brenda Wade sure had a whole lot of friends." Pastor Nichols remarked, looking out over the huge audience as he opened the service.

"Amen," the audience responded.

"I've known Birdie for almost as long as she knew herself, and I can testify that although she traveled far and wide, singing with the Sweethearts of Soul, she never ever really left us in spirit, and we've always claimed her."

Those words set the tone for the service, as speaker after speaker shared a moment or two with the audience. Miss Mattie talked about how stage shy Birdie was, how she got butterflies in her stomach before each performance.

"But once she got up on that stage, all her butterflies flew away, and she sang wonderfully. It was as if this chile was born to sing."

Mrs. Welles, the Sweethearts' junior high music teacher, talked about the time she went to see them at a show, mostly out of curiosity, since she had heard that they had a new lead singer.

"And she totally captivated me. That voice had a life of

its own, running up and down like a roller coaster, just careening all over the place. I only met Brenda once, it was on that same night, after the show. And I found her to be very much like her voice. Special and unique. Beautiful."

Jimmy Dunn, now in a wheelchair, spoke tenderly of the quiet, skinny little girl who had "knocked his socks off" that first night he had heard her sing in the studio.

"She was what we used to call a one-take artist back then. I'm always hearing stories these days about how such-and-such artist or singing group were in the studio for three months, six months, sometimes a whole year even, perfecting one song. Hmph! Not the baby! You show Birdie how to do the song once, just once, she would go home and practice, go into that studio the next day, and nail it to the wall in one take! That's right! One take! They just don't make em like her anymore."

Carl Chance also spoke about what a quick study Birdie had been, how when she joined the Sweethearts she had learned not only her own parts but the group's entire routine in less than a week.

"God only made one like that one, and we'll never see another."

I understand they had to limit the list of speakers, or the service would have run on for at least half a day.

And the music! The Fire-Baptized choir knew they had to come with their A-game, what with the wealth of musical talent in the room, not to mention the fact that this service was for "one of their own," a woman who had once stood in the very same shoes they were standing in today. They *knew* they had to be on point.

And were they ever! Walking the audience in with "Peace Be Still," they sang an entire repertoire of the Sweethearts' favorite songs. With "I'm Going Away," followed by "Standin in the Need of Prayer," "Take My Hand," "Precious Lord," and "God Will Take Care of You," they literally forced the crowd to its feet, so caught up and swept away were they by The Spirit. God was definitely in the building!

At one point, a vocal quartet of little girls from the children's choir, ages eight to eleven, held the Sweethearts of Soul in the palms of their tiny hands with a heart-stirring "Yes, Jesus Loves Me."

As the choir sang the final notes to one of Birdie's personal favorites, "Over the Rainbow," the mourners, who had been following the church's printed obituary program, assumed the service was about to conclude and rose for the minister's final benediction.

But instead of Pastor Nichols, it was Ruth who stepped up to the pulpit.

Ruth, leaning on her walker, spoke.

"We just could not leave without singing with Birdie one last time," she told the gathering.

And with that, Ruthie turned, gestured slightly, and the other three Sweethearts, Venus, Adeline, and Fanya, stepped up and stood around the pulpit with her, leaving the floor mike's stand empty. A stool was placed just behind the stand by an usher, a lone microphone placed on the stool.

First, there was the intro, beautifully played by none other than Mrs. Welles. The audience was quiet, hushed. Then from somewhere came the voice, sweet, high, thrilling.

"How will the stars ever find me if I ever change my name?

"How will my God ever find me if I ever change my name?"

The audience looked around, momentarily confused. But the Sweethearts smiled as the voice of Brenda "Birdie" Wade, piped in through the PA system, filled the room like a mighty cloud of joy.

"I live to be free, I live for beauty in every soul I find.

"Not gonna change me, not gonna change my mind."

The disembodied voice, with a life force all its own, roared up and over the rafters of the church, swooped and swirled through the air like a feather, bounced high above the heads of the mourners like a child's ball, while Ruth, Addie, Venus, and Fanya, bringing up the background, pushed Birdie higher, ever higher.

"They say I'm blind and it's not worth the time to believe in love. They say I'm crazy to fall down and pray to the one I love."

The Sweethearts were sounding like church bells and violins, like trumpets and mandolins, making a joyful noise, pushing Birdie on. The audience was in tears, as were the Sweethearts, the choir, the musicians, everyone. And then they saw it. All in one moment, they saw the bird.

Flying high near the ceiling at first, the little bird suddenly swooped down, flew to the very back of the church, then forward to the very front, hovering for almost a full minute over the heads of the Sweethearts as they sang. It wasn't a pigeon, wasn't a blackbird. Some people in the balcony said it looked like a robin redbreast, the first bird of spring. Singing and twirling and swooping through the air. No matter.

Everybody knew who it *really* was. Saying good-bye.

"Let my devotion move like the ocean, soothe every soul I find. God, never change me, please never change my mind, change my mind, change my mind."

Legs: Reporter's Notes
(An Epilogue)

Whew! See what I mean? Told you. That's just the kinda thing I was talking about at the beginning of this story—or, rather, these stories. They're like one long winding road that splits into two, then three separate paths, then at some point, doubles back on itself and converges into one road again. As Roe would say, this is some hot mess here. Like a DNA double helix. Like family.

And the SOS family is still heavy grieving the death of their Hummingbird. And no matter what anyone says to them, no matter how many people try to convince them that it was not their fault, their sense of collective guilt remains. And it always will. I know a little something about guilt. That's why I still talk to Roe, still beg for her forgiveness each and every day.

But as the old folks say, life goes on. And this is what's going on now—at least it was when I last checked today. Come back tomorrow, it might be some whole new other shit thrown in the mix.

Addie has just said yes to a marriage proposal from William, her contractor boyfriend, who, as it turns out, is a very successful businessman after all. Ruthie, nevertheless, has taken to referring to the man as "Wide-load Willie," though, mercifully, not in Addie's presence. Addie and Venus are excitedly planning the wedding.

"Now, you *know* she gone git worms from that old-ass goat! You *know* he used to baby-sit Jesus for Joseph and Mary!"

I don't even have to tell you who made that remark, do I?

And Venus, Miss Never-fall-in-love-again-professional-virgin Venus, has been having some long, long, long-distance calls almost every night with none other than Jack, the guy from the Heartbreakers who came to their party at Cleo's! Turns out Jack is now a producer in the music biz.

(Lord have mercy. You'd think one Heartbreaker would have been enough. And I ain't nevah lied!)

Fluffy, true to her promise, had called Venus a few evenings after the awards show. She had heard about the accident, and she immediately sent a check for Ruthie's care. She also requested some of Raven's tapes and a recent photo.

Turns out she loves the girl's songs, her message, and her flow, and has signed Raven to an exclusive contract with Music Man Productions, and Fluffy herself will be producing her first CD!

By the way, on April 30th, Venus and Addie became the proud grandmamas of a big, ole, beautiful boy. His name is Raymond Brendan Lights, and they are both trying to outdo each other in totally spoiling the poor little guy for any other woman, ever. Ruthie says she's going to call him "Bright Lights." Venus and Addie are not amused.

Venus and Raven have since discovered that Bobby Lights did not credit Raven as cowriter for the two songs he recorded. Venus was seriously thinking of suing, but Fluffy talked her out of it. For the sake of the family.

"Don't even sweat it, Sis. Let him have the damn songs.

Your baby's got plenty more where those came from."

Bobby Lights is still on the road, though he did come home when Bright Lights—uh, I mean little Ray—was born. Raven, wearing her new motherhood with calm dignity, and with her own contract under her belt ("She's gonna be a star, just like her mom and dad!" boasts Venus), doesn't seem to miss him quite so much these days.

And no one says anything more about a wedding, as far as those two are concerned.

Sadly, Ruthie's daughter, Sunni, is missing in action again. Once she was satisfied that her mother was going to survive, she hightailed it out of that hospital and never looked back. Word on the street has it that she's somewhere in New York, trying to make it as a dancer. But Bad Friday Brown, international man of mystery, is steady on the case, and Ruthie is hopeful.

"Aha!" I teased her one day last week when I went over to see how she was doing.

"You and Bad Friday are still going strong, huh? You go, girl!"

"Oh, I *do* go," she said, laughing, "all the time."

"You know, Legs," Ruth said softly, "when Friday first came to the hospital that day, they took a sample of *his* blood, too."

"And? So what? They took a blood sample from all of us."

"Yes, that's true. But they took a sample of *his* blood. *And* Sunni's. And of course, they already had *mine*."

I cut my eyes sharply to hers.

"Are you saying what I think you're saying?"

"Shhh!" she giggled. "All I'm sayin is they took samples from all three of us. Keep it on the downlow for now, okay? I don't want Addie and Venus to be havin no heart attacks round here." Ruthie smiled at me, winking.

"You got it. Not a word," I said, nodding.

Sometimes, things go deeper than blood. And some-times, blood is all you need.

Amazing, isn't it, how life and death can sometimes turn on a dime? Exactly two days after my visit with Ruthie, I joined Addie and Venus for lunch at Miss Tootsie's, where I found the two new grandmamas happily chattering away over little Ray, about which of them he most resembles, his summer outfits, his winter wardrobe, the best diet for him, the best pediatrician, the best preschool, the best, the best, the best, on and on.

But I was there on a mission. So after taking a seat, exchanging pleasantries, and trying to order from the wait-ress, who was busy fawning all over the two Sweethearts ("I seen yall on PBS! Yall was sharp, girl, sharp!"), I casually dropped the previous day's edition of the *Philadelphia Globe* on the table. It was already opened to the obituary page, where I had circled an item in red pencil.

"Anybody want to tell me what you know about this?"

✳ ✳ ✳

Philadelphia Globe

WELL-KNOWN "SESSION MUSICIAN" DIES IN FIRE

The music community is stunned today upon hearing the news of the death of Barton Coleman, "bass player extraordinaire." Mr. Coleman's body was discovered when the manager at Newark, New Jersey's, Blue Moon Motel smelled smoke and, upon investigating, found Mr. Coleman's room engulfed in flames.

"He had only checked in about an hour before," said the

distraught manager. "I can't imagine what could have happened in such a short time."

Details about the cause of the fire were unavailable as this story went to press, though Mr. Coleman's family affirmed that he was a non-smoker.

Mr. Coleman, 57, a native Philadelphian, began his career in music in the 1960s, playing jazz and rhythm and blues on what was then known as the "chitlin circuit," a series of nightclubs and theaters across the country catering to an African-American audience. He had either traveled and performed with or recorded with just about every major Black artist coming out of Philadelphia and Detroit from the sixties straight on up to the eighties. In the mid-eighties, Mr. Coleman relocated to Hollywood, California, where he became a much-in-demand session player for both recordings and major studio film soundtracks. He is survived by his wife, Terri, two children, and one grandchild.

✳ ✳ ✳

Adeline read the item first, then handed it to Venus, who scanned it quickly. Both were silent.

"Well?"

"Well, what?"

Was it just my imagination, or did they answer me in two-part harmony?

"The bass player?"

"Bass player?" they echoed, still speaking as one.

"Come on, yall. Don't play with me. Is this guy, this Barton Coleman—is he the one who—*you* know—the girl in Baltimore, and, uh . . ."

"Why, yes indeedy, sweetie! I do believe he is! What you think, Ad? Is that him?"

"You know, Vee, now that you mention it, I do think you're right. Why, it *is* him, ain't it?"

Venus Jones and Adeline Lights then turned to me, and I don't know if it was the sun streaming into Miss Tootsie's front window that put that strange glint in their eyes or what it was. I just don't know. I cocked my head and stared at them both.

"What?" they asked in unison. "Don't look at *us*!"

Like I said before, I wouldn't want them sistahs mad at *me*.

✳   ✳   ✳

Anyway, the SOS, Raven, and the baby, are all packed and getting ready to board a first-class flight to California for Fluffy's twenty-fifth wedding anniversary.

"Everybody who is anybody will be there, don't you know," Addie informed me. They will be staying at the mansion with Music Man and Fluffy as honored guests, and they are positively beside themselves. Ruthie, though still recovering, swears she'll be there, "Even if I have to get me some young boys to carry me on that damn plane on a stretcher!"

Unbeknownst to us at the time, PBS had taped the Rock and Soul Foundation Awards program, and it was now being broadcast all over. I had already seen it twice, and despite the fact that I had witnessed the program live, the Sweethearts' performance had me reaching for the Kleenex both times.

The sight of the four of them in that group hug provided one of the most moving moments of the entire evening—and a photo of that moment had been reprinted in newspapers across the country. It had also been featured on such television shows as *Entertainment Tonight, BET News-makers,* and *Access Hollywood.* As a result, the SOS were now very much in demand, so much so that they had had to hire an agent to field gig offers from all over the nation, from Europe, and even as far away as Japan. And the money they were offering was pretty decent, too.

Everybody, from the mailman to the supermarket clerk to the guy who cut the grass to the Asian greengrocer on the corner has seen the PBS special, and the Sweethearts are now the stars of the city.

"They want us to play what they call the 'classic' circuit. Not oldies, not chitlin. Uh-uh. We're *classics,* baby," Venus bragged with a wink.

So not only was Ruthie going to get her big "comeback," all of them would, brass balls and everything. They could hardly wait to begin rehearsals.

"Just wait till I get my shit together. You'll see. I just gotta get back on the boards again, chile. Gotta git back on the boards."

Venus and Addie nodded, smiling broadly.

"The boards," I asked, puzzled. "What boards?"

"The stage, chile," Ruthie sighed, looking at me as if I were certifiably slow.

"The stage boards. Jeez! Don't this girl know nothin bout showbiz?"

"Don't you be worryin bout what she know. At least she had enough sense to know how to put on her red panties that night. Not like some of us," Addie said, cocking that left eye down at Ruth.

Now, besides praying to God each and every day, Venus is convinced that the cause of their good fortune is due to her buying some kind of charm or spell or something from Miss Gustine, the Spirit Woman.

And Addie gives all credit to the Lord, too, but also thinks all their newfound good luck has come to them simply because she fixed that left eye on Frank Flood that night at the awards afterparty.

But Ruthie thanks God for sending me—yes, me—into their lives and bringing them all back together.

In fact, all of them do, even Fluffy. They've taken to calling me their good-luck charm.

And that's why I, honorary Sweetheart of Soul, thank you very much, am packing *my* bags, too.

So hold tight, son, Mama's comin to get you. Mama's comin to Cali! And I'm definitely not setting foot out of this house without my red panties.

Postscript

There is a story told about a bird, a beautiful hummingbird, that sings but once in its life, and the sound of its song is said to be so sweet, it has been known to sometimes still the entire forest. Then it dies, leaving only the memory of its bright and brilliant voice behind.

If you want to find our Birdie again, be still, and listen. Somewhere in our hearts and souls, she sings forever.

Sorrowfully submitted by her beloved sisters,
Ruth, Adeline, Venus, and Fanny Lou . . .
just a few heartbeats away.